# Readers love ARIEL TACHNA's
## *Partnership in Blood* novels

I0675743

"I absolutely love this series."
—Romance Junkies

"I've thoroughly enjoyed the premise for these books and the characters, and recommend them to any reader who enjoys paranormal fantasy; especially those involving vampires, wizards and magic."
— Literary Nymphs Reviews

"…an amazingly well written series that I know that paranormal romantics will enjoy."
—Night Owl Reviews

"[Reparation in Blood] is action packed and full of fascinating and amazing characters. A worthwhile read and fitting end to the series."
—Bitten by Books

"This series is definitely for anyone looking for a new twist on Vampires, and who likes a bit of angst and a bit of adventure mixed into their romance."
—Dark Diva Reviews

"Ariel Tachna has created a truly original version of the vampire archetype…"
—Steve Williams, Suite 101

http://www.dreamspinnerpress.com

# By Ariel Tachna

All For One (with Nicki Bennett)
Best Ideas
Château d'Eternité
Checkmate (with Nicki Bennett)
Fallout
Her Two Dads
Highland Lover
In Search of Fireworks
The Inventor's Companion
The Matelot
Music of the Heart
Once in a Lifetime
Out of the Fire
Overdrive
The Path
Rediscovery
Revelations in the Dark
Riding Double (Dreamspinner Anthology)
Rose Among the Ruins
Seducing C.C.
Stolen Moments
A Summer Place
Sutcliffe Cove (with Madeleine Urban)
Testament to Love
Under the Skin (with Nicki Bennett)
Why Nileas Loved the Sea

THE EXPLORING LIMITS SERIES (WITH NICKI BENNETT)
Exploring Limits • Stretching Limits • Refining Limits
Breaking Limits • Transcending Limits • No Limits

GAMES LOVERS PLAY
Amorous Liaison • Best Behavior • Ride 'em Cowboy

HOT CARGO
Hot Cargo (with Nicki Bennett) • Something About Harry (with Nicki Bennett)
Healing in His Wings

LANG DOWNS
Inherit the Sky • Chase the Stars • Outlast the Night • Conquer the Flames

PARTNERSHIP IN BLOOD
Alliance in Blood • Covenant in Blood • Conflict in Blood • Reparation in Blood
Perilous Partnership • Reluctant Partnerships • Lycan Partnership • Partnership Reborn

AVAILABLE AT DREAMSPINNER PRESS
http://www.dreamspinnerpress.com

# pLycan Partnership

*A Partnership in Blood novel*

## ARIEL TACHNA

Dreamspinner Press

Published by
DREAMSPINNER PRESS

5032 Capital Circle SW, Suite 2, PMB# 279, Tallahassee, FL 32305-7886 USA
http://www.dreamspinnerpress.com/

Lycan Partnership
© 2014 Ariel Tachna.

Cover Art
© 2013 Catt Ford.
Cover content is for illustrative purposes only and any person depicted on the cover is a model.

ISBN: 978-1-63216-672-2
Digital ISBN: 978-1-63216-673-9
Library of Congress Control Number: 2014950199
Second Edition October 2014
First Edition published by Dreamspinner Press, January 2013

Printed in the United States of America
∞
This paper meets the requirements of
ANSI/NISO Z39.48-1992 (Permanence of Paper).

To Rhianne, who let me borrow her werewolves.

# Chapter 1

THE WOLF threw her head back and howled, grief and despair coursing through her as she fled the den she shared with her mate. The scents of home and husband offered no comfort now, only mocked her inability to conceive and provide an heir for the alpha who had given her everything she needed since the moment she laid eyes on his silver-gray pelt. She pushed her body as hard as she could, seeking solace in exhaustion. If she ran until she collapsed, perhaps she could sleep, and if she slept, perhaps she would wake to find this had been only a nightmare, that her body had not betrayed her. That even now she harbored a child within her, a pup who would grow into the alpha who would replace her mate when he could no longer lead the pack.

Her muscles burned as she raced down ravines and up the other sides, but this was pack land, and every inch smelled of her mate. She could not escape the silent reproach emanating from the rocks and trees, his scent a constant rebuke. He might love her, but he had to have an heir. She knew what would happen now. He would have the shaman call the unmated females to him, and he would rut with them until one of them gave him the son she could not. She would be disgraced, humiliated, even if he did not repudiate her. What place could an infertile wolf have in the life of the most powerful, virile wolf in le Morvan? He had to have an heir, and the mother of his heir would be the Consort in the eyes of the pack, no matter what promises had passed between them in the depths of the night. Their mating bond would shatter and she would be outcast, *lowell*, and would spend her remaining days alone—not that she would survive long if she lost her mate.

She leaped toward the top of the ravine, but her body failed her. She missed the ledge and slid pell-mell down the slope to the creek that bisected the valley. She struggled to rise, for the water had taken on the chill of upcoming winter, but her left hind leg would not support her weight. She whimpered in defeat. She would lie here and let the cold drain the heat and life from her body, and then her mate would be spared the humiliation of her infertility and could find someone else to take her place without the shame of replacing her first.

She closed her eyes, muzzle resting on the creek bank barely clear of the water, as she gave up all hope.

She lost track of time as the chill seeped through her, and her mind grew as numb as her body before a warm tongue licking her snout roused her from the pit of her despair. She lifted her head, opening her eyes to meet the frantic gaze of her mate. He whined at her as he waded into the water and nudged her side to get her to rise, but her leg had grown stiff in the water, and even his urging was not enough to allow her to stand.

He shimmered before her eyes, becoming the man she had fallen in love with at sixteen, had pledged herself to mere weeks later, and had stood beside for nearly thirty years.

"Change," he ordered her.

She shook her head, but he was not only her mate, he was her alpha, and his voice could not be ignored for long.

"Change."

She shook herself feebly and became human again. The chill racked her far more deeply in her weaker form, with no clothing to protect her as her thick pelt had done, but she stayed where she was, waiting for him to pass judgment.

He did not speak again but instead lifted her into his strong arms, freeing her from her intended watery grave.

"I'm sorry," she said, tears streaming down her cheeks now that she inhabited human form again. "It didn't work."

"It doesn't matter," Lorens said, his voice distraught. "It isn't worth losing you."

"But the pack, your family's heritage, the future…."

"It doesn't matter," Lorens repeated, kissing her gently. "Nothing is worth seeing you this way."

She buried her face in his shoulder and sobbed.

"We have to get you dry," he said as her shivering increased. "Can you walk in wolf form?"

"I don't know," she said, her voice hoarse from crying and the cold. "I fell."

He set her down and steadied her until she found her balance again. Her leg hurt, but having Lorens at her side gave her the determination she had lacked when she feared her news would shatter their bond. She changed into wolf form and took a tentative step. When her hind leg held her, Lorens changed as well and led her hobbling toward home.

LORENS STARED down at his mate's sleeping face. They had limped home, and he had insisted she take a hot bath before going to sleep. Exhaustion had claimed her the moment she curled up in their bed. He inhaled deeply, wrapping his senses in her scent to calm his restless wolf. He had known what her mournful cries portended the moment he heard them, but it had taken time to find her, time to grow frantic as he searched and searched with no hint of her whereabouts.

They could not go on like this. They had mated young and then waited to start their family, wanting to establish themselves as a couple and as the alpha and his mate before they had children of their own. Then the fertility rituals that had always granted the honor of procreation to the alpha and, more recently, other mated couples of the pack, had failed them repeatedly, and Edine had grown more and more despondent with each unsuccessful attempt.

Something had to give. The pack was dying out, no children being born to replace the elders, many of whom had already lived eighty years or more. Lorens and their shaman, Adenet, had searched the lore of their people to find a solution, to no avail. They had approached other packs, careful not to reveal the desperation of their situation, only to learn that the problem was not confined to their pack—but no one had any solutions.

In desperation, Lorens had suggested to Adenet that they approach the wizards at l'Institut Marcel Chavinier, but Adenet had reacted with all the disdain of their kind for magicians and the rest of *their* kind. They waved their wands and ignored the impact of their actions on the natural forces that surrounded them, sucking the life out of everything they touched. Lorens did not have his shaman's connection with the natural world, so he could not dispute the assertions, but one memory echoed through him.

"Every one of you who has held a child you love in your arms has something in common with the werewolves who celebrate every new birth because they happen so rarely."

Raymond Payet, former president of l'Association Nationale de Sorcellerie and current director of l'Institut Marcel Chavinier, had spoken those words as he accepted the presidency after the magical war that had only served as proof of Adenet's assertions. The man might not know anything beyond what he said, but he had enough awareness of their plight to use it to encourage others to consider a connection to werewolves, and he had enough consideration of their kind as another magical race to include them in his speech.

Maybe it would lead to nothing, but they had nothing now, either.

He tossed a few days' worth of clothing in a suitcase, wrote a note for Edine, and kissed her forehead. He had nothing else to lose.

THE JANGLE of an unknown presence along the edge of the wards at l'Institut Marcel Chavinier roused Raymond Payet from his perusal of the latest round of research proposals he was supposed to be considering. He really wanted to spend the day outside, enjoying the last of the fall sunshine before the gray skies of winter set in. Now he had an excuse.

"Where are you going?" Jean asked.

"Someone's outside," Raymond said. "I thought I'd go see who it is."

"We have a concierge to handle things like that for us," Jean reminded him.

"Maybe, but it's sunny today. Don't tell me you'd rather spend it in here working than out there."

Jean hesitated only a moment, the lingering habit of over a thousand years of avoiding sunlight. With his Avoué at his side, he no longer had that concern. He closed the laptop in front of him. "Let's go greet our guest."

They walked through the halls of the converted fourteenth-century monastery to the courtyard. The grass had faded to brown with the coming of winter and the bushes and flowers had been trimmed back as they fell dormant, but the sun was warm on their faces as they crossed the open space to the gate.

No one was there.

"Where are they?" Jean asked.

"I don't know," Raymond said.

"Can you tell where they were? Do the wards allow you to pinpoint that much? Maybe we can tell who they were by whatever traces they left behind."

"It could have been some hiker in the woods who simply got too close," Raymond reminded him. "It's late in the season for that, but the snows haven't set in yet. The trails are still open, and you know not everyone stays on them."

The relative isolation of le Morvan was one of the reasons they had chosen this location for l'Institut Marcel Chavinier when they founded it nearly a year earlier. It had been far easier to secure the premises on the edge of the natural preserve than it would have been in the heart of Paris or any other city.

"It could have been," Jean agreed eventually. "You didn't answer my question, though. Can you tell where the person was?"

"No. Adèle didn't set the wards with that degree of sensitivity, and we haven't needed it, so I see no reason to have her change them now," Raymond said, "or to try to tweak the work she did."

"Could you?"

"If necessary, yes," Raymond said, "but it's not worth the effort to do so for a hiker or some other random passerby who didn't know where the property line was."

"We posted signs."

"We did, but not on every single tree. It's possible to pass between them and not see them. Stop being an alarmist. Nobody is trying to force their way past our wards and attack l'Institut."

"Not this time," Jean muttered.

Raymond rolled his eyes. "Let's go down to the lake since we've already taken a break."


HIDDEN IN the woods, Lorens fought the urge to change. The moment the two men had come into view, Lorens's wolf had sensed the slimmer man's undead nature—Lorens would worry about how a vampire could walk unharmed in sunlight when his wolf was not straining his control— and had surged against his barriers, fighting to get loose, to attack the vampire before the creature could attack him. If Lorens had been closer to home, where he could have returned on foot—two or four—he might not have fought the transformation so hard, but he had to return to the auberge in Dommartin, and showing up there in wolf form or naked from the change did not strike him as advisable. His wolf had no such concerns.

The provocation of the vampire's presence was almost too much for Lorens's self-mastery. His wolf was such a part of him, so much of who he was, that holding back this way was as foreign as the idea of living without his dual nature.

He sniffed the air, trying to get a sense of the other man, but the distance was more than his wolf senses could cover while he was in human form. He thought he recognized Raymond Payet, but he had only ever seen Payet on television—and even then over a year ago—so he could not be sure. He had no idea who the vampire was, but Lorens was not about to show himself with a vampire present. Lorens might be able to control his wolf at a distance, but up close, hungry, and missing his mate as he was, he would lose control for sure, and that would hardly endear him to Payet or whoever else he might meet. Perhaps Lorens could not identify the men who wandered back inside the monastery walls, but he had not gotten to be alpha of his pack without learning to read body language. Whoever the two men were, their devotion to each other could not be doubted.

Only after they disappeared from sight and smell did Lorens relax. His wolf still was not happy, but without the immediate provocation of the vampire, the animal settled back under his control with a dissatisfied whine instead of an alarming growl in the back of his mind. Lorens would slip out of the auberge after dark and go hunting. That would appease his wolf, and tomorrow he would try again.

He returned to his car and drove back to Dommartin and the auberge. Tomorrow he would pack a change of clothes in his car so he could change and not have to fight his wolf.

His wolf did not like being confined in the sterile, impersonal room at the bed and breakfast any more than it cared for being shut behind Lorens's barriers at l'Institut. He missed his mate, and the absolute misery in her eyes and voice the last time he had seen her made it worse. He had not been able to resist the need to do something—thus the ill-planned dash to Dommartin that had ended with him nearly losing control of his wolf outside l'Institut. He hoped the vampire would be absent tomorrow, but if not, he would decide what to do then.

RAYMOND DID not go looking for Jean the next day when he felt a tickle along the wards. He had considered and abandoned the idea that Jean's presence had anything to do with the absence of their mysterious visitor. At a distance, Jean appeared as perfectly harmless as any other slender man in his twenties. Only someone who knew his supernatural side would have reason to fear him. Jean's edginess had been both annoying and catching, though, and Raymond thought he could assess the situation more clearly alone.

He had not counted on his lover's perspicacity. He had barely reached the door before Jean appeared at his side. "Going for a walk?"

"Going to see who is outside," Raymond answered. No use lying. Jean would sense it.

"Again? Two days in a row is no coincidence."

"You don't know it's the same person. We may get out there and find someone waiting for us."

Raymond did not need to sense Jean's skepticism through their bond to know how he felt. It was clear on his face.

When they walked outside, the area beyond the wards was empty.

"I don't like this," Jean said, stalking toward the perimeter they had laid out. "This isn't the property line. If they made it this far, they're trespassing, even if it's unintentionally."

"What do you propose?" Raymond asked.

"Set a barrier at the property line, something to keep our guest in until we can find him if he comes back."

"The war is over, Jean, and Renaud is in prison. There isn't anyone out to get us."

"That we know about."

Raymond struggled to resist Jean's paranoia. He could separate Jean's emotions from his own, but that did not make them less influential. Not coercive as he had once feared, but enough that he couldn't make a decision without considering Jean's feelings on the matter also. He reminded himself regularly that it went both ways, his strong emotions affecting Jean as well.

"I'll call Adèle," he said after a moment. "I don't know if I can do what you're suggesting. I can do the magic, of course, but I mean legally."

"Find out. I can deal with many things, but not with the thought of you in danger."


LORENS FOUND it easier to fight changing when the vampire appeared along with the wizard the next day. He still kept to the tree line, not ready to show himself, but between hunting the night before and talking to his mate, hearing her in a calmer frame of mind, he was able to settle and study the two men. At this distance he could tell little beyond what he had scented the day before, but the vampire was visibly agitated, gesturing toward the tree line repeatedly as he and the wizard argued about something. In the better light and without the shock of coming face-to-face with a vampire, Lorens could finally identify the wizard as the one he sought. Now he had to decide how best to approach the pair. If he were approaching the king of another pack, the formalities and protocols of his kind would guide his behavior as they would guide the behavior of his host. But Payet was no werewolf, and the other one…. Lorens refrained from even thinking the string of curses his wolf would pile at the vampire's feet if he could speak. Lorens had no reason to trust either of the men he would have to approach if he did not want to go back to his pack empty-handed.

They eventually withdrew and Lorens followed suit, returning to the auberge and his computer. Since approaching the director of l'Institut without also approaching the vampire seemed unlikely, he needed to revise his strategy. That meant finding out as much as he could about the two men and their relationship.


TWO HOURS later, Lorens slammed his laptop closed.

"Chef de la Cour," he muttered. "Of all the vampires in all of France, why did it have to be a chef de la Cour?"

He had learned more than a little about Payet and Bellaiche, the vampire, in his two hours of scouring news articles. Payet had been—and remained, to the extent that he still appeared in the media—an outspoken supporter of the rights and needs of all the magical races.

"Every one of you who has held a child you love in your arms has something in common with the werewolves who celebrate every new birth because they happen so rarely."

That line, from the acceptance speech Payet had given when he became president of l'ANS, resonated deeply with Lorens. Perhaps Payet had never struggled with infertility, but he understood how it could affect the werewolves. He empathized with their plight. He believed l'ANS should help them.

Perhaps Payet's speech had focused more on the vampires than on any other race, but that could be explained by his association with a vampire. From everything Lorens had gleaned from the articles,

Bellaiche was a frequent fixture at Payet's side. They never defined the relationship between them, but Lorens could read between the lines, particularly when more than a few photos of the two of them showed Bellaiche's hand resting on the center of Payet's back. Their "association" was personal. They might use the word "partner" when talking about each other, but the layers of meaning in that word were legion, and Lorens doubted it was as simple as business partners. No, Lorens suspected their partnership was more along the lines of partners in marriage, even if no such legalities bound them together.

# Chapter 2

"MONSIEUR PAYET, there's someone here to see you, but he wants you to come outside rather than meeting with you in your office."

"Why?" Jean asked before Raymond could speak.

"He didn't say," the concierge replied from the other side of the speakerphone. "Only that it was urgent he speak with monsieur Payet."

"Tell him we will come outside," Raymond said, hanging up the phone.

"Are you sure that's a good idea?" Jean asked as soon as the connection went dead.

"Jean, I did everything you asked me to do with the wards, but your paranoia is bordering on ridiculous. Let's go see who is there and what he wants before we decide he's determined to wreak havoc in our lives, shall we?"

Raymond's sarcasm did nothing to appease Jean's unease, but Raymond ignored it. He had no idea what might have triggered this latest round of protectiveness. The months since Renaud's arrest for the attempted murder of their newest faculty member had been quiet, and Raymond saw no reason to believe that was about to change.

They went to the door, expecting to find their mysterious guest right outside, but the portico was empty.

"Where is he?" Jean demanded.

"I don't know, but he's close. I can still feel him along the wards."

"I don't like this," Jean said. Raymond swore he could see Jean preparing for a fight.

"Relax," Raymond said, but he drew his wand nonetheless. He did not need it to cast any spell beyond the most powerful ones, but the sight of it often acted as a deterrent. "We don't know why he isn't waiting for us here."

"I can think of plenty of reasons," Jean muttered, "none of them good."

"Don't jump to conclusions," Raymond repeated as a man stepped into sight from the forest that surrounded the monastery.

Jean's eyes narrowed as he peered at the man across the expanse of field separating them. "Werewolf," he spat after a moment.

"How do you know?"

"He doesn't smell human," Jean replied.

"That doesn't mean he's here to cause trouble," Raymond cautioned. "Remember how you feel when people assume things about you because you're a vampire."

"Werewolves are trouble," Jean insisted. "Nothing but trouble."

Raymond rolled his eyes and took a step forward. "Can we help you?"

"I certainly hope so," the werewolf said, taking a tentative step closer. "I need to talk to monsieur Payet."

"I'm he," Raymond replied. "Why don't you come inside? We'll be more comfortable in my office."

"It would be better if we spoke out here," the werewolf said. "My kind and his don't do well together in close spaces."

Raymond rolled his eyes. He had dealt with the same kind of attitude when the vampires and wizards had first started working together. He had gotten over his own prejudicial attitude. It was time these two did the same. "If you've come to me for help, Jean is part of the bargain. While the title of director is mine, he shares the responsibilities. Jean, your word that you won't harm our guest."

The mixture of hurt and surprise on Jean's face and coming through their bond nearly undid Raymond, but he radiated back as much trust and love as he could. He didn't need the reassurance. He needed to provide it to the werewolf.

"You have my word," Jean said after a moment, his voice tight.

"And yours, monsieur?" Raymond asked.

"I won't start anything with the vampire. If he starts something, though, I will defend myself."

"He won't," Raymond said firmly before Jean could protest.

He didn't really think Jean would start anything unless the werewolf threatened Raymond, but the wizard thought perhaps a reminder of his own abilities was in order, for both of them. Fire might not be his element, but he could wield it well enough when he had to. With a snap of his fingers, he set a flame dancing above his hand—a harmless spell, but one that would prove his power to the werewolf and hopefully remind Jean of his capacity for far more than parlor tricks.

"Shall we go inside?"

At his side, Jean relaxed marginally. The werewolf stood too far away for Raymond to see the effect of his demonstration, but even if it had no effect, having Jean more relaxed would make the upcoming conversation less unpleasant.

The werewolf crossed the open space to where Jean and Raymond waited, though he kept a safe distance from them both even then. Raymond had no idea what had brought him to their door, but it had to be serious for him to overcome his obvious distrust of both wizards and vampires. Raymond only hoped he could help.

Once in his office, he offered the werewolf a seat. "How can we help you, monsieur…?"

"Iserin," the werewolf said. "Lorens Iserin."

"Raymond Payet and Jean Bellaiche," Raymond said, finishing the introductions. "So what brings you to our door?"

"Our pack is dying out," Iserin said, "and I don't know how to stop it."

"People are sick?" Raymond asked, racking his brain for the name of a doctor who might have any experience treating werewolves. He came up with none. He had never heard of werewolves getting sick before. "Have you talked to a doctor?"

"Not sick," Iserin said, "at least not in the immediate or obvious sense. The pack has become infertile. We haven't had any live births in several years, and the past two years, we haven't even had any stillbirths. Without children to carry on our line, we will cease to exist in a generation."

Raymond ignored the mutter of "good riddance" at his elbow, although he pushed his displeasure at Jean's attitude through the bond between them, hoping it would rein him in. "I take it you have explored the avenues open to you in your own lore."

Iserin snorted inelegantly. "And every other lore I could think to consult. I wouldn't be here if I could figure the problem out on my own."

"Not surprising," Jean murmured.

"Excuse us a moment," Raymond said, grabbing Jean's arm and pulling him into the hallway. "Your hospitality leaves much to be desired."

Jean shrugged. "He's a werewolf. A filthy beast. He wants you, and he can't have you."

"What *are* you talking about?" Raymond demanded. "He wants our help."

"That isn't what his scent said," Jean insisted. "Did you see the way he kept sniffing the air? He was checking you out."

"Of all the ridiculous…." Raymond found himself at a loss for words at the utter absurdity of Jean's assertion. "Okay, first of all, your prejudices are showing and I don't like it. Secondly, even if he was checking me out, he can look all he wants. That doesn't mean I have to look back. The last time I checked, I'd made promises to you that I have no intention of breaking, no matter who's looking at me. And before you say something about him being a werewolf or taking what he wants or whatever other inane comment is about to come out of your mouth, how many times do I have to remind you I'm not helpless? Even if he were to come on to me in some tangible way, I'm perfectly capable of rebuffing him, and my magic *will* work on him if he refuses to take no for an answer. Now, I'd like to know what's going on and see if I can help him. We did expand the mandate of l'ANS to include all magical races, and as a branch of l'ANS, we should offer our services to anyone in need. You, however, are going to the réfectoire to find Orlando, and you're going to stay there with him and Alain until I come find you."

"But—"

"No," Raymond interrupted. "No buts. Go sit with Alain and Orlando. I will deal with Iserin."

"Fine, but if you aren't in the réfectoire in half an hour, I'm coming to look for you," Jean insisted.

"Jean, listen to yourself," Raymond said. "You're acting like a Neanderthal, and I don't find it attractive. If I need help, all I have to do is call for it. You'd feel it and be here immediately. Even if everything else I said is somehow false, he can't touch the bond between our hearts. If I needed you, you'd know."

It was the one argument Jean could not refute. His scowl softened a little as he stroked down Raymond's back over the mark that bound them. Letting his hand drop, he turned and walked toward the réfectoire.

Shaking his head, Raymond went back into his office. "My apologies, monsieur Iserin. My partner gets… possessive at times."

"I wondered," Iserin replied. "There was something between you, but the scent is a new one."

"Jean is the chef de la Cour of Paris, the alpha of the vampires there, I suppose you would call him, and I am his Consort," Raymond explained. The werewolf did not need to know the rest. "He has gone to see to some other matters while we discuss your dilemma."

"A wise choice, probably," Iserin replied. "Our two races have a long history of... disagreements."

"I suspected as much," Raymond said with a chuckle, "but working with me, having my help, will mean dealing with him as well."

"He isn't going to like that."

"That's my problem," Raymond replied. "Your problem is your people. If I come around to try to help find a solution, Jean will come with me. Will they accept that?"

"They will if I tell them to," Iserin said. "A werewolf pack is not a democracy."

Raymond nodded. "All right, then. Tell me as much as you can about the problem. The more I know, the better I'll be able to start searching for a solution."

LORENS HESITATED a moment longer, studying the face of the wizard on the other side of the imposing desk. He had taken a huge chance in coming here, a choice that could be viewed as a sign of weakness by his pack, but he did not see any other path forward.

"We haven't had a live birth in three years, and we haven't had any pregnancy go past the first few weeks in over eighteen months. In probably the past six months, we haven't even had any pregnancies."

"How big is your pack?" Raymond asked. "Surely births aren't that common in a relatively small group of people, and werewolves have never been highly fertile, at least not that I've ever read or heard."

"But that's just it," Lorens said. "Werewolves are supposed to be fertile. We were once a pack of hundreds. We have rituals to control that fertility so the pack leader can control the size of their pack, which is why our births have always seemed rare, but this is different. The ritual to grant fertility no longer seems to be working. There are about fifty people in the pack now, twenty of whom are of childbearing age. Six months with no pregnancies would be nothing to worry about if we hadn't seen a steady decrease in numbers."

"Have you changed anything in the ritual?" Raymond asked, going through a mental list of reasons an established ritual might no longer work.

"Nothing," Lorens said. "I've consulted every text in our library about the origins and details of the fertility rituals, and we did everything the way it has always been prescribed."

"Did you change location?" Raymond suggested. "Certain places have far more magical power than others."

"No, the glen where we mate for procreation is the one my pack has used for generations, ever since my ancestors founded it," Lorens replied.

"Has anything changed around the den?" Raymond asked. "A landslide, a forest fire, new construction, old construction demolished, anything that might affect the magical resonance of the area?"

"What does magic have to do with it?" Lorens asked. "We're werewolves, not wizards."

Raymond boggled at the absurdity of the statement. "If you don't think magic is involved, why are you here asking me? I am happy to try to help, but I'm a wizard, and magic is what I do. Whatever solution I could find, magic will be a part of it."

And there was the rub, as far as Lorens's pack—and every other pack he had approached for help—was concerned. Magic had no place in the lives of werewolves.

"We don't practice magic," Lorens said.

"Maybe you don't, but you *are* magical creatures, the same as the vampires are," Raymond said. "Magic allows the vampires to survive far beyond a human lifespan by drinking blood. Magic allows werewolves to change form. Perhaps you don't practice magic the way wizards do, but there can be no doubt that magic dwells within you. Perhaps that is the problem. Perhaps you've lost touch with that magic and so can't consummate the ritual despite saying the words and going through the motions. What other rituals do you do? Have they lost their effectiveness too?"

The light in the wizard's eyes should have been disconcerting, but it reassured Lorens instead. He did not believe the solution lay in magic, but at the very least, the tales of the cruelty and callousness of magical practitioners had proven false. Everything about the man in front of him, from his expression to his scent, proclaimed his honesty and his fascination with the problem Lorens had brought to him. Adenet would not like it, given his insistence that wizards and their magic somehow damaged the inherent life force around them, but Adenet would have to deal with it. Lorens would not survive watching Edine collapse again as she had done when the last ritual failed.

"The only other ritual that could be considered magic is that of turning someone into a werewolf," Lorens said. "We haven't had anyone petition to join the pack recently, so I don't know if it still works or not, but even that is not really magic. It is simply redirecting the life force of the person being changed."

"I don't imagine changing someone simply to see if the ritual still works would be advisable," Raymond said, "so we will have to pursue other avenues of exploration. Who completes the rituals for your pack? Is that something you do, or is there someone else I should consult with?"

"We have a shaman, the spiritual leader of our pack, who conducts rituals at my side, but he was not supportive of my decision to come here," Lorens said. "We will have to persuade him to help."

"Would it be easier to approach a different pack?" Raymond asked. "Perhaps one whose shaman is more open-minded?"

"You would have to convince the king as well as the shaman in any other pack, and my pack is the main pack in France. The others splintered off from us at various times in the past. Leave Adenet to me. I will bring him around, but what are you going to do?"

"First I'm going to do what I do best," Raymond said, "and learn everything I can about lycans, and then I hope I'll be able to study your ritual to see the ebb and flow of power within it. Hopefully that way we'll be able to pinpoint the moment when it breaks down. I study magic. I should be able to trace the lines of power through the words and actions you use. If I can, maybe we can see where that power goes astray. It won't happen overnight, but we didn't win l'émeute des sorciers nor understand the partnerships that arose from that overnight either. We will approach this as methodically as we approach everything here at l'Institut, and we will find a solution if there is one to be found."

"Thank you," Lorens said, rising and shaking Raymond's hand. "Should I stay in Dommartin or return to my pack until you've learned more?"

"You're welcome to stay here at l'Institut for as long as you'd like," Raymond offered. "We have rooms set aside for guests, but it will take me at least a few days to research the problem. I don't know how long you would be comfortable away from home."

"My wolf is happiest on pack lands and at my mate's side," Lorens admitted. "If you don't need me here, I'd rather go home."

"That would probably be easier for Jean as well," Raymond agreed. "He wasn't happy about leaving me here to talk to you without him."

"I am the alpha of my pack," Lorens said. "One of my responsibilities is to bless and support mated pairs. You may not be a werewolf and your mate even less, but I recognize a bond when I see one. I'm no threat to you."

"I'll make sure to tell him that," Raymond said, already envisioning their conversation. Jean needed a reminder of just how capable Raymond was of protecting himself. "Do you have a number where I can reach you? We can make arrangements once I have a better sense of things."

Lorens gave Raymond his number, and Raymond walked him out.

The moment Payet left his side, Lorens slumped against the nearest tree. He had secured Payet's help. Now he had to hope it made a difference.

# Chapter 3

"WHAT THE hell was that?" Raymond demanded. "From the minute Iserin showed himself, you were like some... God, I don't even know what the word is. You are the most civilized, controlled man I know, but all that vanished the moment he appeared."

"He's a monster, an animal," Jean replied with a shrug. "He doesn't deserve any better."

"He was a guest at l'Institut," Raymond retorted, herding Jean ahead of him toward their bedroom. It would seem his vampire needed a lesson in humility, but while Raymond had no qualms about giving him one, he would not do it where others could see. "And as such, he deserved our respect and our attention to his problems."

Jean scowled, opening his mouth to reply, but Raymond flicked his wrist, aiming a clean sock from the drawer at Jean's mouth. Jean grabbed it and pulled it free. "What was that?"

"If you're going to talk nonsense, I'm going to put a sock in it for you," Raymond retorted. "When you're ready to talk sense, I'll take it out."

"You know I'll just pull it free."

"Maybe," Raymond said. He would only get one chance at this. If he miscalculated his spells, he doubted he would catch Jean off guard a second time. Hoping to lull his prey into complacency, he sat on the edge of the bed and pulled his shoes off. "I just wish you would look at the drivel you're spouting and realize how asinine it is."

"Werewolves have a long history of taking what isn't theirs."

"There you go again," Raymond said. "You've never met Lorens Iserin before today. He may be a werewolf, but that doesn't make him like any other werewolves you may have met. Couthon wasn't like any other vampires, but how would you feel if someone judged you by his actions? Deal with him and his actions."

"He was sniffing around my Consort," Jean said. "That's not exactly the path to my good graces."

"Your Consort who happens to be one of the more powerful wizards in France," Raymond reminded him. "Iserin didn't try anything. He has his own mate and it was their problems that drove him here, but even if he had made a pass at me, he wouldn't have succeeded. You keep forgetting who I am and what I'm capable of."

Jean's expression suggested he was tired of the conversation already, but Raymond could not let it go quite yet. When Jean came to bed, stripped to the waist, Raymond took his chance. The ties from the heavy bed curtains that had once been necessary to protect Jean from stray rays of sunlight provided the bonds Raymond needed to pin his lover to the bed. The moment the cords circled his wrists, Jean fought them, but even his preternatural strength could not overcome Raymond's magic. The ties pulled tight, leaving Jean spread-eagle on the bed, glaring at Raymond with all his might.

"You think this proves something?"

"Yes, as a matter of fact," Raymond said. "I think it proves you're not as invincible as you think you are, and it proves that ingenuity will serve even when magic won't. I can't cast a spell on you and have it work, even one to shut you up when you're being an idiot, but I can cast one on the bedding to hold you here until you're ready to listen to sense. I'm going to dinner and to make some calls so I can see about helping Iserin and his pack. When I get back, maybe you'll be ready to reconsider your prejudices."

The blast of anger and betrayal that flooded Raymond's mind nearly undid his resolve, but Raymond refused to budge. He could send someone else to work directly with the werewolves, but he could not let Jean's biases poison everyone around them. L'Institut's primary focus might be the partnerships that brought vampires and wizards together with extraordinary results, but their full mandate included research into magical conundrums across the spectrum. Lorens's infertility fit the bill.

Raymond sent back a wave of love, devotion, and determination, hoping Jean would understand. Their relationship had taught them both much when it came to compromising, but on this one issue, Raymond could not budge.

"WHERE'S JEAN?" Martin Delacroix, one of the researchers working at l'Institut, asked when Raymond came into the réfectoire for dinner. Martin had joined the staff of l'Institut six months earlier on sabbatical from Canada and had found his partner in the chef de la Cour of Autun.

Raymond had come to consider him a friend, but some things were too private to share even with the men he had fought beside during the war.

"He's tied up at the moment," Raymond said. Thierry would have detected the lie in his voice, but Martin did not know him that well yet. "Is Denis joining us tonight?"

"Not tonight," Martin said. "He was meeting with his Cour. Renaud's trial starts in a few days, and Adèle wants some of the vampires to testify about Renaud's former leadership and Denis's coup d'état. She thinks the defense will try to use losing his position as grounds for losing his mind, and she wants to combat that as thoroughly as possible by proving he'd lost touch with reality well before Denis deposed him."

"That makes sense," Raymond said. "How is Pascale taking all of this?" Pascale Auboussin, Adèle's vampire partner, had been turned against her will by the former chef de la Cour of Autun a few months earlier, triggering a frantic hunt for the culprit that had ended in Martin and Denis becoming partners as well. Raymond fully expected to have to testify when it all went to trial, since he and Jean had been part of the chase that had resulted in Renaud's capture.

"As well as can be expected, I suppose," Martin said. "We don't see a lot of her when Adèle is on police business, although Denis asks after her every time. Adèle always assures us she's adjusting. It has to help having a wizard for a partner. It gives her the freedom to go about a mostly normal life again."

"Yes," Raymond agreed. "Give them all my best if you see them this evening. I'm afraid I'll be up to my elbows in werewolf lore tonight."

"Werewolves?" Thierry asked as he and Sebastien joined them at the faculty table. "That's not your usual fare."

"No, it's not, but I had an unusual visitor today, and if I'm going to help him, I'm going to have to learn more about werewolves," Raymond replied as he turned back to Martin. "I don't suppose you're an expert in their mythology and just haven't mentioned it before."

"Sorry," Martin said. "The closest I've come is a footnote to an article I read about a couple of witches—British ones, I think—mating with werewolves and being turned in the US. I could probably find it again if you think it would help you."

"Unless they were involved in the fertility rituals of their new packs, it probably wouldn't be useful," Raymond said. "Thank you, though. I'll keep it in mind if it comes to that. If nothing else, I could try to contact them and talk to them as one user of magic to another."

"They are, or were—I don't know what being changed to werewolves might have done to their abilities—either way, they were witches, not wizards," Martin said.

"What's the difference?" Sebastien asked. "Isn't it just a matter of semantics?"

"Yes and no," Raymond said. "It's a question of how we draw power. You've watched Thierry work. His power comes from the earth, from the stone itself and his connection to it. Mine comes from water, Alain's from air, Adèle's from fire, and so on. We make a connection with the elements and we channel power through that. A witch, on the other hand, doesn't associate with the elements so much as with the life force of all creation. They use a lot more herbs and potions along with their magic and a lot less pure magic. Not that they can't cast a spell if they need to. They can be quite powerful, but they get their energy from a different source and channel it in a different way."

"How do you know if you're a witch or a wizard?" Sebastien asked.

"It isn't mutually exclusive," Raymond explained. "With the right teacher, I'm sure I could learn to draw power the way they do, and I'm sure they could each find a resonance with one of the elements, but they made their first magical connections through incantations and rituals and I made mine with water, and so I became a wizard and they became witches. It's not worth learning a new way of doing magic when there's still so much to learn about my own methods. I would imagine they feel the same way, although I would never refuse to teach a witch who was interested in our methods."

"It tends to be a traditional thing as well," Martin said. "You see a lot more British witches than wizards, probably a legacy of the Druidic and Celtic traditions, whereas Europeans or people of European descent tend to lean more toward wizardry than witchcraft. Québec is an interesting mix for that very reason. The farther east you are, the more likely you are to find wizards, but as you move west into the English-speaking portions of the province and then into Ontario and the rest of Canada, you find more and more witches and fewer wizards."

"Interesting," Sebastien said, "although I don't guess it really makes much difference to me. I have a wizard and I'm happy with him. The rest is just fascinating trivia."

"About the witches, anyway," Raymond agreed, "but not about the werewolves. I've got a werewolf pack asking for help, and I don't even know where to start."

"By showing them the door," Sebastien muttered.

Thierry turned his head to stare at his partner so fast Raymond would have laughed if the reaction had not stunned him almost as much as it did Thierry. Raymond had thought Jean's reaction stemmed from some personal experience that had soured him on werewolves, but Jean and Sebastien had not been on speaking terms for nearly four hundred years, so they almost certainly had not had the same experience.

"Why would you say something like that?" Thierry asked.

"Because werewolves are filthy, stinking animals," Sebastien replied. "No good ever comes of associating with them."

"You didn't even meet the werewolf today," Raymond said. "How could you have the slightest idea what might come out of that conversation?"

"They're werewolves," Sebastien repeated as if that statement told Raymond everything he needed to know. Maybe it did not tell him everything, but it did tell him one important thing. Whatever was driving the vampires to react so strongly to the werewolves, it appeared instinctual, not experiential.

"Not the most open-minded attitude there," Thierry commented. "You sure you want to judge an entire race without meeting one first?"

Sebastien had the good grace not to answer that question, but Raymond could tell he hadn't changed his mind. If the reaction was really going to be this strong, though, he had a different problem. He couldn't endanger the partnerships of any of the paired wizards and vampires by asking a paired wizard to work on this project, but given how thoroughly his life had become entangled with Jean's and with the research going on at l'Institut, the vast majority of his contacts had vampire partners.

"I don't suppose you know any unpartnered wizards with an interest in werewolves, Thierry?"

"Not off the top of my head, but I could ask around," Thierry offered. "I take it you think this isn't going to be a theoretical problem."

"When are they ever?" Raymond replied. "If I'm going to keep my word to Iserin, I'm going to need someone who can move freely within his pack, and from the tenor of Sebastien's and Jean's comments, someone with a vampire in tow isn't going to work out, since the werewolves aren't any happier about the idea than the vampires are."

"I'll ask around," Thierry agreed. "If all you need is eyes and ears on the ground, you could ask Eric and Vincent. I don't think they have any particular background where lycans are concerned, but they're levelheaded, reasonably powerful, and aren't saddled with a vampire."

"Saddled?" Sebastien said, his voice a low growl.

"In this case, yes," Thierry said. "If you'd swallow your attitude, we could volunteer, but since you've got something stuck in your craw, we have to pass on this one."

"Something stuck...."

"Argue about it later," Raymond said when Sebastien sputtered to silence. "That's a good idea, Thierry. If nothing else, I know no one will get anything over on those two. They didn't survive behind Serrier's lines for over two years by being weak or fools."

Thierry might have argued with the "fools" part of Raymond's statement, especially where Vincent was concerned, since Vincent had genuinely sided with Serrier and not changed sides until late in the game. Eric, though, had managed to spy for the Milice through the entire war and live to tell about it. Thierry figured that made the man either brilliant or stupidly lucky. Regardless of which it was, they would be sufficiently wary of any underhandedness that might come from the werewolves, and could gather information for Raymond until they could find someone to take over the project.

"Do you want to call them since you know the details?" Thierry asked. "I don't mind checking in with them, but all I can really do is have them call you."

"I'll call them," Raymond said. "First thing tomorrow morning. I have some other things to take care of tonight."

Like an incredibly angry vampire tied to his bed.

They finished eating and Raymond excused himself, citing business to attend to, although from the look on his friends' faces, he doubted he had actually fooled any of them. Deciding it didn't matter— the others had partnerships of their own and knew what they entailed— he climbed the stairs of the Abbot's Lodge to the old abbot's quarters, which had been transformed into an apartment for him and Jean. If it was slightly less ornately decorated than Jean's apartment in Paris, Raymond chose to attribute that to the year they had lived there compared to the two hundred years Jean had spent filling his apartment with museum-quality pieces. They had left most of the apartment in

Paris intact since they still spent a fair amount of time there when Jean dealt with the Cour, but they had moved Jean's beautiful four-poster canopy bed with the thick black velvet curtains to l'Institut. Raymond hoped Jean would not decide to send it back to Paris after Raymond's stunt tonight.

When he had made the decision to force Jean to examine his behavior, he had assumed Jean was acting out of the stubbornness and sense of righteousness that made him such a good leader. Now, having watched Sebastien have a nearly identical reaction at the mere thought of werewolves, even without the provocation of their presence, Raymond wondered if something deeper had been triggered by putting the two magical races together. Perhaps it was not a question of stubbornness but of some deeper instinct Raymond could not understand and Jean might not be able to control. They had talked more than once about what Jean called the beast within him, the instincts that drove him to feed. Perhaps the incident today stemmed from that as well, in some way that currently eluded Raymond.

One way or another, he owed his vampire an apology.

Raymond opened the door to their bedroom, half-convinced Jean would have found a way to free himself and would be long gone—but his vampire lay much as he had when Raymond left him, arms stretched above him on the bed, eyes closed, body motionless except for the rise and fall of his chest.

"I'm sorry," Jean said, eyes still closed, before Raymond could speak. "I promised you I would always support you when you became president of l'ANS after the war, and I broke that promise today. I can't work with the werewolves. That's beyond me. But I won't say or do anything in their presence that will undermine your work with them."

The sincerity in the softly spoken words and in the bond between them nearly took Raymond to his knees. Of all the outcomes he had imagined as he climbed the stairs to their rooms, this had not even figured on his list.

"I apologize as well," Raymond said. "I should have known you wouldn't act the way you did without reason. I still don't understand the reason, but I watched Sebastien react the same way to the mention of werewolves, and he didn't even meet Iserin today. I shouldn't have thought the worst of you."

He leaned forward and took Jean's lips with his own, kissing his lover with all the undimmed passion that had sprung to life between them on a fateful night two and a half years before. That passion had only grown stronger as they committed to one another and to a life together. Immediately Jean strained at the bonds holding his hands in place, but Raymond didn't cast the spell that would release his partner. He had plans for the evening now that Jean had apologized—plans that would be derailed the moment Jean's hands were free. Instead Raymond focused on all the love he felt for the man beneath him, investing it in the kiss as he showered his devotion on his lover. He wanted Jean to *know* to the depths of his being how thoroughly Raymond desired him, how deeply Raymond needed him.

Jean opened beneath him, giving Raymond access to his mouth. Raymond felt the slight graze of Jean's fangs, but that only heightened his need and his determination to make their loving all about Jean for once. He took his time, exploring Jean's mouth again as if they had not kissed countless thousands of times since they had become lovers, as if they had not made hard, fast love that morning before rising to face the day and its myriad tasks. No, he wanted to make this time like the first time all over again.

The thought made him smile. Jean had come to him flushed with magic and need, overloaded with power from the spell they had cast to rein in the wild magic from the Rite d'équilibrage gone wrong, and Raymond had given in. That night he had told himself he had no choice, that the magic was too strong, but he had known better even then. Now, with Jean as his partner and a brand on his skin proclaiming him Jean's Avoué for anyone who would ever see it, he didn't even try to pretend he had been anything but a willing participant in a series of events that had gone off course the moment they began the Rite d'équilibrage.

"Don't fight me," Raymond said as he broke their kiss and rose to strip away the sweater, shirt, and trousers he had donned against the late fall chill. He finished undressing Jean as well, not wanting anything between them. "You told me our first night together that you could only ever let go of everything else and simply be Jean when you were with me. Let me remind you how good that can feel."

"Raymond," Jean hissed in protest, but Raymond ignored him, stretching out at Jean's side so he could press their bodies together and lick and nibble his way along Jean's jawline and up to his ear.

Before meeting Jean, he had always imagined a vampire would smell of earth and decay, like fallen leaves on the forest floor, but like every other preconception he had of vampires, he had learned differently as he had gotten to know Jean. No, if anything, his lover smelled more like spring rain, fresh and crisp, with only a hint of the power of summer storms to come. Raymond buried his face in Jean's shoulder-length brown hair where it cascaded over the pillow and simply breathed as the silky strands covered his face. He could lie that way for hours, wallowing in the contact, but the lure of Jean, bound and helpless to stop anything Raymond might do to him, was too tempting to resist for long. Raymond nuzzled the spot behind Jean's ear that matched one of Jean's favorite places to feed from Raymond.

Raymond had asked him once if it would not be easier to feed from his pulse point, but Jean had assured him that while it was quicker, he preferred to linger, drawing out the pleasure between them for as long as possible. Their Aveu de Sang protected them both from the effects of overfeeding, but that had not always been the case between them, and Raymond had benefited more than once from Jean's self-control.

Tonight, Jean would benefit from his.

He sucked on that little patch of skin, knowing Jean would remember the same conversation and the same nights of lovemaking.

Jean squirmed on the bed, pulling pointlessly at his bonds. He might have the strength to break the bedframe that held the ties in place, but with magic supplementing the strength of the ties themselves, those would never give. He had tasted the breadth of Raymond's power as they worked together for various magical rituals. He knew better than to underestimate the spell that held his arms in place, and since he didn't want a broken bed, he had no real choice but to lie back and give Raymond control of their lovemaking.

The teasing pressure below his ear drove him wild. He loved to sink his fangs into Raymond's neck at that exact spot when he took Raymond from behind, either spooned against him lovingly or fucking frantically in a rush for release. Now, though, it was Raymond's teeth on his skin rather than the reverse. Raymond's incisors would not pierce flesh and draw blood, but the pressure made Jean's fangs drop with the need to reciprocate, to join with his lover in the most intimate way known to his kind. "Please."

"What?" Raymond murmured against his ear. "Do you want to bite me? You just fed this morning."

"It's not about being hungry," Jean said. "It's about being close to you."

Raymond knew that. More than once, he had found release from nothing but Jean's fangs in his flesh, usually with those fangs in the spot on his chest he refused to let heal, the intimacy of giving of his body to nourish his partner more powerful than anything he had ever known. Tonight, though, he wanted something different. He wanted to be the one to create the intimacy between them rather than let Jean do it through the exchange of blood.

"Then let me be close to you."

How was he supposed to resist a request like that, Jean wondered before deciding he wasn't supposed to resist it at all. He was supposed to give his Avoué what he needed, the same as he had always done and had sworn to always do. Usually Raymond was perfectly happy to follow Jean's lead, but tonight he needed to be in charge, and Jean ceded to that desire with grace. "As close as you want."

The contact of skin against skin was as electric as it had ever been, not at all dulled by familiarity or routine. Raymond stretched against the full length of Jean's body, not pushing aside the cloth that separated their legs yet. The time would come for that, but for the moment, he wanted to make the most of the anticipation. He kissed his way up Jean's bound arm, tracing the lines of muscle apparent beneath the pale skin. That was the only thing about Jean, other than his fangs, that might give away his nature. Even in the height of summer, his skin remained kissed by Artemis, not Apollo.

"What are you laughing at?" Jean asked beside him.

"Nothing important," Raymond said. "Just being fanciful. Stop trying to read my mind and enjoy what I'm doing to you."

Jean closed his eyes and relaxed on the bed again, concentrating on the brush of Raymond's lips and tongue over his skin rather than on whatever stray thoughts populated his lover's busy brain. He could count the number of times since they had made their Aveu de Sang that Raymond's brain had been completely still, and he treasured every one of them. That would not happen tonight. Tonight Raymond would make sure Jean's brain shut down instead. Jean silently promised to return the favor the next chance he got.

Raymond kissed over the curve of Jean's bicep and the bend of his elbow to the slender forearm and the long fingers Jean used with such wicked acuity to drive Raymond wild.

Jean moaned when Raymond sucked on his fingers, each in turn, lingering over them with the same diligence he showed each time he sucked Jean's cock. Jean jerked against his bonds, trying to reach for Raymond to pull him closer, but the ties held him fast, creating a sense of helplessness he had not known since he had become a vampire and learned to control the beast inside him. His instincts railed against his confinement, but he inhaled deeply, drawing in the scents of home and his Avoué, the two things guaranteed to settle him. Here in their rooms, with Raymond at his side, nothing could harm him. His wizard would never allow it.

Raymond thought Jean needed a reminder of his abilities, but Jean never forgot. He had witnessed too much at Raymond's side to ever forget how much power his lover could command with a twitch of his fingers or the flick of his wand. Raymond rarely doused them in rain showers when they were making love anymore, not like he had when they first consummated their Aveu de Sang, but magic surrounded them, intertwined with the fabric of their daily lives. The problem was not discounting Raymond's abilities but fearing to underestimate the werewolf's perfidy. Raymond would insist Jean had no reason to judge the werewolf as he had done, and Raymond might even be right—but some reactions strained Jean's control, and the sight of the werewolf sniffing around his Avoué had been more than he could take.

He pushed that aside. The werewolf was gone and Raymond was here with him, safe and sound and completely in control. Jean relaxed and gave in to that. He hadn't lied all those months ago when he told Raymond that everyone else expected him to play some role or another and that only with Raymond could he let down his guard. Nonetheless, he had fallen into the habit of taking charge in the bedroom the same way he took charge in the Cour, not keeping his guard up—an impossible task given the bond between them—as much as remaining in control of their interactions and, most especially, of himself.

Raymond had reminded Jean more than once that Jean didn't have to be in control, even of the beast within him, around Raymond. He could give in even to that nightmare and Raymond would hold his own against it. If experience was any guide, he would not only hold his own but revel in every minute of it. Tonight, though, it would not be a question of Raymond holding his own but of Jean giving in, totally and completely, to the man he had pledged himself to for all eternity. He might find another lover after Raymond passed from this life, but he would never have another Avoué.

Raymond felt Jean's capitulation in his body and in his mind. The moment it came, he abandoned his teasing of Jean's fingers for another kiss, more voracious this time. Jean responded ardently but made no move to wrest control from Raymond, not even to play his fangs across Raymond's tongue as he so often did when they kissed.

Raymond debated releasing Jean's hands—Jean had given in, which was what Raymond wanted—but he decided against it. If Jean's hands were free, he would try to return the pleasure Raymond was lavishing on him. While Raymond was not opposed to that in principle, tonight he needed to focus on Jean, on how much he loved the vampire, and he needed Jean to focus on how much he could trust Raymond to take care of himself and of everything else. In the Cour, with the other vampires, with the rest of the world, Jean would always be the strong one, but here with Raymond, he could let down those walls, and Raymond intended to take down every single stone until nothing was left but the core of the man he had bound himself to for the rest of his life.

He abandoned Jean's mouth for the delights of his neck and shoulders, kissing his way over every inch, bringing a flush of desire to the alabaster skin. Normally that tinge of color only accompanied Jean feeding from him, but Jean had feasted that morning, enough apparently for the effects to linger even half a day later. Raymond smiled and traced his fingers over the pale-pink flesh. Jean would never let anyone else see him flushed this way.

He looked up and met Jean's eyes. His pupils were dilated, his face as flushed as his chest, but he was not out of his mind with need yet, and that was what Raymond wanted. "Trust me."

"I do," Jean swore. "No one else would have gotten close enough to tie me up this way even if they'd had the strength or power to do so."

"I know," Raymond said, "but you're still holding back, still guarding yourself. Let go."

Jean took a deep breath, trying to do as Raymond asked, but even with his Avoué, he could not release that one small part of himself he kept chained. He had killed the night he was turned because he hadn't known how to control himself. He had sworn then never to let go again. He knew what Raymond wanted, but he wasn't sure he could give it to his lover, even bound as he was, even knowing Raymond could escape with a whispered incantation if he needed to. He had spent over a thousand years keeping his demons in check. To loosen those reins now went against every tenet he had lived by all those years.

Raymond found one ruched nipple and drew it into his mouth before sucking on it lightly. Jean squirmed a little beneath the contact, a soft moan escaping his lips. He wanted to run his fingers through Raymond's dark hair, maybe not guiding his actions as much as encouraging them, but he couldn't move his arms. He settled for arching his back as best he could, pressing his chest into the tender caress.

Raymond shifted so he could see Jean's face. His lover's desire was easily visible in the taut set of his features, but Raymond wanted more than that. He wanted Jean wild with need, completely unfettered for once.

Taking a chance, he bit down on the nipple in his mouth with more force than he had ever dared before. Jean reared up within his bonds, thrashing on the bed as he tried instinctively to reach for Raymond. Raymond watched as he took a deep breath and subsided, but he could feel the effort it had taken.

"Stop fighting yourself."

"You don't know what you're asking."

Raymond thought he did. The one time Jean had lost some degree of his infamous control, Raymond had ended up covered in fang marks and fucked six ways to Sunday, and he had loved every minute of it despite Jean's later remorse. Raymond had convinced Jean to stop being quite so careful with him after that, but Jean had not let go that way since. Raymond intended to drive him to it again.

"So show me." He pulled away from Jean long enough to run his hands over the bedposts that anchored Jean's arms. "There, now you don't have to worry about breaking the bed. You can't get free. You can't hurt me. Whatever monster you think dwells inside you, it can't do any damage tonight, so let it go. For one night, stop fighting whatever internal battle you live with every day and just *be* with me."

"You'll hate me for it."

Raymond closed his eyes and focused on the presence in his mind that never fully went away, the bundle of emotions that was the core of Jean's being. In his mind's eye, he cradled that precious gift, wrapping it in the strength of his magic and his love. "I could never hate you. You read my emotions in my blood and through our bond, but I can do the same, remember? I know you. That 'monster' is part of you, not something to be rejected but something to be embraced."

Raymond could feel Jean struggling with his assertion and decided words alone would not be enough. He would have to prove the truth of his assertions by pushing Jean until he lost control and then loving him still.

To that end, he returned to Jean's chest, focusing on the opposite side from before, licking and sucking, nipping and even biting occasionally. He could feel Jean fighting to overcome a millennium of self-conditioning. "What do you want?"

"My hands free," Jean said, an honest answer, but Raymond knew it went beyond that. The one time Jean had come close to losing control, he had wanted far more than just his hands free. He had wanted Raymond at his complete mercy, submissive to his every whim. Raymond had ended up covered in love bites and as thoroughly fucked as he had ever been. He intended to return the favor tonight.

"When you stop holding back, we'll see," he offered, biting sharply at Jean's nipple before latching on to the patch of skin directly above it and sucking at it until he raised a bruise. Jean cried out in surprise, but the pulse of desire through their bond grew stronger and Raymond felt the walls around Jean's beast crumble just a little. He kissed his way back up to Jean's neck, gentling the contact again. He could provoke Jean's temper and make him lose control that way. If he could draw Jean's beast to the surface, he could tempt it free through his submission as he had done the last time, but he really wanted Jean to let go of his own accord. The end result might be the same, but Raymond suspected Jean's reaction in the morning would be completely different if he chose to let go instead of being pushed into it.

Jean could feel the instincts he had fought so long to control surging to the fore, lured by the willing body of his Avoué and the possibility of freedom, but the vision of the man Jean had killed swam before his eyes. He might not be able to drain Raymond the way he had done that long-ago victim, but he had sworn never to be that monster again, and not even Raymond's insistence that he would love Jean no matter what could assuage all his fears. Resisting grew more difficult as Raymond combined gentle caresses with rough bites to both goad and lure him out.

"What do you want?" Raymond asked again.

*To fuck you senseless.* "You."

"You're still holding back," Raymond said, as if Jean was somehow not fully aware of the internal walls Raymond was dismantling with each passing second. "Tell me what you really want."

"To fuck you," Jean snapped, losing that much control. He took a deep breath and tried to draw back, but Raymond would not let him, swooping down on Jean's cock and drawing it deep into his mouth. Jean reared up as much as he could within his bonds, fighting in earnest now. He needed to flip Raymond beneath him, to drive into his willing body and take what belonged to him.

Raymond felt the surge of lust and anger and need through their bond. He let his treat slip from his lips and kissed Jean's stomach lightly. "Stop fighting yourself and tell me what you need."

"You beneath me, ass in the air, begging for more until you come so many times you pass out."

"That's more like it," Raymond said with a grin, "but you're still holding on to your control. By your fingertips, maybe, but you are." He reached for the lube on the table by their bed and smeared some over his fingers.

He nudged Jean's knee, not entirely sure Jean would spread his legs and grant Raymond access to his body, but Jean acquiesced, allowing Raymond to kneel between his thighs. Raymond lowered his head again and licked at Jean's sac as he teased around his lover's entrance with his fingers.

Jean moaned and pulled at the curtain ties again, but Raymond's magic held, leaving words as his only recourse. "You realize what's going to happen when you finally let me go, don't you?"

Raymond had a pretty good idea, but the more Jean dwelt on it, the closer he would come to letting go and giving Raymond what he wanted. "Not at all."

"Liar."

"Tell me," Raymond said. "What's going to happen when I finally let you go?"

Raymond swore he heard the bed frame creak as Jean strained to pull his arms free. Raymond lifted his head long enough to check Jean's wrists, but the spell he had used to strengthen the cords had also cushioned the twined threads so that no abrasions appeared on Jean's pale skin.

"I'm going to fuck you harder than you've ever been fucked," Jean swore. "You won't be able to sit for a week without feeling me inside you."

"How is that different from any other night?" Raymond teased, working his fingers deeper into Jean's passage until he found Jean's sweet spot. "You never go that long without making love to me again anyway."

"So deep you'll feel me all the way to your throat."

"I already know what it feels like to have you in my throat," Raymond reminded him before suiting actions to words and taking Jean all the way inside his mouth and down his throat. Jean thrust hard, nearly tripping Raymond's gag reflex, but Raymond drew back and then went deeper in concert with Jean's motions so that he controlled their lovemaking again despite Jean's attempt to take over. He swallowed hard as Jean thrust again, and squeezed the tip of his cock at the same time he pressed Jean's prostate.

"Putain," Jean cursed, fighting not to climax right then. He had more self-control than this, damn it, except that Raymond didn't want him in control tonight. Raymond wanted him to let go. Raymond wanted him wild with lust and need. Raymond wanted the beast within him that was never entirely sated.

Jean looked down into the glittering hazel eyes of his Avoué and stopped fighting—his orgasm, his beast, all of it. For the first time since Grégoire had coached him through caging the creature within him, he consciously let it go.

The sudden rush of salty fluid nearly choked Raymond, but he drew back enough to swallow it all. He kept up his attentions to Jean's gland, knowing he could rouse his lover again in moments, but the actions were more automatic than conscious. He was too caught in the realization that Jean had given him what he wanted. All the walls were down, the wild surging passion completely unfettered.

Now he had to tame it to his hand.

He sucked and fingerfucked Jean until the vampire was hard again. On most nights that would have taken a minute or two, given that Raymond had not found his release, and so his passion would keep Jean's high, but tonight, with Jean's inner demons unleashed, it took mere seconds. Raymond was tempted to linger and make Jean come this way a second time, purely for the power of it, but that wasn't what either of them needed. It would be too easy to turn their lovemaking—for that was what Raymond was determined it would remain, no matter how primal it became—into a power struggle.

Lifting his head, he met Jean's eyes. "If you want to fuck me, you'll have to get me ready."

"Let me go, then."

Raymond shook his head before scooting around on the bed and offering his ass to his lover. "Surely you can be more creative than that."

Jean's fangs pierced the skin of Raymond's buttocks before he could take a breath. He had expected it, of course, but the roughness of the bite was more proof that Jean had abandoned his civilized façade. He had bitten Raymond there on more than one occasion, but always before, he had taken the time to lick and prepare the area rather than simply taking as if it were his due. Raymond did not complain, though. He had long since learned the pleasure to be found in his vampire's bite, and he already knew that when the beast was sated—and it would be, because Raymond would not consider any other outcome—the bond between them that would not let Jean hurt him would reassert itself and Jean would bathe every bite mark with his tongue, speeding their healing and soothing any lingering aches.

Jean sucked hard, heedless of finesse now that he finally had Raymond within reach of his fangs. He needed blood on his tongue. He needed *Raymond's* blood on his tongue. The taste of it, the absolutely unshakable bedrock of love that permeated the life-giving elixir, soothed Jean's demon so that while it clamored to be joined with his Avoué in body as well as in blood, Jean stopped fighting the ties that kept him from speeding that process along. That in itself was a revelation. When Jean had been newly turned and out of control in his ignorance, nothing had assuaged his bloodlust, not even his first victim's blood and climax, not even his death. If Grégoire had not been there to stop him, Jean would surely have rampaged, continuing to feed from and drain everyone he met.

Perhaps the time spent under his control had tempered it, but Jean suspected he had Raymond to thank for this new state of affairs. Releasing his fangs' hold on his lover's body, he turned his head to the target of his desire and ran his tongue along Raymond's crease. Raymond shifted, straddling Jean's chest so his ass opened for Jean's attentions. For one wild second, Jean imagined sinking his fangs into the sac that bumped his chin, but that would hurt his Avoué, and to his surprise, even the monster within him had no interest in anything that would hurt Raymond.

"I love you," Jean choked out.

The sentiment came as no surprise, but Raymond hadn't expected to hear the words with Jean trussed to the bed and his demon in control. If anything, he had expected invectives until he agreed to release Jean's arms.

"I love you too," Raymond said, starting to turn around so he could kiss his lover.

"Don't move."

That was more along the lines of what Raymond had anticipated. He settled for kissing Jean's stomach softly and reaching back to spread his cheeks so Jean could rim him more easily. Jean took immediate advantage of the offer, leaving Raymond the one moaning and struggling not to come.

"Now who's holding back?" Jean goaded.

"Bite me," Raymond begged, knowing that was all it would take to send him over the edge, as aroused as he was by all the foreplay and by feeling Jean's first climax through their bond.

Jean turned his head just enough to keep his fangs from piercing anything critical and licked the sweaty skin once before driving his fangs as deep as he could. Blood rushed into his mouth as Raymond's cock twitched and covered his chest with spend. The surge of rapture in Raymond's blood and mind nearly triggered Jean's release as well, but he fought it back. If they climaxed together, it would be over, and he had not had nearly enough of his Avoué's blood or passion yet. For the first time ever, he sensed the possibility of true satiation within reach, not merely enough to hold him for a few days but enough to leave him completely satisfied. He would not let a little thing like timing keep him from achieving it. For once, self-control coincided with his demon, making staving off his release far easier than it should have been. The monster inside him might be slavering for sex and blood, but it had enough sense to realize the best way to get it was to wait for Raymond to be ready again.

A few thrusts of his tongue sufficed to start Raymond hardening against him again. "Let me loose."

"Not yet," Raymond said breathlessly, pulling away from Jean's mouth and reaching for the lube again. This would never have worked if Jean had been free, but since he was not, Raymond hovered just outside the reach of his lover's mouth and pressed slick fingers to his own entrance, adding to the moisture from Jean's tongue.

"Oh, merde," Jean groaned, his fingers itching to replace Raymond's in the tight heat, but the ties held, leaving him helpless to do anything but watch and plot revenge. "Just one finger. I want to feel it when I finally get inside you."

Raymond was tempted to challenge the assertion and ask Jean why he thought he would be getting any closer to Raymond's ass than he had already been, but any such comment would be sheer bravado when he wanted Jean inside him nearly as much as Jean wanted to be there, to judge by the emotions coming through their bond.

Raymond prepared himself slowly, drawing out the moment for both his own benefit and for Jean's titillation. The longer this went on, the more comfortable Jean would become with allowing the other side of his nature out from behind his iron control and the more convinced he would be, Raymond hoped, of Raymond's desire for every aspect of Jean's personality.

When he had thoroughly slicked the channel, he spun around and positioned himself over Jean's cock. "Is this what you want?" he teased.

Jean thrust up as if he could join their bodies already, but Raymond hovered out of reach. "Is this what you want?" Raymond insisted.

"Ride me," Jean ground out. He had no control left other than that which came from needing to hold out until Raymond released him so he could finish sating himself on his lover's body. The beast within him had surfaced and would only be satisfied by glutting itself. The rounds of sex and the little bit of blood he had taken so far had only whetted his appetite. Raymond would not know what hit him when Jean was finally free again.

Raymond slid into place, groaning at the stretch of Jean's erection inside him. As familiar as the feeling was, Jean usually delighted in stretching him first so that he was filled perfectly. Without that foreplay between them, he was tighter than usual, the stretch almost enough to burn.

"Am I hurting you?"

Raymond smiled down at the vampire on the bed beneath him, all wild eyes and bared fangs… and full of concern despite it. Raymond concentrated on the sense of well-being and joy that came from being joined with Jean in any way and pushed it out through their bond. He could say words he did not mean, but the emotions between them could not lie.

He started moving, riding Jean hard and fast now that Jean had stopped fighting his instincts. Raymond wanted to sate those desires and then fall asleep in Jean's arms, content in the knowledge he had proven his point.

Jean's demon was not so easily sated, though.

"Don't come," Jean ordered as his release threatened. "We aren't done yet."

Raymond nodded and held back as he felt Jean flood his insides, easing his passage as, still fully hard, he continued to press up into Raymond's downward movements.

"I don't know how much longer I can wait," Raymond said as Jean continued to drive up into him as if they had just started.

"Then come here and let me bite you," Jean said. "I need to taste you."

Raymond leaned forward, offering his chest or his neck, whichever Jean preferred. Jean's fangs sank into the muscle of his chest immediately, reopening the healing incisions that had not faded completely since the last time Jean had lost control of himself. Raymond cried out at the sudden redoubling of their connection, losing control of his climax and his magic. Mist coated their bodies as Jean surged inside him again, a second burst of fluid joining the first.

Raymond collapsed on top of his lover, knowing Jean would welcome his weight despite his slighter build. Taking a deep breath, he ran his hands over the cords holding Jean's arms to cancel the spell.

He sighed in relief when Jean pulled him into a tight embrace.

Only as he snuggled closer did he realize that Jean was still completely hard. He looked up at Jean questioningly.

"You told me to let the beast go," Jean said. "I need you."

Even as exhausted and wrung out as he was, Raymond felt his body react to the heat in Jean's voice.

"What do you need?"

Jean rolled to his knees and flipped Raymond onto his stomach, tugging on his hips until he lifted his ass into the air in submissive offering. Jean mounted him instantly, plunging back inside the now well-stretched passage with all the force his earlier position had denied him. He needed to take, to rampage, and the only field of battle available to him was the body beneath him, his to take. He threw his head back and let the wild power within him guide his motions.

As good as it felt, though, it was not enough. Raymond was not pleading beneath him. Jean traced the place where they were joined, watching the muscle contract and release around his cock. He wished wildly that his dual nature could give him a dual body so he could ravish Raymond even more thoroughly. He pressed a little harder with his finger, working the tip past the muscle alongside his cock. Raymond reared up at the sudden added girth, but Jean felt no protest through their bond.

He could add another finger. He could pull out and thrust his whole hand inside Raymond. He could just keep going, his wrist, his forearm, his elbow. Just climb all the way inside his lover's body.

Then his gaze landed on the brand in the center of Raymond's back and the demon inside him calmed, focused on only one thing.

Treasuring, not taking, their Avoué.

Jean slipped his finger free, then pulled back the rest of the way. He turned Raymond onto his back with gentle hands and joined their bodies again but did not resume the wild thrusting. He needed something else instead. Covering Raymond's body with his as best he could given the difference in their sizes, he licked the marks on Raymond's chest and let his fangs slide home.

There.

Satiation lay there, in the sweetness of the blood directly above Raymond's heart, in the unshaken and unshakeable bedrock of love and desire he could taste, in the absolute mindlessness that accompanied it. He had done his worst and Raymond loved him still.

Jean lost track of how long they lay that way, Raymond's blood trickling into his mouth, the stickiness of Raymond's spend between them, their hearts and minds as open to each other as Jean had ever felt them. In those moments of connection, Jean felt something he had resigned himself to never knowing again. He knew peace. For the first time in a thousand years, he felt like himself again, no inner demon driving him to do something he would regret. No expectation to be in control. Just himself, the poor monk in training with a thirst for knowledge and experience that his sequestered life would probably never give him.

He had more knowledge and experience than he had ever imagined possible in his little cell in tenth-century Paris. And now, once more, he had peace.

He licked carefully at Raymond's chest, stopping the bleeding.

"I love you."

The words were so inadequate, but Jean had none better. Fortunately Raymond did not need better. He could sense everything Jean was feeling, and the wave of joy and devotion that came through their bond told Jean everything he needed to know.

He rolled to the side, dislodging his cock from its berth. Raymond hissed slightly, but he turned immediately into Jean's embrace and rested his head on Jean's shoulder.

"You should sleep."

Raymond smiled at him. "So should you."

Jean started to reply that vampires did not sleep when he realized he did indeed feel sleepy. Another first since he was turned. He pulled the covers over them and shook the bed curtains to make sure the morning light would not disturb them. Pressing one last kiss to the top of Raymond's head, he closed his eyes and slept.

# Chapter 4

"YOU WANT us to what?"

"First, come to l'Institut and hear me out," Raymond said, "but I'm hoping you and Vincent will be willing to spend a few days, maybe a little more, with the local werewolf pack. They're having issues with their rituals not working and have asked for our help."

"You're far more qualified for something like that than Vincent or me," Eric said. "I'm an engineer and he's a mechanic. We aren't researchers."

"I know," Raymond said, "but I have a vampire for a partner, and that apparently precludes me from participating in this process. The werewolves don't want Jean around any more than Jean wants to be around them. I swore Jean and the werewolf were going to come to blows right there in my office."

"Jean?" Eric said. "He's the most controlled of all the vampires."

Raymond smothered a grin, thankful Eric could not see him. Jean had been anything but controlled the night before. "Apparently mixing vampires and werewolves is like throwing gas on an open flame, which not only eliminates me as an option but also most of the people I work with on any kind of a regular basis. I don't think the werewolves have any ulterior motive in asking for help. I think they've reached a level of desperation so extreme that they're overcoming their own fears and prejudices in asking for help, but if I'm going to send someone into a situation that could be volatile, I'd rather have it be people I know can take care of themselves. You and Vincent proved that beyond doubt by surviving the war as you did. I can tell you what to check for, and you can report your findings so I can evaluate what to try next."

"We'll have to see if we can get some time off work," Eric said. "Unless Anne-Marie wants to draft us on official ANS business, of course. The Milice was disbanded, but we're still technically on call with l'ANS."

"I haven't talked with Anne-Marie," Raymond said, "but you're probably right that I should. It will make it easier to get the help we need, once we know what that is."

"We'll come for dinner," Eric said. "You can feed us and give us a better idea of what kind of time commitment you think we're talking about, as well as the details of what you want us to do. In the meantime, we'll mention it at work so they won't be caught off guard if Anne-Marie does agree to call us in."

"Thank you," Raymond said. "We'll have dinner in the Abbot's Lodge. That way we can talk without worrying about being disturbed."

"WE'RE INVITED to l'Institut for dinner," Eric told Vincent as soon as he hung up the phone.

"Invited or summoned?" Vincent asked with a wry grin. He ran the towel over his scalp-cut hair, freshly washed from his post-work shower.

"Invited," Eric said. "You know Raymond can't summon us anymore. He stepped down from that post almost a year ago."

"I know," Vincent said, "but there are invitations and then there are *invitations*. You know as well as I do that an invitation from Raymond is still tantamount to a summons."

"Whatever it is, he thinks it's important," Eric went on. "We're having dinner in their private dining room rather than in the réfectoire."

Vincent whistled softly. "Did he give you any details?"

"Just something about werewolves having trouble with their rituals not working and vampires and werewolves not getting along," Eric replied. "Not really anything concrete, but it sounded somewhat open-ended."

"Oh, that's going to go over well at the garage," Vincent said, sarcasm heavy in his voice. "We're already shorthanded, and Antoine only gives us our five weeks of vacation grudgingly. He's going to be a bastard over anything else or any kind of change in the schedule."

"I reminded Raymond we don't work for l'ANS and can't just drop what we're doing because he called," Eric said. "If he needs us for much more than a long weekend, he's going to have to get Anne-Marie to request our participation officially. I can't afford to lose my job and neither can you. Raymond will just have to understand that."

"Hey," Vincent said, wrapping his arms around Eric's waist, "this is Raymond we're talking about, not Serrier. He's not going to flip out on us if we say no to something he asks. We left that behind two years ago."

"I know," Eric said, "but I had a rough night last night, and not even making love this morning has completely dispelled the sick sense of being back at his mercy again."

"He's dead," Vincent reminded Eric. "And so are Aguiraud, Blanchet, and all the rest. They can't hurt us anymore."

"I keep telling myself that," Eric replied, leaning back against Vincent. Eric was a large man, but Vincent was even broader through the shoulders, giving Eric the rock he needed to lean on when the memories and flashbacks got to be too much. "Sometimes I'm more successful at believing it than others."

Vincent tightened his embrace, wrapping his lover in as much security as he could provide. "We're safe now. Just remember that."


"TELL US about this problem and why you think we can help," Vincent said after they had finished dinner. "I mean, you've got to have people better qualified for this."

"Yes, but most of them have vampire partners," Raymond said, "and while I think that's to their advantage in most situations, when it comes to dealing with werewolves, it's definitely a problem. Vampires and werewolves aren't a good mix."

"Which rules you out directly. It rules also out Thierry and Alain, but only a relatively small percentage of wizards have vampire partners. You have to know people at l'ANS. People who wouldn't have problems with taking off work."

"I know plenty of people," Raymond agreed, "but I'm not sure how many of them I'd trust in a situation I can't get a real sense of. Maybe it's Jean's reaction to them rubbing off on me, but I feel like I need someone with enough paranoia to watch their backs. You stayed alive in Serrier's camp for two years when he killed as many of his own people as the Milice raids did. Eric spied for two years and survived. If anyone knows about watching their backs, it's you."

"You realize you're the only person in France who doesn't consider that a mark against us."

"You realize I'm the only other living person in France with a mark to match yours." Never mind that it was covered now by a different mark, one that would change everything if more people knew about it. He was still keenly aware of the scar Serrier had inflicted as proof of his lieutenants' loyalty.

"If we agree to do this, what do we do? We aren't researchers," Eric said.

"I know that, but you are reasonably powerful wizards, and Vincent's affinity with earth could prove particularly useful. The werewolves have stopped reproducing. Their fertility rituals are failing, and it's been getting worse. My first thought, and where Vincent could be even more useful than me, is that something has disrupted the magical resonance of the den they use for their ritual. If some portion of the power is in the place and something has changed, it could be part of the problem. If that's the case, solving their problem could be as simple as finding another place within their territory that has enough inherent power to support them again. Or it might be possible to determine what caused the disruption and restore it."

"That's not a simple undertaking," Vincent said. "It's certainly not something I could do on my own."

"But could you tell me if that might be part of the problem?" Raymond asked. "If they let you into their sacred space, could you diagnose a problem if there is one?"

"Probably," Vincent replied after a moment. "Maybe not to tell you what the problem is, but I should be able to tell you if there's any inherent power in the place and if anything is blocking it."

"If that's your first thought, what else have you considered?" Eric asked.

"I haven't," Raymond admitted. "I don't know anything about werewolves beyond the barest bones of lore, certainly not enough to have any real sense of how they function and how their rituals work. I'd love to be able to go in and observe, but even if they were willing to allow me in, they wouldn't let Jean come, and that means I won't be going either."

"Then they aren't as desperate for help as they say they are," Vincent said.

"That may be," Raymond agreed, "but I'm not sure it's something they can control. It was too immediate, almost like a reflex. I know sending you two isn't a long-term solution, but it's an initial gesture of goodwill while I do more in-depth research and try to figure out other avenues for research."

"If it's really just to check out their den and maybe look around their territory for anywhere with a better magical resonance, a weekend would probably be enough," Vincent said. "If they could wait until Friday evening for us to arrive, we could have a look around and go home Sunday night and not have to miss work. It wouldn't be a solution necessarily, but it would give you a place to start."

"That's already more than I have now," Raymond said. "Should I let Iserin know to expect you on Friday, then?"

"Tell him Saturday morning," Eric said. "Friday is our anniversary, and we already have plans."

That would make it the anniversary of a number of the couples in Raymond's circle, he realized with a jolt. He and Jean had resisted the burst of wild magic that had escaped after a Rite d'équilibrage gone wrong, which had pushed many of the wizard/vampire partnerships into becoming intimate—but he knew of several couples who counted that night as the beginning of their relationship. It also meant his and Jean's anniversary was only a few days behind.

"WHAT DID Eric and Vincent have to say?" Jean asked when he returned that evening. He had hated missing dinner with the two wizards, but Denis Langlois, chef de la Cour in Autun, had specifically requested Jean's presence at a Cour function, and Jean had not wanted to refuse. They needed a sympathetic chef de la Cour in Autun, and if missing a dinner with Eric and Vincent was the price Jean had to pay to keep Denis in power, Jean would pay it.

"They're willing to help as far as they're able," Raymond said, "but there are limits to the time they'll have available and to what they'll be able to do for us. As they pointed out repeatedly, they aren't researchers."

"Do you need to go?" Jean asked. Everything inside him rebelled at the thought, but Jean did his best to ignore that reaction. He had promised to support Raymond, and if that meant finding a way to deal with the werewolves, he would find a way.

Raymond knew what the offer cost Jean, so he shook his head. "Not yet. It might come to that eventually, but I want to talk with Anne-Marie first. Maybe she knows someone I don't or who I've forgotten, someone with an interest in werewolves who could start immediately instead of waiting for me to research everything. I could do it. I could read and study and learn what I'd need to know in order to help them, if a solution lies within our methods of magic, but it would take time. I don't know what pushed Iserin into seeking help now. The pack has about fifty members, he said, so short of a natural disaster, they aren't in danger of dying out tomorrow. Whatever it was, though, it had to have been serious for him to overcome an obvious disdain for wizards, not to mention his distrust of you."

"Iserin is the alpha," Jean said, consciously pushing aside his instinctive derision so he could help Raymond think through the problem at hand. "If he doesn't have an heir, he may be feeling pressure from within to step aside for someone who does have one or for someone younger who might have a better chance of having one."

"Why do you say that?" Raymond asked. It made sense, but it seemed an odd insight from Jean after everything he had said earlier.

Jean shrugged. "Because I can't imagine a werewolf pack is any less cutthroat than a vampire Cour, and that's how vampires would react in a similar situation. At the first sign of weakness, they look to play it to their advantage. Why shouldn't wolves be the same?"

Raymond resisted the urge to point out how ridiculous Jean's reaction to werewolves was given the parallels he was now drawing. Jean was applying his formidable intelligence and millennium of experience to the werewolves' problem, which was what Raymond really wanted. He would take the high road and not point it out.

"Can we afford to wait until this weekend to send someone to start helping?" Raymond asked. "I don't want him to lose his seat because we're slow responding."

"Call Anne-Marie in the morning," Jean said. "I might be able to answer that question if everyone concerned were vampires and I knew all the circumstances surrounding the situation. I haven't a clue where werewolves are concerned. But I would think he'd appreciate as much haste as we can make."

"BONJOUR, RAYMOND," Anne-Marie Valour, current president of l'ANS, said when Raymond called the next day. "What can I do for you?"

"I'm hoping you know someone who's as fascinated with lycan lore as I've become with vampire lore," Raymond admitted. "The local werewolf pack has come to me for help, and I don't even know where to begin."

"Oh, thank God," Anne-Marie said with a breathless laugh. "I have been looking for something to do with this kid for the past two weeks."

"What kid?" Raymond asked, not sure he liked the sound of that.

"Our new intern," Anne-Marie explained. "He's just out of college, newly come into his powers, although he seems quite strong for such a late bloomer, and he's obsessed with werewolves. Every conversation ends up scattered with analogies to werewolf lore or pack laws or other such things. I swear if he could find a werewolf pack, he'd beg to be turned just so he could live all the stuff he's read about for however long he's had this obsession."

"Maybe I shouldn't take him," Raymond said. "I don't want to be responsible for some kid who's too young to look out for himself and gets into trouble because of it. I need someone with a good head on his shoulders, not his head in the clouds."

"I didn't say he wasn't smart," Anne-Marie replied. "He's sharp as a tack. As long as his enthusiasm doesn't get the better of him, he'll be fine."

That was what worried Raymond.

"I guess I could meet with him anyway," Raymond said. "I can ask him some questions, get an idea of what we might need to do to help the werewolves, and see about finding someone other than your intern to actually do what needs to be done."

"Is there a reason you wouldn't do it yourself once you know what the problem is?" Anne-Marie asked.

Raymond sighed. He was getting tired of this conversation already because it made Jean look bad, but he was sure it would be repeated another dozen times at least. "I can't take Jean with me. Werewolves and vampires don't mix well, and you know Jean won't want me to go without him. Eric and Vincent are going to check one thing for me, but they can't really take time off indefinitely, and they don't know what they're doing any more than I do right now."

"Marc should be able to answer the 'what you're doing' question, but it might be worth keeping Eric and Vincent on call," Anne-Marie said. "For a little extra muscle, if nothing else."

"Are you authorizing me to call them up?" Raymond asked. "When I talked to them yesterday, they seemed to feel that was the only option for being away from work for more than a weekend."

"Meet Marc and see what you think," Anne-Marie said. "I'll leave it up to you since you've met the werewolves and have a better idea of the situation than I do. If you want Eric and Vincent there along with Marc, I'll sign the paperwork."

"Thank you," Raymond said. "When would be a good time for me to come to Paris to meet him?"

"He's here regular hours," Anne-Marie said. "Since he isn't working with anything vampire related, I didn't see a reason to put him on the alternate schedule."

"If he can't carry on a sentence without referencing werewolves, you'll want to keep it that way, even after I'm done with him," Raymond said. "I really wasn't kidding when I said vampires and werewolves don't mix. I thought Jean and the werewolf were going to come to blows in my office, and you know Jean is usually more controlled than that, even when he's wishing he could murder someone."

"I will remember that," Anne-Marie said. "When shall I tell him to expect you?"

Raymond looked at the calendar with his schedule of seminars and meetings at l'Institut. This was important, but so were his commitments to l'Institut, its faculty, and the vampires and wizards attending the current educational seminar. He refused to miss the session he was scheduled to present this afternoon. "Tomorrow morning," he said. "I'll come around ten."


MARC ALWAYS dressed up for work, too excited by the prospect of working for l'ANS to do anything that might give his employers a reason to reconsider his employment. When he found out he would have a meeting with Raymond Payet, former president of l'ANS and hero of l'émeute des sorciers, he spent an hour staring at his closet, trying to pick the perfect suit so he would look professional but not pretentious and, more importantly, more than ten years old. His mother insisted he would be grateful for his youthful looks when he turned forty, but at twenty-three, he would have appreciated looking more than fifteen. It was hard to make a strong first impression when the person he wanted to impress saw him as a little kid.

He settled on a conservative dark suit, light wool since it was October and cold enough to justify it without looking like he had chosen the most expensive suit in his closet just to impress monsieur Payet. Of course he had, but he hoped it would not be too obvious.

Marc rode the Métro to work rather than cast a spell because that seemed less pretentious too. He knew monsieur Payet would be arriving from Burgundy, so he would use a displacement spell, but *he* was a war hero, not some newly awakened kid with no experience to his name except what he had managed to earn in the past year. Marc figured that hardly counted compared to a wizard of monsieur Payet's fame and ability.

He arrived well before the allotted ten o'clock meeting time, not wanting to be late, but of course that got him there ridiculously early, and he had cleared his desk the day before, not wanting anything to interfere with his meeting.

"Go away," Fabienne, the administrative assistant for madame Valour said when Marc wandered past her door for the third time. "Raymond isn't here yet, and you're annoying me."

"I just don't want to make him wait," Marc protested. "I mean, he's a hero!"

Fabienne sighed. "There's no denying his contributions in defeating Serrier. I was there, in case you've forgotten. But he's just one man."

"He's one of the most powerful wizards alive," Marc insisted. "Maybe one of the most powerful wizards ever!"

"He's still just a man," Fabienne said. "I fought beside him and then I worked for him for a year, and let me tell you something I learned about him in that time."

Marc leaned forward, eager for whatever insight the vampire could offer.

Fabienne leaned in to meet him until her face was barely an inch from his.

"He hates it when people fawn over him," she said. "I understand that you want to impress him, but you won't do that by being some adoring little puppy yipping at his heels and driving him mad. If he's coming here to meet with you, he thinks you can be useful to him in some way. So prove him right. Maybe you aren't as powerful a wizard as he is. Maybe you didn't fight in l'émeute des sorciers like he did. Maybe you don't have a vampire partner, and maybe you'll never have one, but you have something he needs or he'd still be out in Dommartin with his research projects and his books. Take a deep breath, get a cup of coffee, and stop acting like you're going to jump out of your skin the second you meet him. Believe me, it won't impress him."

Marc took a deep breath as Fabienne had directed, not that it did anything to settle the mix of nerves and excitement assailing him. He had already drunk so much coffee he was afraid to drink more for fear he would have to excuse himself a dozen times during the meeting, but Fabienne's advice was sound. It did nothing to mitigate Marc's awe at the thought of getting to meet monsieur Payet, but Marc did his best to pull himself together.

A shimmer of magic resonated from the office behind Fabienne's desk, and then the door opened and madame Valour looked out. "Oh, good, you're here, Marc. Come inside and meet Raymond."

"Remember what I said," Fabienne whispered as Marc walked past her desk and into the office.

Marc had seen pictures of monsieur Payet in the news and even on the Presidents' Wall of l'ANS, but they had all been static, carrying none of the charisma of the man in person. Marc swallowed down the immediate adulation and offered his hand. "Marc Gourlin. It's an honor to meet you, monsieur Payet."

"Thank you for making the time to see me," monsieur Payet replied. "I'm sure Anne-Marie keeps you very busy. And please, call me Raymond. You must know by now that we're not a formal bunch unless we're dealing with people from outside the magical community."

"Yes, sir, er, Raymond," Marc said, reminding himself of Fabienne's advice again. Whatever monsieur Payet—Raymond— needed, Marc already knew the opportunity would be second to none. He refused to mess that up by alienating Raymond. "Madame Valour didn't give me any details about what you needed to speak with me about."

"Madame Valour?" Raymond asked, turning to Anne-Marie.

"I am old enough to be his mother," Anne-Marie said with an indulgent smile. "You can't force informality on people any more than you can force friendship."

Raymond shrugged and turned back to Marc. "Well, I'm not old enough to be your father," he told Marc, even if that was perhaps not strictly true. "Have a seat and we'll talk."

Marc took the seat Raymond indicated and waited.

"Anne-Marie tells me you have a passion for werewolves."

"Oh yes!" Marc said. "When I was younger, I always wanted to find a werewolf pack and petition to join, and I figured my chances were much higher if I knew as much as I could about them and their ways."

"Have you ever actually met a werewolf?" Raymond asked. "I ask only because when we first formed the alliance with the vampires, we found that much of what we thought we knew, on both sides, was completely false. Fortunately for us and the outcome of the war, the reality was much brighter than legend and lore painted it."

"No, I haven't actually met one," Marc said, "but I've done enough reading to have seen contradictory information in places and to feel like I have an understanding of the agendas that may have led to certain comments or stories that don't fit the overall picture."

Raymond nodded. "Well, you're still a step ahead of me, then. I've met a werewolf, but I know next to nothing about them except what he told me. That's where you come in."

"Me?" Marc squeaked. Realizing how young that made him sound, he took another deep breath. "What do you need me to do?"

There, that sounded more professional.

"Lorens Iserin, the alpha of the Morvan pack of werewolves, came to l'Institut earlier this week asking for our help," Raymond said. "I'd like to give it, since I truly believe anything that fosters the bonds between the magical races can only benefit us all, but werewolves have never been my area of study, so I'm already at a disadvantage. Add to that the fact that the alpha and my partner don't get along, and I'm going to be of little practical help in this situation."

"What kind of help?" Marc asked. The rest was interesting, but that was the crux of the matter, the situation where his obsession might actually be useful.

"Their fertility ritual has stopped working."


"MINCE, HE'S little more than a child," Raymond said to Anne-Marie after Marc had scurried off to check his sources for any details of werewolf fertility rituals. "He'll end up joining the pack instead of helping us solve their problems."

"He had some good suggestions," Anne-Marie reminded him. "Some good lines of research both theoretical and practical."

"I heard them," Raymond said, "but there's no way I can send him to Iserin by himself. He'd get lost in everything he wants to know and doesn't yet, and we'd never see him again."

Anne-Marie chuckled. "And he would be happier than he's ever been. He isn't your responsibility, Raymond. He's twenty-three, despite looking like he's about fifteen. If he chooses to go to le Morvan and never come out again, we can't stop him."

"Maybe not, but I'd still feel responsible because I was the one who sent him there."

"So send Eric and Vincent to keep an eye on him," Anne-Marie said. "You wanted them there anyway."

"You'll call them up?" Raymond verified.

"The paperwork is already ready," she said. "All I have to do is sign it. They'll have it this evening and can go to le Morvan whenever you're ready to send them."

"Thank you," Raymond said. "I owe you for this."

"You really don't," Anne-Marie said. "The werewolves might have approached you, but the mandate to represent and help all magical races is in my hands now and has been for a year. I may not have a vampire partner the way you do, but I believe in the integration the partnerships represent. Helping the werewolves is another step in that. If they'd approached anyone but you, the first reaction would have been to send them here to me anyway, and I would have done exactly what you've just done. I would have asked Marc for help."

Raymond was not entirely sure that reassured him, but he could not argue with her logic. "Then I guess I'll go back to l'Institut and Marc can come out there when he's ready. I want to talk through his research with him before I contact Iserin. Jean is rubbing off on me despite my best efforts, and I'm having trouble trusting the situation."

"I'll make sure he gets out to you tomorrow," Anne-Marie said. "Is there a time that's better than another?"

"I have a seminar in the morning," Raymond said, "but any time after lunch is fine. I'm supposed to be meeting with Martin to discuss the progress of his research, but he's at l'Institut full-time. I can meet with him tomorrow evening or even the day after."

"I'll send him down in the afternoon, then," Anne-Marie said, "even if I have to tie him to his chair to keep him here until then."

Raymond chuckled. "He is enthusiastic, isn't he? He can come earlier. There's more space to walk off his energy, if nothing else. I just can't meet with him until after lunch. He can terrorize my staff."

"Very generous of you," Anne-Marie said with a laugh. "I'm sure they'll thank you for it. Give my regards to everyone. Maybe I'll come for a visit with Marc. I haven't seen Thierry, Sebastien, Alain, or Orlando in months. You've stolen all my best people. I should be angry with you."

"I didn't do it on purpose."

"I know you didn't. You inspire loyalty, whether you believe it or not, and they responded to that. I wasn't the least bit surprised when they all ended up out there in the country more than here in Paris."

Raymond had been, though. He hadn't thought of Alain and Thierry as his friends, and while Jean and Orlando had been friends before the alliance, Jean and Sebastien had not been. No, the presence of the other two couples at l'Institut and frequently at their dinner table still astonished Raymond. He figured that was not all bad. It kept him from taking them for granted.

"We'll look for you tomorrow, then," Raymond said. "Come for lunch, if you'd like. Our chef always makes more than we could possibly eat. I think he still forgets not to include the vampires in his head count when he's planning for meals."

Anne-Marie smiled. "I'll see if Fabienne will let me away from my desk long enough. Give Jean a kiss for me and tell him to bring you to Paris more often."

"I will," Raymond promised and cast the displacement spell to return to l'Institut.

"How did it go?" Jean asked when Raymond walked back into the office they shared.

Raymond shrugged. "He has enough theoretical knowledge to sink a ship and not enough practical experience to fill a thimble. I hope we don't end up regretting this."

"You worried about regretting the alliance too," Jean reminded him. "Your research and all your knowledge, not to mention your experiences with Serrier, make you understandably cautious, and I know I'm not helping this time with my reaction to Iserin, but think about all the good that came out of an alliance you wouldn't have made if Marcel hadn't insisted."

Raymond nodded and pulled Jean in for a quick kiss. The mark on his back—Jean's mark, not the hated scar from Serrier's spell—tingled for a moment, a living testament to their bond. "I know. I've been reminding myself of that, but that was my life and future I was gambling with, and I went into it wary enough to protect myself. You didn't see this kid, Jean. He's so wrapped up in the werewolves that he won't have any protective instinct. He said he used to dream about becoming a werewolf, but he's a wizard now. We have no idea what would happen if they tried to turn a wizard."

"It's his risk to take," Jean pointed out, "just like it was Laurent's risk to take when Blair tried to turn him as a way to save him. It didn't work for Laurent, but that doesn't mean werewolf magic is as incompatible with wizards' magic as vampire magic is. And even if it is, even if he tries and doesn't survive it or survives but loses his magic or any other outcome, it's still his choice to make."

"I know," Raymond said, "but I'm the one who brought the situation to him."

"Ah, love, you can't take the weight of the world on your shoulders. As broad as they are, they aren't broad enough for that."


MARC PORED over his books, searching for every detail he could find about lycan rituals and fertility, but unlike other topics, the information was relatively sparse and general. The thought of being able to add to that information with firsthand experience thrilled him. Oh, the articles he could write!

He chided himself for being overly enthusiastic. He had not discovered anything yet, and if he could not find a solution, it would not matter what the rituals had been. Werewolves would die out within a generation and all Marc's fascination would amount to nothing.

Deciding to try a different tack, he pulled out a sheet of paper and started writing down everything he knew about werewolves and magic. If nothing else, it would give him a place to start asking questions when he finally met the alpha and the pack shaman. He only hoped the shaman would be willing to discuss their esoterica with him. Werewolves were reputed to be distrustful of outsiders, especially of magical practitioners.

He knew lycans used a ritual to choose the time of their fertility, specifically that the alpha chose the time so that pack numbers could be controlled. He knew the ritual usually took place in a special den reserved for pack rituals—mating rituals, changing rituals, fertility rituals. If there were others, Marc had not come across references to them, although he would not be surprised to learn there were more. He knew the alpha oversaw them while the shaman conducted them, except when they changed someone or accepted someone new into the pack. Only the alpha could accept a new pack member, although the shaman would stand as witness, and a changing required four pack members for the four directions. Usually it would be the alpha, the shaman, the mate of the person being changed, and either the alpha's heir or another senior werewolf in the pack.

None of that helped him, though, except to add to his sense of the shaman's importance in his search. He stared down at the notes on the page and felt a sense of failure wash through him. He had not even filled a page with his thoughts and had nothing concrete to take to Raymond tomorrow. He would have to hope the pack would be willing to let him observe their rituals and study the flow of the magic as it happened.

# Chapter 5

LORENS HUNG up the phone and looked around the living room of his small farmhouse. He might be the king of his pack, but that title did not come with a palace. Of course with just him and Edine, they hardly needed more space than they had.

He wanted to count the news from l'Institut as progress. Payet had several suggestions and potential solutions, most notably looking into whether the den they had always used for their rituals had somehow lost its magical resonance. The thought still made Lorens vaguely uncomfortable since he had never thought of their rituals as magic, having always focused on them as the Goddess's blessings, but he was desperate enough to try anything.

Now he had to convince Adenet.

"Edine said you wanted to see me."

Lorens summoned a smile for his childhood friend and shaman. "I did something you aren't going to like," Lorens said, gesturing for Adenet to have a seat. "Do you want anything to drink? Tea? Coffee? Cognac?"

"Is this a cognac-drinking offense?" Adenet asked with a hint of a smile.

"Maybe," Lorens said. "I went to l'Institut Marcel Chavinier earlier this week to meet with the director, monsieur Payet. Whatever the solution to our current problems, the answer doesn't lie within the wisdom of the pack. We have searched and searched to no avail. We have to have outside help."

"Maybe, but wizards? Really, Lorens? You know how I feel about wizards!" Adenet protested. "We've talked about this before."

"Who else would you suggest I ask?" Lorens asked. "Seriously, Adenet. Who else could I have turned to?"

"There are other packs, farther afield. In Africa, in Canada," Adenet said. "Other resources we could explore before we went to *wizards*."

"And while we do that, while we delay on the vague hope some other pack isn't dealing with the same problems we are, I have to watch Edine suffer," Lorens replied. "You didn't see her after the last ritual failed. She's better now, but she had given up hope. She had given up on our life together. You don't have a mate. You don't know what it's like to see your other half suffering that way. I couldn't just sit around anymore. I had to *do* something. Anything."

The words stung even though Adenet knew Lorens did not intend them as a reproach. Adenet had no mate, a lack he felt every time he joined Lorens in blessing a newly mated pair, but while his wolf was happy to cavort and play with the others in the pack, he had yet to find the one on whom his wolf would fixate, the one who would be Adenet's center for the rest of his life. He had enough experience as shaman to understand the alpha's compulsive need to protect and soothe his mate. Even the lowest-ranking wolf felt that way about his or her mate. For Lorens, the need would be enough to drive him to any number of desperate acts to assure Edine's happiness.

"What did they say?" Adenet asked. He might resent Lorens taking the decision out of his hands, but now that it was made, he would make the best of it.

It was what he did.

"He had some ideas," Lorens said. "He suggested letting one of his wizards examine the den to see if something had disrupted the flow of power there and if he could restore it. I couldn't think of anything that had happened in the area that should have changed anything, but it seems a harmless enough avenue of exploration."

"Harmless?" Adenet repeated. "You're talking about letting wizards into our most sacred space to do Goddess knows what while they're in there, and you think it's harmless? They could fix it so we never have a successful ritual again, of any kind. And then where would we be?"

"You make it sound like they're out to destroy us, Adenet," Lorens said. "All they have to do is not help us and that's going to happen anyway. There's no reason for them to speed the process up. I wasn't going to send them in there alone. I'd planned on us going with them."

"And how do you plan on making sure they don't fuck anything up once they're in there?" Adenet asked.

"I figured that was up to you," Lorens said. "You're the one with the connection to the den. You'd be able to sense if they were doing anything that might damage that. They might be wizards, but we're wolves. We could stop them if we had to."

Adenet was not so sure, but arguing with Lorens never got him anywhere. "Is that it, or do they have other suggestions?"

"They have a wizard who is apparently something of an expert on werewolves," Lorens said. "He's coming as well to see if he can help."

Adenet snorted. "This 'expert' is going to come in, wave his wand, and make our problems magically disappear? I know Edine is hurting. I know that's making you insane with the need to fix things for her. But you've got to think this through too, or you're going to start losing the respect of the pack—and if that happens, someone's going to challenge you for the throne. How do you think it would make Edine feel to watch you fight for your position? How do you think it would make her feel if you lose?"

"Do you really think I would?" Lorens challenged.

"Not today, no," Adenet said, "but if they start to lose trust in you, it won't just be one challenge. It will be a challenge today and another next week and another after that until you're worn thin because you're too kind to kill your challengers. It makes you a good king, but it would put you at a disadvantage if the pack decided to replace you. They'd keep at it until they won, and they wouldn't hesitate to kill you because they couldn't risk people rallying around you later and trying to put you back on the throne."

"Then help me put this to our people in such a way that they'll see the rationale behind it," Lorens said. "If we present a united front, they'll accept it without looking more closely into it. Most of them know next to nothing about the details of our lore. It's not their role and so they trust us to manage it. As long as we bless them when they find their mates and help them procreate when they're ready, they don't care about the rest."

"When do these wizards arrive?" Adenet asked with a resigned sigh.

"Saturday morning," Lorens said.


MARC ARRIVED at l'Institut the next day before lunch, even knowing Raymond would not be free when he arrived. Marc wanted to get a feel for the place and maybe meet some of the other heroes who worked there. He reminded himself of Fabienne's advice, figuring none of the other veterans of l'émeute des sorciers would want him fawning over them either. That would not stop him from doing it internally, but he could temper his outward reaction.

Given how early he was and that the sun was shining despite the cool temperatures, Marc chose to wait in the courtyard. The benches beneath the overhanging branches of a number of old trees would be relaxing spots in the summer, Marc imagined, but with the breeze coming off the lake, he preferred to walk rather than sit. He had made nearly a full turn of the area when he caught sight of a slender, dark-haired figure sitting on one of the benches near the lake's edge, staring out across the wind-ruffled water.

Marc did not disturb the man's ruminations, but the man turned at his approach nonetheless.

"I'm sorry. I didn't mean to disturb you."

"You didn't," the man replied. "If I wanted to be left alone, I wouldn't have come out here, but with winter closing in, I prefer to be outside rather than confined inside. There are few enough days of sunshine left before winter sets in with all its dreary clouds and snow. I'm Orlando St. Clair. I don't think we've met."

"Marc Gourlin," Marc said, offering his hand. "I have an appointment with monsieur Payet this afternoon, but I got here a little early."

"Monsieur Payet?" Orlando said with a smile. "He'll never let you call him that."

"No, he didn't want me to," Marc agreed, "but it's hard enough to call him by his name to his face. I'm not sure I can do it when he isn't around."

Orlando's smile widened. "Fair enough. So what project is he working on now? Alain and I haven't had a chance to talk with him and Jean recently. Everyone is so busy these days."

"I'm not sure how much I should say," Marc admitted. "He didn't tell me it was classified, but I wouldn't want to abuse his trust."

"That's very wise of you," Orlando said, "but unless he specifically said not to discuss it with anyone, you're safe discussing with the staff at l'Institut. Who do you think he relies on for help when he has a new problem to dissect?"

"I've never really thought about it," Marc said. "Until yesterday, I never figured I'd get a chance to meet him, much less work with him, and now...."

"Now you're as in awe of him as the rest of us are," Orlando said. "You just haven't learned to hide it as well."

Orlando's comment surprised a laugh from Marc. "And here I thought I was managing."

"Raymond is my friend, and his partner, Jean, is the brother I never had before I was turned. I've learned to hide my awe of both of them, but every day I remember I owe them my happiness, if not my very existence. I'm not sure I would have survived the war if it hadn't been for them and a few others. But enough of that. Tell me about Raymond's new project."

Marc could not imagine how his poor musings could be nearly as interesting as anything he might learn from the vampire sitting next to him—about the war, about monsieur Payet, about vampires and everything l'Institut represented—but he reminded himself again of Fabienne's advice. "Well, I'm something of an amateur enthusiast where lycans are concerned," Marc explained, "and Raymond thinks that could be useful to him. I guess we'll have to see what he thinks of my research, but I found a new, well, really an old article, just new to me, as I was looking stuff up yesterday, and I think it'll be useful."

"Lycans?" Orlando asked, feeling the monster within him stir. He pushed it down with all his might. He had spent over a hundred years at the mercy of a vampire ruled by his appetites rather than his conscience. He would never allow that beast any dominion of his actions or thoughts. "I wasn't aware there were any in the area."

"I'm not sure where they are," Marc answered honestly, "but Raymond said a pack approached him for help. I assumed they were in the area, but maybe not."

"And they could be without me knowing about it," Orlando said. "So tell me about this new-to-you article. Think of it as a practice run before you present it to Raymond. I can't promise to have any insights, but at least you'll have talked through it once."

"The problem, as I understand it, is that the werewolves' fertility rituals have stopped working," Marc explained.

"And the article you found?" Orlando asked.

"It doesn't deal specifically with fertility," Marc replied, "but it does talk about the shaman's role in the pack and the way the shaman relates to the spiritual and magical world."

"What's this about magical worlds?"

Marc thought he had seen Orlando smile earlier, but that was nothing compared to the expression that lit the vampire's face as a blond man joined them, sitting on the bench on the other side of Orlando. "Alain, this is Marc Gourlin. He's here to help Raymond with a new project and was practicing his presentation on me. Marc, my partner, Alain Magnier."

"Nice to meet you," Alain said, offering his hand.

Marc shook it, feeling his heart beat faster as he realized who he was meeting. He had not recognized Orlando's name, but he knew the name Alain Magnier. "It's an honor," Marc said. "Truly an honor."

"I just did what needed to be done," Alain said, "but you're welcome."

"I didn't mean to embarrass you," Marc said. "I won't mention it again. I was telling Orlando about an article I found yesterday. Did you want to hear it as well?"

"I'd be happy to listen," Alain offered.

Marc nodded and picked back up the thread of his thoughts. "As I was saying, the article dealt with the role of the shaman in the werewolf pack and his—or her, but usually his—connection to the magical and spiritual energies. There weren't any details of the rituals themselves, but it postulated that a strong shaman meant a strong pack and a weak shaman led to a weaker pack."

"Don't say that to a werewolf," Orlando said. "They won't stand for it."

"Have you ever met a werewolf?" Marc asked excitedly.

"No," Orlando said, "but that's how any vampire would react. It seems like a logical extrapolation."

"Maybe," Marc said. "But however I choose to word it, it suggests I should talk to the shaman and that we should consider his magical connection and how strong it is. If we can work on that somehow, maybe the problem will solve itself."


"I COULD see that being an explanation if it were only Iserin's pack having problems," Raymond said after Marc finished laying out his theory over lunch an hour later. "It certainly makes sense if they have a shaman who perhaps inherited the position rather than having any actual gift for it, but that doesn't explain why other packs are having the same problem. Surely not every shaman in France has a poor connection to the elemental magic."

"That's the other part of it," Marc said. "I don't think they connect to the elemental magic, not the way we do. I think they connect to the life force around us."

"The witch versus wizard conversation," Raymond murmured. "It's certainly possible. One of my researchers told me about a British witch who was part of a lycan pack in New York. Depending on what we find, or rather if we don't find anything useful, it might be worth contacting him as well."

"You don't want to contact him now?" Marc asked.

"He is a *British* witch," Raymond said with a chuckle. "He already has one strike against him for being a witch—the alpha was clear about the pack's attitude toward the rest of the magical community. We may be wizards, but at least we're French wizards. As conservative as the pack seems to be, the double mark against him could well be too much."

"I thought it was just vampires they didn't like," Jean said.

"Oh, it's definitely vampires," Raymond said, "but they seem to be resistant to any outsiders. I remember not so long ago another group of magical beings who felt the same way."

"Just as long as you don't try to convert them the same way you converted me," Jean said, his voice a possessive growl.

"I'm not converting anyone," Raymond said. "Marc is. And I didn't convert you. Orlando and Alain did. You believed in the alliance, in the partnerships, long before I did."

Jean didn't argue since there was some truth in Raymond's words, but Alain and Orlando alone hadn't been enough to convince Jean. It had taken Raymond and his restless, tortured soul to do that.

"How am I supposed to win them over?" Marc asked.

"With sincerity, honesty, and the best effort you can give," Raymond replied. "Their problem is a real one. If you can help them solve it, the rest will take care of itself."

"And if I can't?"

"Then you can't, but you'll know you've done everything you can to help them. As much as we wish there were, there isn't a solution, or at least not an immediate one, to every problem. Even with magic, sometimes people die. They get sick. Things happen that we can't control. Yes, this is a magical problem. Logically there should be a magical solution, but sometimes there just isn't."

"Wizards can't be turned into vampires," Jean said. "Vampires can only have one Avoué. There's no reason why that should be so, yet it is. We deal with it and go on."

"That's kind of cynical," Marc said.

Raymond shook his head. "It's not cynical, just realistic. Knowing that doesn't stop us from trying to find solutions and explanations. It just means we accept the limits of reality. I don't know why their rituals aren't working, but the answer may not lie within our power. If that's the case, we have to accept that just like they do."

# Chapter 6

"WHY ARE we doing this again?" Vincent asked as he and Eric tramped through the woods of le Morvan.

"Because Raymond asked us to," Eric replied as he stepped over a fallen tree on the path that would lead to where they were supposed to meet the werewolves.

"We aren't spies or fugitives anymore," Vincent continued to mutter. "Why couldn't we drive up or cast a spell to get there like normal people?"

"Because Raymond said the werewolves wanted us to do it this way," Eric repeated. "I don't know what their issue is, but I know we owe the Milice for keeping us both out of prison. Marcel is retired, so that leaves Raymond. If he had spoken out against us, we would both still be in jail and you know it, so if he asks me to do something that isn't illegal, I'm going to do it, even if it's inconvenient or awkward or cold—putain!"

Vincent could not stop the chuckle that escaped him. "You were saying?"

Eric glared down at the log that had tripped him. "I was saying I will do whatever Raymond asks," Eric repeated. "I might make him take me to the doctor when it's over, but I'll do what he asked first."

"Messieurs Simonet et Jonnet?"

Eric only barely refrained from drawing his wand. Vincent was less successful. Eric brushed his hand down Vincent's arm, lowering the weapon. They would defend themselves if necessary, but the man in front of them did not seem like much of a threat.

"Yes," Eric said. "That's us."

"Tell your friend to put away his weapon. We allow no instruments of violence in our Grotte de rassemblement."

"Our wands are not weapons," Eric said, even as he gestured for Vincent to do as the werewolf asked. "They are the tools we use to cast our magic. If we can't take them with us, we can't do what we came to do."

"Very well, but do not think we are defenseless because we do not carry wands," the man said.

"We?" Vincent asked.

Three other men stepped into view, much burlier than the one who had greeted them. Eric could feel Vincent tense beside him, but Eric ignored it, focusing on the new arrivals. "Messieurs," he acknowledged with a nod of his head.

"Lorens Iserin," the tallest of the three men said, "and this is Adenet Silaire, the shaman of our pack."

"And your other two friends?" Vincent asked.

"Two of our Guardians," Lorens replied. "They accompany me on official business."

"This way," Adenet said shortly, interrupting the introductions. He led them deeper into the woods, the thick undergrowth pulling at the legs of their jeans as they walked. Eric tucked his hand into his pocket so he could finger his wand. He would not draw it unless absolutely necessary, but he could cast a displacement spell even with the wand hidden as long as he had contact with the wood.

VINCENT WALKED into the den, finding it more of a grotto than the cave he had been expecting, with a rock ledge overhanging a portion of the area while a circle of trees delineated the rest. Every inch of the grove was immaculately tended, not a blade of grass out of place, to the point that it felt nearly sterile after the wild teeming overgrowth they had walked through to reach the den. Vincent approached the cliff face that formed the grotto, preferring to have the rawest portion of the land under his hands. He doubted the werewolves flanking him would appreciate him disturbing the carefully manicured plants to bury his fingers in the dirt. The stone had been partially carved in places, but it remained bare stone connected to the earth, and that was where Vincent would make the best connection with whatever power dwelled here.

The moment he laid his hand against stone, everything around him faded, all his senses focused inward on the world revealed to him by his elemental connection. Only Eric's hands on his shoulders, augmenting his strength, kept him grounded. He took a deep breath and tried to parse the sensations that flooded his senses. He struggled to find his balance as he moved through the magical landscape revealed by the ancient power in the ground, but as he followed its lines and plumbed its depths, he could feel how it had grown wild, diffuse. The latent power of the grotto had been neglected as completely as the physical aspect had been tended.

"Well?"

The werewolf's voice at Vincent's elbow shattered his concentration, breaking his bond with the earth around him and leaving him feeling bereft. He dropped his hand back to his side and turned to face them. "There is power here," Vincent replied, "but no channel for it. It's wild, desperate for attention, like a garden left to go to seed. I thought you said you did your rituals here."

"We do. At least once a month on the full moon," Adenet said. "I don't understand. This den has never been as well tended as it is now."

"Physically," Vincent agreed, "but not magically."

"Can you help us?" Lorens asked. "You were able to sense the power. Can you help us use it?"

"I don't know," Vincent replied. "I could channel it for my own use or for the use of other wizards. I know how to do that. I've never tried channeling magic to anyone of a different race, but even if I do that now, it doesn't solve your problem because I won't always be here."

"We can't *do* magic," Adenet insisted. "We aren't wizards."

Vincent did not have to hear the lycan say he had no wish to learn. His attitude was clear in every line of his body.

"Once upon a time, someone tended the magic in this place," Vincent said slowly. "I don't know how and I can't tell when, but someone in the past did enough magic to create the remnants of power that remain. I don't know why you can't make that connection anymore, but it's clearly been lost. Raymond sent me to help. I'm willing to try to jumpstart your connection again, but at some point, that has to come from you. I don't know your rituals, and I'm not sure I could perform them even if I did."

"We have to try, Adenet," the alpha said. "What do you need us to do?"

"Give me your hand," Vincent said to the shaman.

Adenet approached reluctantly and let Vincent guide his hand to the same place he had touched before. The moment Vincent's fingers connected with the cliff face, the connection slammed back into place with even more power and a sense of joy at being allowed to flow again. Vincent nearly drowned in the outpouring, only Eric's hands on his shoulders keeping him from going under and merging with the stone beneath his touch.

Vincent tried to focus on guiding the power into the hand beneath his, offering it to the werewolf, but he could get no sense of whether it was successful. The magic he had summoned with his touch eddied around him and the werewolf standing next to him, but Vincent could discern no welcoming reply from the shaman.

"Can you feel it?" Vincent asked. It took all his concentration to speak through the power that glutted him. "It's there for you to command."

"We don't do magic," Adenet repeated, tearing his hand out from under Vincent's. "There's nothing for me to feel. I'm a shaman, not a sorcerer."

"Then you need someone who knows more about your rituals and how power flows through them," Vincent said, dropping the connection with the elemental magic regretfully. He lived and worked in Paris, but he felt most fully alive when he had bare earth beneath his hands and feet. "I can offer you raw power, but you have to be able to do something with it."

Adenet shot a look of pure hatred toward Vincent before nodding curtly to the alpha and leaving the grotto.

Vincent sighed. "I didn't mean to upset him."

"Adenet has been against the idea of bringing outsiders in from the beginning," Lorens said. "He will do what I order because I am the king of his pack, but that doesn't mean he likes it."

"That doesn't change the fact that I can't channel magic the way you need it to be channeled," Vincent said. "Whatever the problem with the fertility ritual is, it isn't your den. It must be in the ritual itself."

"We usually do our ritual at the full moon," Lorens said, "but that's still two weeks away. I will speak with Adenet and see if we can try again sooner. Perhaps if someone observes, he or she can see where the ritual goes wrong. Monsieur Payet suggested he could see the lines of power within a ritual."

"If anyone can, it would be Raymond," Eric agreed. "I'm sorry we couldn't do more."

Lorens shrugged. "You did what you could. We know more than we did an hour ago, even if I don't like the results. Now I have to convince Adenet to allow someone to observe the ritual. Could either of you do it? I can order Adenet to allow a wizard to observe, but he will never agree to having a vampire in our grotto. It goes against every instinct we have."

"Jean would never let Raymond come without him," Eric agreed. "Their partnership is the core of Raymond's strength."

"You say that so casually," Lorens said. "It doesn't bother you to have vampires around?"

"The ones we're around are all too besotted with their partners to be interested in anyone else," Vincent said. "There's nothing to be bothered by. Raymond found a wizard with some interest in your kind. His familiarity might make it easier for him to do what needs to be done, and he doesn't have a vampire partner, so he wouldn't set your shaman's teeth on edge the way Raymond would. I still think Raymond would be the best one to help you, but if that truly isn't an option, we'll try something else."

"I will speak with Adenet and let monsieur Payet know," Lorens said. "Thank you for your help. My Guardians will see you out."

Eric raised an eyebrow at Vincent, who shook his head, gesturing for Eric to follow the Guardians. Only after they were well away from the boundaries of the den did he clear his throat.

"You don't need to walk us all the way back," Vincent told them. "We can return home from here."

"Our king ordered us to escort you to the border of our lands," one of the Guardians insisted.

"We understand, but we weren't planning on walking," Eric said. He met Vincent's eyes and cast the displacement spell that returned them to l'Institut's outer wards.

"You realize Raymond's going to get complaints about that," Vincent said as they walked inside.

"Your point?" Eric asked. "We waited until we were outside their sacred space, but I wasn't hiking all the way back out. I have other things to do with my weekend."

"Problem solved?" Raymond quipped from the doorway.

"Not even close," Vincent said. "I'm pretty sure all we did was alienate the shaman."

"Maybe you'd better come in and tell me what happened."

RAYMOND LEANED back in his chair, having listened to the full account of Vincent and Eric's afternoon. "Nothing disrupted the magical flow, which is good, I guess. We don't have to go searching for a new location for their rituals or try to convince the shaman or the rest of the pack of the necessity of moving their rites."

"That's where the alienating part comes in," Vincent said. "If the problem isn't with the grotto, then it has to lie either in the ritual itself or in the person conducting the ritual. If they swear they haven't changed the ritual, then the logical conclusion is that the shaman is the problem."

"I was under the impression he wasn't new to his post," Raymond said, "and from what Iserin told me, they had successful rituals until a few years ago. The population has dwindled over time, but I got the impression that hadn't happened just in the past few years but over the last few generations."

"Like maybe some previous shaman introduced a change that led to the problem? Although that doesn't account for it being more widespread," Vincent said. "Still, if that's the case, we might be able to win Silaire, the current shaman, back over by making it clear the error isn't his. But that means we have to find what the error is and figure out how to correct it."

"Which is where Marc will come in," Raymond said. "Of all of us, he knows the most about werewolves."

"Can he follow the spell lines the way you would?" Eric asked. "That's not the easiest skill to master."

"I don't know," Raymond replied, "but we're going to find out."

"ALL MAGIC leaves a trace," Raymond explained to Marc when he arrived at l'Institut the next day. "The challenge is learning to reveal and interpret those traces."

"And you want me to do this?" Marc asked.

"I can't attend the werewolves' ritual," Raymond said. "I could barely keep Jean and Iserin from coming to blows in my office, and Jean won't let me go out without him, so that rules me out. Vincent and Eric could do the spell, but they know nothing about werewolves or how the magic should flow in the ritual, so they wouldn't be able to interpret what they're seeing even if they saw it. You at least know what *should* be happening."

"In theory," Marc said, "and assuming the research I've done over the years is accurate, but are you really sure you want to trust me with this? Surely someone else—"

"There is no one else," Raymond interrupted. "At least not right now. The spell to make the magic visible is a straightforward one."

He cast it with a simple command, and the room lit up like fireworks, reflecting both the layers of the wards around his office and the echoes of the spells he had cast over the course of the day. He was quite sure his back glowed as well, but Marc couldn't see that given the way they were facing, and Raymond didn't turn to reveal it. Marc would ask questions Raymond had no desire to answer.

"I never knew…." Marc walked slowly around the room, tracing the lines of magic with his fingers. They had no solidity for him to touch, but he followed them nonetheless, learning their contours. "I can guess the ones along the walls are wards or protection spells, but I don't know where to begin with the rest."

"Look at the colors, the patterns," Raymond said. "Some of it is my magic and some was done by others. See if you can find the patterns and identify my magic."

Marc studied the threads of magic as directed, looking for similarities. The wards along the walls were too complex, so he turned to the other spells in the room.

"Is that your signature?" he asked after a few minutes, pointing to a pattern of golden light shot through with blue and green veins.

"Yes," Raymond replied. "The distinctive pattern and hues of blues and greens are unique to me, but you will find those themes with any wizard who associates with water."

"What would mine be?" Marc asked. "Reds and oranges, I would think, for fire. Browns and yellows for earth, but what about air?"

"Air is the hardest one to identify by sight because it can be a mixture of any of those colors or none at all," Raymond replied.

"How can you see it if it's none at all?" Marc asked.

"Cast a spell," Raymond directed. "Something simple like a levitation spell on the coffee cup there."

Marc did as he was directed.

Raymond repeated the revealing spell and a new band of magic appeared, clear like crystal and yet visible. "That is what an affinity with air looks like in its purest form," Raymond explained. "If there are colors in the signature, the wizard almost always has a secondary affinity—not as strong as with air, but enough to explain the colors."

"So I can see the magic using your spell," Marc said, "but that doesn't help me figure out what is or isn't going on during the ritual."

"Tell me about the ritual," Raymond said. "All the detail you can. Then let's think about how the magic should flow. If you know what it should look like, you can compare that to what it actually looks like, and that will hopefully give us some answers. Vincent assures me the grotto they use for their rituals will provide a wellspring of power, so now we need to see how they're directing it."

"Keeping in mind that everything I know is theoretical and that werewolves are a fairly private race so details are scarce, fertility rituals are traditionally done in March," Marc said, "around the feast of Ostara. Beltane is more typically associated with fertility, but that's when the pups should be born, not conceived."

"Two months?" Raymond verified.

"Yes," Marc said, "werewolves have the gestation period of their lupine half, not their human half. Typically it's sixty days. Again traditionally, only the alpha mates with the females—and once he is mated, often only with his mate—because it strengthens the pack to have the pups born from the strongest females and sired by the strongest male. I don't know how traditional this pack is in that respect."

"I got the impression they weren't," Raymond said. "The number of pups being born was so small—and getting smaller over time—that I got the idea they had opened the ritual to anyone who chose to participate."

"And it isn't Ostara, so they haven't limited their rites to the traditional time either," Marc said.

"Could that affect the potency?" Raymond asked.

"I suppose," Marc said, "but if it's been some years since the ritual worked, surely they would have tried at Ostara as well."

"That would be a question for the pack," Raymond said. "So they gather at Ostara and do what?"

"That's the problem," Marc said. "I don't know. They call on the Goddess and they mate, but beyond that, the texts I read didn't say."

Raymond sighed and rubbed his temples. Why did werewolves and vampires have such an ingrained antipathy? This would be so much simpler if Raymond could observe the ritual himself.

"At a guess, then, since the goal is fertility, there should be visible magic around the shaman and around the couple or couples who are trying to conceive," Raymond said. "From my understanding of what they said, the shaman isn't casting a spell so much as channeling power. There may not be a visible imprint, but even elemental magic is visible, usually as the pure color of its element, if it's limited to one, or as pure gold if it's all the elements mixed together."

"It would probably be gold, then," Marc postulated. "They aren't wizards. They wouldn't be tied to an element."

"True," Raymond said, "but they would be channeling the magic in their den, so it could be more earth magic than anything else simply because of availability. There are very few magical loci in the world. The only one in France to my knowledge is Notre-Dame. There is magic everywhere, but its exact composition varies with the elements. That's why when we do a Rite d'équilibrage, we summon the elements that aren't already present in the place."

"Could that be the problem? A shaman with no earth affinity and so he's stymied by the absence of his element?" Marc asked.

"If it were a wizard, I would say that was a strong possibility, but Iserin insisted they weren't wizards and didn't do magic, so I doubt they have affinities the way we do. Anne-Marie has assigned you to l'Institut for the duration of this project," Raymond said, "and from what Eric and Vincent said, we have until the full moon for their next ritual, so that gives us two weeks. Spend this week here practicing the spell I just taught you. Learn to identify your own magical signature so you don't mix that up with what you see during the ritual. A few days before the full moon, we'll send you to the pack so you can begin to learn the signatures there. Hopefully that will make it easier to make sense of what you see during the ritual. They may not be wizards, but werewolves change form. That requires some kind of magical resonance."

"I'll do my best," Marc promised.

"I know you will," Raymond replied. As Marc left the room, Raymond realized he even believed it.

# Chapter 7

"ADENET?"

"Go away."

"You can't avoid me forever. You have to come out to hunt eventually."

"I can try."

"Your wolf won't let you starve yourself to death. He has enough sense to know this isn't your fault even if you don't."

Adenet ran his fingers through his wavy brown hair. He hated that Lorens knew him so well. He couldn't hide anything from his alpha for long. How he had managed to hide the one secret Lorens had not yet discovered, he didn't know, but he would do everything in his power to keep it that way.

"Go away," he repeated.

"No."

Adenet growled low in his throat, his wolf rising at his agitation, but of the two sides of himself, his wolf was even more susceptible to Lorens's influence, the call of the alpha impossible for his lycan side to ignore. He unlocked the door and slammed it open.

"Fine. Happy now?"

"No," Lorens said, coming into Adenet's house and closing the door behind him. "You're upset. Of course I'm not happy."

"What do you expect?" Adenet demanded. "That wizard came in, made his pronouncements with no proof I could see, implied we didn't know what we were doing in tending our den, and then blamed me for the fertility ritual failing. I wasn't about to thank the bastard. How do we even know he was trying to help us? He could have done something to make sure the ritual would never work again."

"I suppose he could have," Lorens agreed, "but why bother? Why go to all that trouble when we're already dying out? This pack used to be three hundred strong. Now we're down to fifty, and nearly half of those are elders. In another twenty years, there will be nothing left if we don't find a solution. If they had it in for us, they could simply let nature take its course. It's not like damaging the den would make that happen any faster."

"He's a wizard," Adenet replied. "Who knows why they do anything? At least he's gone now." The pained look on Lorens's face caught Adenet's attention. "He is gone, isn't he?"

"Yes, they both are," Lorens replied, "but since we still don't have a solution to our problem, they, or someone, anyway, will be coming back again. I don't believe the problem is with you, and I told the wizards that, but there is undeniably a problem. Something has caused the ritual to stop working. If it isn't you and it isn't the den, then it must be something in the ritual itself. The wizards think they might be able to figure out what if they can observe and follow the flow of power."

"No!" Adenet said immediately. "We've never allowed outsiders to attend our sacred rites. Ask anything else of me, Lorens, but don't ask that. Please, by the Goddess, don't ask me that."

"What other choice do we have?" Lorens demanded. "Give me a viable alternative and I'll take it, but our pack is dying, and the other packs in France are right behind us. We don't have time to waste." The memory of Edine's mournful howls and of finding her in the creek half-frozen and sapped of her will to live haunted him. He had to find a solution, for her sake if not for his own.

Adenet's shoulders slumped in defeat. "I don't have one. You think I would have let the wizards anywhere near the grotto if I did?"

"No, I know you wouldn't have," Lorens said, "but that makes them our only hope now. We can impose whatever limits on their observation that will make you more comfortable with it. We don't have to let them inside the circle. We can limit it to one wizard attending. We can do whatever you want to make it easier, but we need to do this."

Adenet nodded. "When do you want to do the next ritual?"

"You've always said the full moon was best," Lorens said. "That gives us two weeks. It'll give you time to get used to the idea and maybe to meet the wizard and get more comfortable with the idea of having him or her around for the ritual. You used to say you could sometimes sense ill intent. Maybe if you meet the person ahead of time, you'll be able to reassure yourself on that count."

Adenet didn't reply, not wanting to tell Lorens he had lost that ability about the same time the fertility ritual had stopped working entirely. As much as he resented the necessity, the suggestion wasn't a bad one, though, not entirely. He might not be able to sense people's intentions the way he once had, but he had learned a few things about lycan—and human—behavior in his tenure as shaman.

"Tell the wizard to arrive three days before the full moon," Adenet said. "I will meet him and decide if we will allow his attendance."

"I'll call Payet and let him know," Lorens said. "You should meet him someday. If you could get past him being a wizard, I think you would have a lot to talk about."

"Like what?" Adenet scoffed.

"All the same things you talk with other shamans about when you gather," Lorens said. "Payet seemed just as fascinated with old lore as you are."

Adenet didn't want to admit to any curiosity about any wizard, much less that one, but Lorens's comment had been effective. "Is there any chance he would come?"

"Only if we are willing to allow his partner to accompany him," Lorens said. "And if his partner is willing to let him anywhere near us."

Adenet frowned. "What aren't you telling me?"

"His partner is a vampire," Lorens said. "The alpha of the Parisian vampires."

Adenet's wolf surged against his barriers, fighting to get loose so he could protect them from the undead monster.

"Change," Lorens said, sensing Adenet's turmoil.

Adenet shook his head, determined to retain the control he had mastered when he left puberty, but the provocation was too strong and his wolf won out. With a full-body shiver, he shifted, a large black wolf taking the place of the man who had stood there seconds ago. The wolf threw his head back and howled his anger and frustration at being denied a target for his aggression. The open door and the lure of the wild beckoned, and with his lupine half fully in control, Adenet lunged for freedom.

The chill of the evening pinched Adenet's nose, but his thick pelt protected the rest of his body as he surged forward, sniffing out any scent of intruders in his territory. He was shaman of the pack, his duties to guide and nurture the wolves who lived within his purview, but at that moment, he understood the fire of the Guardians to protect no matter the cost. He avoided the sacred grotto, but he found the trail the wizards had used to enter pack lands and then to leave again, the stink of their magic so strong at one point that his rage got the better of him. He clawed at the fallen leaves, destroying the trace of footprints and releasing the clean scent of earth and loam again until he could no longer smell them.

Only then did he turn and head toward home at a much slower pace. The grotto would have to be cleansed as well before they could do another fertility ritual there, but he had time for that. The new moon was tomorrow night. He would tend the grotto then so the waxing moon would bring new life to the space. And the new wizard, whoever that ended up being, would have to observe from outside the circle of trees. Adenet would not allow any taint to influence the outcome of the fertility ritual.

In wolf form, his primal side ascendant, Adenet cringed at the thought of the fertility ritual. Like all the other males of the pack, he participated in the ritual, hoping some union would bear fruit and bring a new pup to the pack, but his wolf hated the obligation. Perhaps if he had a mate of his own he would feel differently, but the instinct-driven copulation brought about by the ritual felt empty to him. The bodies of the females beneath him were not at all the connection he sought in either form. More than once he had worried that his lack of interest had negated the ritual's effectiveness—but it had worked until three years ago, and Adenet's feelings dated back to the first time he joined in as more than the shaman, when he realized he was more interested in the other males than in any of the females. He had participated then as now, though, because they could not afford to do otherwise.

The Goddess had not seen fit to send him a mate, so he would do his duty to the best of his abilities, the way he had always done, and pray that this time it would be enough to bring the blessing of new life to the pack.

JEAN LOOKED up when the door to his office opened and Orlando came in.

"Bonjour," Orlando said. "I haven't seen you in weeks. Not just us, anyway."

"I know," Jean said. "Do you want to stay in here and visit or go outside?"

"Go outside," Orlando replied immediately.

Jean laughed. "I should have known. Next time I'll just meet you at the lake unless it's snowing."

"I don't mind the cold as long as the sun's out," Orlando said. "After so long without it...."

"Yes, I know," Jean said. "The chill will keep the wizards inside and we can talk uninterrupted."

"Do we need to talk?" Orlando asked, his face showing his concern.

"Nothing bad," Jean assured him quickly. "Just nothing I want random people overhearing."

The concern on Orlando's face didn't not fade, leaving Jean to curse under his breath. He had not wanted to start this conversation with Orlando's instincts on high alert. It would be a delicate enough discussion without his best friend probing for more details than Jean was willing to give. He would have enough trouble admitting that he, the master of self-control, had chosen to relinquish that control and set free his demons even for a few minutes. He had no intention of admitting he had done so while tied to the bed after Raymond had gotten the best of him. Some things were too private to share even with Orlando.

"Stop worrying," Jean ordered. "It's nothing bad, just private, and you are, to my knowledge, the only other vampire who might understand."

Orlando nodded and waited until they reached the stone bench next to the lake that bordered one side of l'Institut's property before asking, "Is this about your Aveu de Sang?"

"Yes," Jean said, reminding himself that his bond with Raymond had never been a secret from Orlando and Alain, even when he had tried to keep it that way. Orlando hadn't given them away then. Jean could trust him with this new secret now. "I think I might have found a new side benefit to having an Avoué."

"Really?" Orlando asked. "What?"

"I think our Avoués can help us control the beast inside us," Jean said.

"How?" Orlando asked, his voice as eager now as it had been concerned earlier.

"I don't know how," Jean said. "I just know it worked. Having the werewolf here threw me off-balance. Raymond calmed me down."

"That's not exactly the same thing," Orlando said. "I mean, I'm glad he helped you calm down, but that could just as easily be his emotions coming through your bond—assuming he wasn't bothered by the werewolf the way you were."

"It was more than that," Jean said through gritted teeth. He had not wanted to talk about this. He had hoped Orlando would take him at his word or would offer corroborating evidence without hearing the full story from Jean's perspective, but that had clearly been wishful thinking.

"What do you mean?"

"Raymond knew how upset I was, how badly I was fighting to stay in control," Jean said. "That's no surprise, but instead of trying to help me win that fight, he goaded me into losing control. I hadn't given free rein to the monster inside me since the night I was turned, but I did it at his insistence—and I still didn't hurt him."

"Sebastien told me we were incapable of hurting our Avoués."

"Well, apparently that's the case even when we're otherwise completely out of control," Jean said. "And when we were done, I slept. Not just closed my eyes and rested beside him, Orlando. I slept. For the first time since I was turned."

"You have a theory on why that happened, I'm sure," Orlando said.

"Maybe," Jean replied. "For the first time ever, even counting the first night and the man I killed because I didn't know how to stop, the beast was sated. I'd had all the blood I wanted, not just enough to hold me until the next time, but all I wanted."

"All the sex too, I imagine," Orlando teased.

"No such thing," Jean said flippantly, hoping the heat he could feel rising over his cheeks was not visible. "But you know as well as I do what any kind of extended feeding with your Avoué entails. The point, though, is that it's possible to calm those instincts completely rather than just keep them in check like I've always believed was my only choice."

"And you think this is a benefit of an Aveu de Sang."

"I don't see how any other one person could have given me everything Raymond gave me that night," Jean said. "I can't drink him dry, so I could feed until I no longer wanted more, and the bond between us lets us make love far longer than we could do without it. Maybe a vampire could get the same effect by moving from person to person over a short period of time, but that's not terribly practical."

"No, probably not," Orlando agreed. "What do we do about it? You can't exactly go around telling people what you've discovered since no one else knows about your Aveu de Sang."

"It's not as important to keep it secret now as it was when we formed the bond, but that's not the only reason to wait before saying anything. I had this experience once under very specific circumstances. It was enough to make me ask questions. It's not enough to prove anything."

"You're asking me to test it too, aren't you?" Orlando said slowly.

"There's no one else to ask," Jean said, "unless you know another vampire with an Avoué that I don't know."

"You could try asking Sebastien. He doesn't have an Avoué now, but he did. And didn't you tell me monsieur Lombard had an Avoué once as well?"

Jean winced at the idea of approaching either of the other vampires with any part of the information he had shared with Orlando. Monsieur Lombard was too much like the stern abbot of Jean's youth for him to feel comfortable sharing such personal details, and Sebastien and Jean had only been on speaking terms again for three years after avoiding each other for nearly four hundred because of Sebastien's Avoué.

"I suppose I could," Jean said, "but unless they tried it when their Avoués were alive, they can't help me. You can."

"You of all people aren't really asking me this, are you?" Orlando replied. "After everything I've shared with you, you can't be asking this of me."

Jean winced again. "I'm sorry, but I don't see another option."

"You could leave well enough alone," Orlando said. "Why is it so important to know this? It doesn't affect anyone but you and me. You already know the outcome for yourself, and I don't want to know the outcome for myself, so I don't see the point in it."

"Because if Thierry is right and if our partnerships are indeed meant to help balance us all, this is additional proof of that."

"But that's not about the Aveu de Sang at all," Orlando said. "Any pair could test that. You could ask Sebastien and Thierry to test it."

"Because I think the Aveux de Sang are the logical extension of the partnerships," Jean said. "It only makes sense. Vampires might be able to create the bond now, but magic had to be involved at some point in the past to create the spell, and that means a wizard."

"Ask someone else," Orlando repeated. "I can't do this."

Jean opened his mouth to plead his case again, but before he could begin, Alain appeared at the edge of the rise leading down to the lake. "What's wrong?" he demanded.

Jean sighed and let it go. He knew from experience how the conversation would go. If Orlando was protective of his partner—and there was no doubt of Orlando's protectiveness—Alain was ten times as protective of Orlando.

"It's nothing," Jean said. "I didn't think through a favor I asked, but now that Orlando pointed out the error of my logic, I've changed my mind. I can find the answers I need another way."

"Orlando?" Alain asked.

Orlando just shook his head, so Jean took that as his cue to leave them alone.

"What did he ask?" Alain asked when they were alone.

"He thinks the Aveu de Sang would protect us if ever I lost control and let the monster inside me free," Orlando said. "It's a reassuring thought if he's right, but he wanted me to do that deliberately to test his theory, and I can't. I won't be the monster who turned me."

"You couldn't be like Thurloe," Alain said, squeezing Orlando's hand comfortingly. "You don't have that kind of malice in you, no matter what instincts lie dormant."

"You've never seen me at the mercy of the bloodlust we all feel," Orlando protested.

"Yes, I have," Alain reminded him. "After we rescued you from Serrier, when Jude reanimated you, you didn't know where you were or who I was at first. You were barely conscious. I certainly wouldn't call you in control. You weren't careful like you usually are when you feed from me. You lunged at me like some creature out of my childhood nightmares. Then you tasted my blood, and the minute you did, you calmed down. It took a little longer for you to recognize me, but not for the bond between us to keep you from hurting me."

"So you're saying I should do what Jean wanted?" Orlando asked.

"That's up to you," Alain said. "If you don't want to be out of control, then you shouldn't do it. If you want to try it, either to reassure yourself or because you want to help prove Jean's theory, that's fine with me. One of two things is going to happen if you do what he wants. You're either going to feed from me or you're going to make love to me, and I don't see anything to complain about in either of those outcomes, but I wouldn't ever want you to do something that would make you uncomfortable about being with me. The choice is yours."

"We have a seminar to teach this evening," Orlando said. "We can't do anything about it until after that. Let me think about it."

"You don't have to decide right away," Alain said. "You don't have to decide at all. My feelings on the matter aren't going to change. As long as you keep feeding from me and keep making love with me, I'll be happy."

"Those two things won't ever change," Orlando promised as he leaned over to kiss Alain. They kept the contact light, knowing they had to stand up in front of a group of wizards shortly and talk intelligently about the history of the partnerships and the alliance, but Orlando could feel the passion that simmered beneath the surface, waiting for the right moment to break free.

Could he develop a different relationship with the primal side of himself so that, instead of suppressing it, he dealt with it much as he did his hunger and his desire for his wizard? Could he continue to control it when he needed to, but still let it free at other times? He had always dismissed such a thought because he had never known of any vampire who had found that balance. Thurloe had been completely in thrall to his primitive side, to the point of torturing and killing those around him with a sadistic glee that had left Orlando sick to his stomach more times than he could count. After his escape from Thurloe's clutches, Orlando had spent most of his time with Jean, the perfect picture of complete control. They had hunted together enough times for Orlando to know that Jean did not give in to his bloodlust when he fed. They had never crossed the line from friends to lovers, but Orlando doubted Jean would relinquish control in that arena any more easily than at any other time. He was chef de la Cour of Paris. Any slip in his control could cost him his position. He had to be the consummate player at all times.

Except that now he had made an Aveu de Sang. If that were known, he would be outside le jeu des Cours, above it for his Avoué's lifetime. Orlando had always understood that as an indication of the rarity of the bond, but now he wondered if the roots of that custom, lost as so much had been in the depths of the past, were tied to Jean's theory. If a vampire with an Avoué could relinquish control safely, he would have an unfair advantage over the other vampires in the game of appearances and one-upmanship that ruled the very existence of the vampires.

"Let's go inside. We can worry about the rest later."

# Chapter 8

"I'VE BEEN thinking about what Jean said."

Alain had suspected as much. Orlando had been unusually quiet on the drive home instead of discussing the seminar, the reactions to their presentation, and the reactions to their partnership the way he did most evenings after they had done a teaching stint at l'Institut.

"And have you made a decision?"

"Not completely," Orlando replied. "I know I'm not supposed to be able to hurt you, even if I'm out of control. But if I did, you would find a way to stop me or to get away from me, wouldn't you?"

"It won't ever come to that," Alain said with utmost confidence.

"But if it does," Orlando pressed, "you won't let me hurt you, right?"

"I won't let you hurt me," Alain promised. He stood by his assertion that it would never come to that, but if his promise would assuage the last of Orlando's fears, Alain would make it and more.

"I don't even know if I can do it," Orlando said. "I've spent so long perfecting the art of staying in control no matter what that I'm not sure I can let go that way."

"If you can't, you can't," Alain replied philosophically. "Or maybe you can't this time, but you'll be able to next time. It could be that learning to let go will be like learning control in the first place, something you have to practice. Just remember that I love you. Nothing else matters."

Orlando nodded but made no move to initiate any intimacies. Alain debated letting it go for a moment but decided against it. The matter was clearly preying on Orlando's mind. It would be far better to work it out now than to let it fester.

"What are you worried about doing to me that we haven't already done hundreds of times?" Alain asked softly. "We've made love in pretty much every configuration I can think of, and I've loved every one of them, so that won't be a problem. I'm pretty sure the only places you haven't bitten me are places that would hurt, so you wouldn't do it even while out of control since you can't hurt me, and I've loved every moment of our time together, even the first moments after Jude reanimated you, because I'd been afraid I'd never feel you feeding from me again. What do you want to do that you haven't done?"

"I don't know," Orlando said. "It's just... Thurloe did such terrible things to me and to other people. It didn't scar my body, but it scarred the rest of me. And then Jean rescued me, and I spent a hundred years with almost no other vampires. Jean's so in control of himself it's scary. Until the war began, I'd only had those two examples of how to be a vampire. I never let myself consider any other path because if my choices were to be like Jean or to be like Thurloe, there wasn't any question of which choice I'd make."

"But you aren't Thurloe," Alain pointed out. "You don't want to do those kinds of things. My question was, what do you want?"

"To make you feel good," Orlando said immediately.

"You have always made me feel good," Alain promised, "from the first time you bit my wrist at Père Lachaise. That isn't going to change, but that's for me. What do *you* want?"

"I don't know," Orlando said, his voice betraying his agitation.

Upsetting Orlando defeated the purpose, so Alain tried a different tack. "What's your favorite part of making love?"

Orlando brightened immediately. "Seeing you completely exhausted and sated when I'm done with you."

Alain smiled and reached for Orlando's hand. "I've never seen you that way. Satisfied for the moment, maybe, but never completely, never so wrung out you couldn't move if your life depended on it. You've made me feel that way on countless occasions, but I've never seen you that way. I'd like to."

"But—"

"No," Alain said. "Don't use me as an excuse. Yes, you've left me wrung out before, but that doesn't mean I wouldn't have given more if you'd asked for it. You can't drain me dry, Orlando. You can drink from me until another drop would make you ill. And all it takes to make me ready for another round of sex is knowing that you still want me. If you aren't comfortable with the idea, I won't push it, because I do know some small part of what you went through with Thurloe—but don't hold back because you're somehow worried about what letting go would do to me. You won't hurt me, and I've already promised that if somehow you do, I will stop you or get away."

"I... I'll think about it," Orlando said after a long pause.

Alain accepted the delay as he had learned to accept all of Orlando's hang-ups. Each time before, Orlando had come around given enough time. Alain would give it to him now as well.

"You *are* still going to make love with me tonight, right?" Alain said. "All this talk about feeding and sex has gotten me worked up." He sent a surge of need through the bond between them. Not that he thought Orlando was unaware of it, but when Orlando got wrapped up in his own worries, he tended not to pay as much attention to Alain's emotions as at other times. Alain was not above distracting him from his concerns with a little old-fashioned lust.

"I still don't know why you want me the way you do," Orlando said with a shake of his head, "but yes, I will make love with you."

"I love you," Alain said. "I don't need another reason."

Orlando was keenly aware of the miracle implicit in that statement. He might not be able to let go completely the way Alain seemed to want him to do, but he could spend the next several hours making sure Alain did not regret being with him. "Let's go upstairs."

Their bedroom was the one room of their house they had completely finished, and it was their haven. Alain took his time now, opening the volets to let the moonlight stream in. He was tempted to open the windows and let in the night breeze as well—but even with a heating spell in place, he was not sure he could maintain a comfortable temperature for himself, and he did not want to give Orlando something else to worry about as they made love.

He undressed swiftly and laid his clothes over the arm of his wingback chair in the sitting area of their room. Orlando had already removed his sweater and shirt by the time Alain turned back to face him, but he still wore his trousers. "Let me," Alain said, moving to Orlando's side.

Orlando dropped his hands to his sides, ceding control to Alain. Alain wondered for a moment if this was what Orlando needed—for Alain to take control and hold on to it until Orlando had none left—but that was what Thurloe had done to him, and Alain refused to do anything that might recall the years Orlando had spent at the mercy of his maker. He topped when Orlando wanted him to, but that was as far as Alain was comfortable pushing the matter. No, he could not push Orlando into losing control, but he might be able to seduce him into it.

"My beautiful angel," Alain murmured as he kissed Orlando's neck, running his hands over the smooth skin of his vampire's chest.

Orlando made an instinctive sound of protest, which Alain ignored. They had discussed the matter at length. They would gain nothing by hashing it out again. Instead Alain focused on the man beneath his hands, on proving his words through his actions. He continued to nuzzle Orlando's ear as he sought the dark nubs on his chest and tweaked them repeatedly until Orlando moaned softly.

"What do you want?" Alain asked. "More? Or should I do something else?"

"Whatever you want," Orlando said.

"No," Alain insisted, "what do *you* want?"

Orlando waited so long to reply that Alain almost prompted him again. "More."

Alain rewarded the reply with a nip to Orlando's earlobe and more stimulation to his nipples as requested, rubbing and tugging on them until Orlando had arched completely into the caresses, gasping with each movement of Alain's fingers. Only when he felt a hint of discomfort through the bond between them did he stop and turn his attentions elsewhere, running his hands down Orlando's flat belly to the waistband of his slacks. The button gave beneath his insistent fingers, the zipper following suit, so that Alain could push away all the fabric between him and his lover. Orlando stepped free of his pants and boxers and turned in Alain's arms so they stood face-to-face.

Alain framed Orlando's face with his fingers and drew him into a kiss that started out tenderly but grew hotter with each passing moment. Orlando's fangs scored Alain's tongue as they tangled their bodies together, and Alain felt Orlando's immediate withdrawal.

"Don't pull back," Alain said. "Whatever you want."

Orlando shook his head. "I don't want that. It hurts, and I won't do that to you. I don't *want* to do that to you."

"Are you sure?"

"I'm sure."

Alain searched Orlando's face and the emotions he could feel through their bond and accepted the truth of Orlando's statement. "Then what do you want?"

"Take me to bed," Orlando said.

Alain spun them around and backed Orlando toward the bed, not stopping until Orlando had fallen backward onto the expanse of mattress. Alain followed him down, aligning their bodies from tip to toe.

Orlando tilted his head to the side, kissing the brand on Alain's neck.

"Bite me?"

Orlando took his time, licking over the marked skin so his saliva could prepare the area for the touch of his fangs. Alain shivered in delight and need. He loved everything he and Orlando did together, but Orlando's fangs in his neck, especially through the mark of their bond, drove him wild like nothing else.

Far too soon, Orlando moved his head. Alain opened his mouth to protest, but Orlando silenced him with a kiss, the taste of Alain's blood still strong on his tongue. "You keep telling me to do what I want," Orlando said when he broke the kiss. "I can't do everything I want to do if I'm feeding from your neck the whole time."

"Just don't stop because you think you should," Alain said.

Orlando rolled Alain onto his back and nibbled his way down Alain's neck to his collarbone, trying to do as Alain had asked and listen to the needs inside him that he usually ignored in favor of Alain's favorite ways of making love. To his surprise, the voice had only one desire: to drive Alain wild with a combination of feeding and fucking that would leave him a sweaty, sated mess on the bed.

If Orlando ended up just as sweaty and sated beside him, even better.

Suddenly the prospect of doing what Jean and Alain had asked didn't seem so daunting. Giving in to the need for blood, Orlando latched on to the patch of skin above Alain's collarbone, tasting the passion and love in Alain's blood as it rose to match his own. Without releasing the hold of his fangs in Alain's skin, Orlando traced the lines of Alain's muscles with one hand, learning again the contours of his lover's body. He knew every mark by touch, sight, and taste, but he sought them out again, lavishing pleasure in every way he knew how. Alain's nipples tightened beneath his fingers. Alain's cock jumped at the hint of nails as Orlando passed over it. Alain's sac drew up as Orlando cradled it in his palm. Every touch added to the desire Orlando could taste in Alain's blood, and with each new burst of flavor, the voice inside him grew more insistent. "More."

Orlando closed the punctures on Alain's shoulder with a quick flick of his tongue so he could change position and reach other parts of Alain's body. He sucked on one of Alain's rosy nipples for a few moments, but he needed blood. He was tempted to bite right there, his fangs framing the areola.

"Do it," Alain said softly. "Whatever you're hesitating to do, stop worrying about it and do it. If I don't like it, I will tell you. I promise."

Orlando hesitated a moment longer, but the lure of loving Alain without reservation was stronger than his fears. Twice before, he had lost time that could not be regained because he had held on to pointless fears. He had only a finite amount of time with Alain. He would not lose any more precious moments to his past.

He licked carefully around Alain's nipple. He might want blood, but he did not want to hurt Alain, so he took his time preparing the skin. The process delighted Alain as much as it did him, to judge by the way Alain moaned and squirmed beneath him. Finally convinced he could do this without hurting his lover, Orlando sucked Alain's nipple back into his mouth and let his fangs touch the pale skin on either side. He pressed gently, enough for the tips to penetrate but not enough to truly feed. Not yet. He had to see how Alain would react.

"Do it," Alain begged, his hands tangling in Orlando's hair to urge him on.

The gesture that would once have sent Orlando into a full-fledged panic now gave him the reassurance he needed. He sank his fangs to their hilt in Alain's chest, titillating his lover's senses at the same time he satisfied his own need for blood.

"Putain! Oui, Orlando. Just like that."

Orlando could feel Alain's heart racing beneath his lips as he sucked life-giving blood into his mouth. Each press of his fangs brought his lips and tongue in contact with Alain's sensitive teat, sending lust spiraling through them both.

*Make him come.*

The thought echoed through Orlando's mind, crystallizing his desire to taste not just passion but orgasm in Alain's blood. Orlando was nowhere near that stage himself, but he had learned a trick or two about making Alain lose control in the two years they had been lovers. He sucked harder as he coated his palm with the fluid already pooling on Alain's stomach. He closed his hand around Alain's cock and shunted it up and down the straining length in time with the pull of his lips. Within seconds Alain was thrashing on the bed, begging Orlando for more.

It would be easy to do, but it seemed Orlando's inner voice had a mischievous side. He wanted to hear Alain plead with him nearly as much as he wanted to taste Alain's climax. He kept the pace just slow enough to leave Alain teetering on the brink of release without pushing him over the edge. The string of profanity from Alain's lips as he realized what Orlando was doing only added to the headiness as Orlando reveled in the sheer power of the moment.

"Please," Alain said finally, that simple word tipping the scales.

Suddenly giving Alain what he needed became the only thing in the world that mattered, everything inside Orlando—his rational mind and the devil on his shoulder—aligning to bring Alain surcease. He moved his hand faster and sucked more purposefully on Alain's chest, his only concern now to augment the rapture he could taste bubbling up in Alain's blood. Then it exploded onto his tongue as Alain found his pleasure.

He licked across Alain's nipple one more time, closing the fang marks on either side. He had learned how sensitive Alain was there after an orgasm. Once his passion was roused again, Orlando could resume his attentions if he wanted. For now, he would focus elsewhere.

The smell of sex permeated the air as Orlando skated his lips over Alain's damp skin, the light sheen of sweat only adding to the pleasure Orlando found in knowing how good he had made his lover feel. He lapped at the puddle on Alain's stomach, only a hint of the salty flavor coming through.

He needed more.

Before he could drive his fangs into Alain's lower belly, Alain sat up halfway, reaching for Orlando.

Orlando lifted his head to meet Alain's eyes.

"Turn around," Alain said. "Let me make you feel good too."

Orlando shifted on the bed until his hips were level with Alain's head. Alain urged him to get on his knees and straddle Alain's face so his cock bumped against Alain's lips.

"Perfect."

Orlando agreed completely. He had Alain spread out beneath him to feast on and he had Alain's mouth on his cock. What more could a vampire want?

The simple and immediate answer was blood, something Alain could provide. Orlando lowered his head again to resume his task of licking Alain clean, not wanting to risk any chance of infection in the marks left by his fangs.

Alain did not waste any time either, drawing Orlando into his mouth. Orlando paused in his task to savor the sensation of the head of his cock sliding through the moist heat into the constriction of Alain's throat. Alain's hands on his hips kept him from driving too deep or lingering too long, a long-established concession to Orlando's fears of hurting Alain as he had once been hurt.

When Orlando had removed all trace of Alain's release and his lover's skin was glistening from his tongue, he zeroed in on the throbbing pulse point where Alain's hip and thigh joined. He had exhausted his patience and now he needed blood.

Alain groaned around Orlando's cock as Orlando prepared the spot he had chosen. He knew what was coming next. He had lost track of how many times Orlando had licked places on his body with that careful determination. A slight pinch would be followed by the most intimate sense of connection he had ever known with any lover. Not even the taste and feel of Orlando's cock in his mouth could rival the sensation of Orlando's fangs sinking into his flesh, binding them together.

His nerves tingled as the sharp tips of Orlando's fangs pierced his skin. The familiar zing along his nerves was as addictive as any drug, a heady sensation that set his body on fire and started his sated cock hardening again. Even before they were lovers, Orlando's feeding had been a sensual experience. Now that Alain knew with absolute certainty what would follow, it was as erotic as any touch to his cock or ass. Alain moved his leg, wanting to give Orlando a better angle to access the sensitive skin.

The implicit invitation triggered Orlando's sense of mischief again, so instead of driving his fangs deep as he would usually have done, he lingered with only the tips embedded in Alain's skin, licking around the marks, tracing Alain's iliac crease with his fingers, driving his lover mad with the anticipation. Orlando had worried once that his need for blood would repulse Alain. He had quickly learned the opposite was true, and more than once had brought his lover pleasure from nothing more than feeding.

Alain felt Orlando's glee through their bond and knew exactly what that portended as Orlando teased him with only the barest of penetration. Another time he might have protested, but Orlando's sheer delight in what he was doing silenced any sound of dissent Alain might have made. He had urged Orlando to relinquish his usual control and to do what felt right and good to him. Alain could not doubt how Orlando felt at the moment. Alain had never been passive by nature, though, and he was supposed to be returning the pleasure Orlando had lavished on him moments ago.

He lifted Orlando's hips with his hands so he could pull free of the cock in his throat and tongue the length instead. When Orlando was desperate for release, Alain would offer his mouth again, but Orlando was not the only one who knew how to tease a lover.

Orlando hissed in protest as Alain pulled away, only to groan as he felt the slide of Alain's tongue down his shaft toward his sac. His entire body clenched as he wondered if Alain might continue, but for the moment, Alain focused on his cock and balls, not his ass.

Even now, after two years as lovers, Orlando realized he had tensed against the thought. He pushed the awareness aside. Tonight he would focus on what felt good, and everything Alain was doing felt incredible. As his lover's ministrations stoked the flames of need inside him, the need for blood grew as well, and the teasing pinch of his fangs in Alain's groin was suddenly not enough. He turned back to his task with ferocious determination, driving as deep as he could. A spurt of blood filled his mouth as he found the thick vein and drew from it hungrily.

Alain cried out at the sudden thrust of Orlando's fangs, but Orlando knew his lover's sounds by now and recognized it for the encouragement it was. The reawakening desire he could taste in Alain's blood pushed the limits of Orlando's control.

"What are you waiting for?" Alain asked, replacing his mouth with his hand for a moment so he could urge Orlando on. "What do you want? My hand? My mouth?"

Orlando could not reply with his fangs buried in Alain's flesh, but he angled his hips so the tip of his cock bumped Alain's lips again. Alain opened for him, letting him slide deep. One of Alain's hands remained on his hips, but loosely, steadying him rather than directing him. The other slid over the curve of his ass, squeezing and kneading the smooth skin.

Orlando shuddered, the sensation so welcome and so fraught at the same time, but he reminded himself Alain had never hurt him. When Alain traced his crease with one teasing finger, Orlando moaned and shifted his knees farther apart, offering Alain access to his entrance. He bucked frantically into Alain's mouth as he swallowed mouthful after mouthful of hot blood, nearly out of his mind with need. Alain's finger circled his entrance, teasing along the rim. That contact tipped the scales and Orlando gave in to his need for release, shooting down Alain's throat in sharp, short spurts.

Closing the marks on Alain's thigh quickly, Orlando turned his head, capturing Alain's cock in his mouth. His fangs drew back without any thought on his part as he sucked hard on his lover's erection.

"Not yet," Alain protested. "If you make me come now, we'll be done, and you aren't done. You're still wild for more. Take what you want."

Orlando reared back, breath coming in harsh pants as he struggled to make sense of Alain's words and the urges of his body and soul. He lifted off Alain's torso so he knelt at Alain's side.

"Look at you," Alain teased. "You're flushed and sweaty and your eyes are as dark as I've ever seen them. You've been holding out on me."

He had been holding out on himself, Orlando realized as he stared down at Alain. Alain's lips were swollen from being stretched around Orlando's cock. His eyes glittered with desire and love. His hair was tousled and sweaty, much as Alain said he looked. He was the perfect picture of wanton desire, but he was still coherent enough to speak, and the devil on Orlando's shoulder found that unacceptable. He wanted Alain so far beyond words that it would take him hours—no, days—to recover.

Then he wanted to go there himself.

When Orlando nudged his knee, Alain parted his thighs willingly, making space for Orlando to settle between his legs. Orlando delved into Alain's crease, finding Alain's entrance with unerring precision and probing at it gently. With nothing to ease the way, Alain's body resisted despite Alain's best attempt to relax. Orlando had no desire to hurt him even that much, though, so he pulled his hand away to return moments later slick with gel. Alain shivered with delight as Orlando breached him, playing his body like a symphony.

The touch was nothing new. Orlando had prepared him this way more times than he could count, often dragging it out for the sheer pleasure of watching Alain come undone at his hands, but it felt different this time, more... Alain could not think of the right word, not with Orlando's fingers strumming across his prostate and driving him out of his mind with need. That was not so unusual, but the echo of the same wildness came through their bond, making him hope Orlando had finally done as Jean had suggested and abandoned any level of control. Alain forced his eyes open, not sure when they had fallen closed, wanting to see the expression on Orlando's face.

"Now," Orlando said, pulling his hand away and moving between Alain's legs. "I need you now."

"I'm yours," Alain gasped as Orlando nudged his entrance. "Always yours."

Orlando thrust deep, not waiting for Alain to urge him on. They had passed that stage some time ago, but Alain didn't need tenderness now. He needed the deep, powerful, unfettered joining he had not realized was missing between them until now.

Moments or hours later, Alain could not have said which, Orlando's passion finally crested, taking Alain with him, the connection between them so strong that Alain swore he felt their souls touch. He gasped at the feeling, sure nothing they had shared on any physical plane could ever surpass that moment of connection, of unity. In that moment, they were one.

Orlando collapsed on top of him, Alain's arms coming up to cradle him. As Alain lost consciousness, he realized Orlando had not fed from him at the end, and yet Orlando lay completely limp, his eyes closed and his breathing even. Alain rolled Orlando to his side, but the vampire's eyes stayed shut, and Alain breathed a sigh of contentment. It had worked.

# Chapter 9

"MERDE," MARC muttered as his attempt to localize and follow a thread of magic failed once again. It had looked so easy in Raymond's office.

"Tracing spells?"

Marc turned to see a wizard he had met only in passing standing behind him. "Sort of. I'm trying to learn how to read magical signatures and lines of power. I have to observe and analyze the werewolf ritual in a few days, and I'm still making a mess of it."

"L'Institut might not be the best place to try that, you know. I'm Martin, by the way."

"Why not try it here?" Marc asked, filing the name away.

"Because there are so many magical signatures here that it's easy to lose the thread even when you know what you're doing," Martin said. "Hundreds of wizards have come through here, doing magic as easily as they breathe, and I would guess that few if any of them actually ended their spells and cleaned the area behind them. There's no reason they should, after all. They weren't trying to hide what they did, nor were they working in an area where having a clean slate would be expected. You'll have far better luck going somewhere fairly isolated."

"Like where?" Marc asked. "I work at l'ANS when I'm not here. That would be even worse."

"Probably," Martin agreed. "Why don't you come to Denis's apartment tonight? I'm pretty much the only wizard there, but we could see if someone else wanted to come too so you'd have two different signatures to follow. I don't know how werewolves work. Would there be multiple signatures?"

"Probably not," Marc said. "Unless something has happened to change this, it's usually one shaman per pack. If the shaman is new, there might be some residual signature, but there should only be one active line of power."

"Then this is even less the place to practice," Martin said. "Take a walk with me and let's try something different."

Marc figured he had nothing to lose, so he followed Martin down one of the paths into the woods. When they passed outside the wards that surrounded l'Institut, Martin stopped. "Now cast your spell and see if you can find the lines of power delineating l'Institut's barriers. Don't worry about who cast them or anything like that. Just find where they are."

Marc cast the spell and watched as the woods lit up with a wall of magic. "That's...."

"Impressive," Martin supplied. "And yes, it is. Adèle did them. The point is that you see them. You don't have to identify every piece of every spell to know they're there. Now, Raymond will probably come running when I do this, but watch them now."

Martin cast a harmless spell on the wards. With the revealing spell in place, Marc could see the thread of Martin's magic and the way the wards absorbed it, spreading it along the surface. "That's amazing. I've never seen anything like that before."

"Most wizards haven't because they never bother to look," Martin replied, "but it's easy enough to see when you do. And you could follow the lines of power from both me and the wards."

"Yes, clear as day," Marc said.

Raymond appeared suddenly behind them, wand drawn. "What's going on?"

"Marc was trying to learn how to use the revealing spell in the courtyard of l'Institut," Martin said. "There's no way *you* could make sense of that, much less someone new to the spell, so we came out here where there are fewer competing influences. He also needed to see magic interacting with magic, not just magic interacting with nature, since we don't know what the werewolf ritual will entail. So I cast a spell on the wards so he could see the overlap."

"Warn me next time, okay?" Raymond said. "I get a jolt every time there's activity along the wards. It's unsettling."

"We can go somewhere else and practice," Marc said, his hero worship kicking in enough that he didn't want to trouble Raymond.

"No, Martin is right. This is a much more logical place to practice what you're likely to need to do than anywhere inside l'Institut. Now that I know what's going on, I can ignore it."

"You could stay and help," Martin suggested. "Your magic probably interacts differently with the wards than mine does."

"Why would it do that?" Marc asked.

"Why do you think it would?" Martin countered, ever the teacher.

Marc thought for a moment. "Because this is Raymond's home. Even if he didn't create the wards, they're his in a way that's different from the way everyone else looks at them."

"Very good," Raymond said. "Adèle's magic probably would interact with them the same way mine would, but you're right that very few others would get the same reaction."

"Can I see?" Marc asked, struggling to contain his excitement at Raymond's praise. "I mean, if you don't mind."

Raymond cast a spell toward the wards, but this time instead of spreading out along the wall of magic as Martin's spell had done, Raymond's magic twined with the wards and then passed through.

"So it... I don't know, recognized you?" Marc extrapolated.

"Something like that," Raymond agreed. "Adèle set the wards to recognize certain wizards' magic—hers, mine, the other full-time staff—so that their magic doesn't trigger an alert. Martin should really be added, but since he's only here for a year, I didn't have her alter the wards."

"Couldn't you do it?" Marc asked. "I mean, you're the most powerful wizard in France."

"Don't believe everything you hear," Raymond said. "I'm a powerful wizard, yes, but there are others with as much strength or more. Marcel would be a perfect example, and he didn't need a vampire partner to increase his abilities. More importantly, though, raw power isn't enough. Adèle has a gift for working with wards and magical shields that I don't have. I chose to develop different skills in my life. I can create a ward if I have to, and it will hold, but hers are works of art. I wouldn't damage that with my magic unless I had no other choice, especially not when she lives just a few kilometers away and comes to visit frequently."

Marc filed that away for future reference. "I hope I'm not getting in over my head with the werewolves," he said after a moment. "There's so much I don't know, and I'm still so new to magic. Are you certain I'm the right choice?"

"Necessity is the mother of invention," Raymond said, his tone philosophical. "You're our best choice at this juncture because of the antipathy between werewolves and vampires, and because of the protective nature of vampires toward their partners. I could find another unpartnered wizard. I could send Eric and Vincent back, even, but they don't have your background with werewolves. They have no concept of what they should see during a ritual."

"I'm not sure I do either," Marc protested. "I mean, I've read everything about werewolves I've been able to get my hands on since long before I was old enough to be reading some of it, but a lot of that stuff is pretty generic. It says things like the fact that they have a fertility ritual and it usually takes place at Ostara and things like that, but it doesn't say what they actually do. Besides, well, I suppose they have to have sex at some point."

"Kind of hard to be fertile without it," Raymond said, trying not to smile. "But that presumes the females are in heat or in season or whatever the term is for werewolves at the moment of Ostara. If they aren't, they would either need to repeat the ritual each time a female is ready or the magic would need to linger."

"Or the ritual brings them into their fertile period," Martin suggested. "My sister used to talk about how just living in proximity to other women affected her cycle. Something as powerful as a fertility ritual connected with the moon, especially if this is a regular occurrence, could easily influence their cycles."

"The way Iserin described it, I got the impression the ritual 'turned on' their ability to be fertile, for lack of a better expression, so it's possible mating would occur as part of the ritual. Is that going to be a problem?"

"I'm not a kid," Marc muttered.

"I didn't say you were, but that doesn't mean you're comfortable with watching complete strangers have sex. I still think you're the best choice for this, Marc, but if you don't feel you can do it, I need you to tell me so I can find someone else."

Marc took a deep breath. "No, I'll do it."

ADENET STOOD in front of his closet in only his underwear, trying to decide what to wear to greet the wizard Lorens hoped would solve their problems. Adenet had no illusions it would work, but he would do as Lorens asked. Even though he was the least susceptible to the alpha's power of anyone in the pack, he still couldn't refuse a direct request without far more reason than the nebulous edginess that had assailed him since Lorens had told him when the wizard would arrive.

The two who had come to explore the grotto had done no damage that he could tell, so he could not even use that as part of his argument. After they departed, he had cleansed the area to the best of his abilities, but he had no real way to check if they had left less tangible evidence of their passing. He hoped not. They had enough problems without the wizards' magic interfering more. He would make that very clear to this newcomer. He could observe from outside the circle of trees that included the grotto, but Adenet would not allow any of his magic to taint the fertility ritual. They had no idea what kind of impact that might have. He shuddered at the possibilities that ran through his mind: birth defects, twisted powers, abominations in every possible variation.

Growling at himself for his hesitation, he grabbed a suit and tie, the better to present an aura of authority.

"Are you ready?" Lorens asked when Adenet joined him at the central square of the village where most of the pack lived.

"As ready as I'll ever be," Adenet muttered. "I hope we don't regret this."

"We have nothing else to lose," Lorens reminded him. "Unless you want to see the pack die out?"

"Don't ever question my loyalty," Adenet snarled, fighting the urge to shift. "I may not think this is the right path forward, but I'm standing here beside you anyway because you are my alpha and you have made this decision. If you're right and I'm wrong, I will work with the"—he shuddered even as he spoke—"wizard for as long as it takes to see our pack built back up to what it once was." He wanted to ask Lorens if he had any idea what Adenet sacrificed every time he participated in the fertility ritual, not just as the shaman but as man and wolf as well, coupling with the females in the hope that someone would conceive, but Lorens would not see it as a sacrifice. Adenet had no mate, no reason not to participate other than his own inclinations. Lorens knew from their youth that Adenet had enjoyed the company of men, but Adenet had never said more. As long as he had no mate, it did not matter. He was free to participate in the ritual like everyone else. Lorens never saw how forced Adenet felt.

"I'm sorry," Lorens said to Adenet's surprise. "You didn't deserve that. Blame it on my frustration with the situation."

Adenet wanted to resent the ease of Lorens's apology, but he was no more proof against the alpha's charisma than any of the other wolves, male or female. They knew dominance when they saw it, and Lorens was in his prime. "Just remember that everyone else is as frustrated and worried as you are, okay?"

The sound of a car approaching put an end to their conversation. Adenet had put his foot down at the thought of allowing the new wizard to simply pop into pack lands like courtesy and protocol meant nothing, and Lorens had agreed with him. If this wizard intended to stay with them for an extended period of time, he would respect their customs and their limits or he would return to l'Institut.

The man who got out of the slightly battered Peugeot 206 was younger than Adenet had expected, given the age of the two wizards he had already met. He expected someone of similar age, someone his own age, not this… puppy they had sent.

The wizard approached slowly, palms up in front of him so everyone could see he did not have his wand in his hand. Adenet frowned when he felt his wolf sit up and take notice. His wolf ignored humans unless he considered them a threat, but his wolf's interest did not feel like threat assessment this time. It felt like….

Adenet pushed his wolf back behind his carefully constructed barriers. He did not have time for this. The wizard would be here for a few days, observe the ritual, and then go slinking back to l'Institut in defeat because he could not help them solve their problems, and Adenet would be left here just like before, alone and caught in a life he had not chosen, without anyone to care for him. If only Adenet just let his wolf loose, he could convince the wizard to—

Adenet cut off the train of thought as soon as he realized his wolf had gotten the better of him again. Forcing himself back under control, he strode forward, a step behind Lorens. His wolf protested when Lorens offered the wizard his hand. Adenet ignored the sinking feeling in the pit of his stomach. This could not happen, for too many reasons to count.

"Welcome to Breugnet," Lorens was saying. Adenet forced himself to pay attention. "I am Lorens Iserin, alpha of the Morvan pack."

"Thank you for your kindness in welcoming me," the wizard said, offering Lorens a deep bow before shaking the outstretched hand. "I am Marc Gourlin, and I am entirely at your disposal."

Only Adenet's surprise that a nonlycan would know the words of a formal greeting, even if he did add a little to them, kept him from growling in protest at the thought of the wizard—Marc—at anyone's disposal but his.

Lorens accepted the comment as it was intended and gestured for Adenet to step forward. "My shaman, Adenet Silaire."

"At your service," Marc said, bowing to Adenet almost as deeply as he had to Lorens. Adenet returned the bow without offering his hand. He could not touch the other man right now, not with his control over his wolf so tenuous.

"Welcome to Breugnet," Adenet made himself say.

"Normally my mate and I would extend our hospitality to you, but given your own background, perhaps you would enjoy the company of our shaman more?" Lorens proposed once the introductions were complete.

"My house is small in comparison," Adenet protested, ignoring Lorens's sharp look. "You would be more comfortable in Lorens's home."

"I'm sure it will be fine," Marc said. "I don't need a lot of space, and you're really the one I need to talk to and get to know for me to do my job."

Adenet's stomach sank. If Marc had accepted his protest, he could have overruled Lorens, but with Marc insisting, Adenet had no real choice but to accede. "Then I will show you to your room."

He wondered wildly how long it would be before he could shift and go for a long, long run. He had a feeling he would be doing a lot of that over the next few days.


MARC COULDN'T have said later what he had expected a werewolf's home to look like, but as he looked around the small house, he could definitely say he hadn't expected it to look quite so normal. He was no expert on architecture, but the house was clearly not new, built of rough-hewn stone with a tile roof like all the other houses in the hamlet that sheltered the werewolves. The inside had been modernized—somewhat, anyway. Someone had installed electricity and plumbing at some point, but the interior walls were the same stone as the outside, only smoother and covered in places with decorations of various kinds: paintings, photos, even an old tapestry depicting two wolves howling at the moon. The furniture was plain, utilitarian, and of indeterminate age, nothing remarkable. When the shaman showed Marc to the room that would be his for the duration, he found a simple bedroom with a bed, a nightstand, and an armoire. Exactly what one would expect to find in a bedroom in a house too old to have closets.

"Thank you," Marc said, realizing the werewolf was waiting for him to say something. "I'll just unpack a little, if that's all right."

"Faites comme chez vous," the werewolf said, although Marc would not have described his voice as welcoming despite the words. "I have business to attend to."

"Is it something I could help with?" Marc asked. "Or maybe something I should observe?"

"You are here to observe the ritual on the night of the full moon," Adenet replied shortly. "Nothing else in our pack is your concern."

Marc flinched at the sharpness of the reply and retreated into his room to unpack. He had put away the last of his clothes when a strange sound in the other room caught his attention. Even knowing the shaman would probably snap at him again for intruding, Marc could not stifle his curiosity. He opened the bedroom door and peeked out in time to see a huge black wolf standing on the threshold of the open door. Marc's breath caught as the magnificent animal turned to stare at him. Eyes the color of rich amber met his, leaving Marc with the impression of such intelligence that he knew this must be Adenet in his wolf form. He took a step forward involuntarily. The desire to see if the wolf's fur was as soft as it appeared was more than he could resist. The wolf whined softly before turning his head and bounding away into the woods.

Marc collapsed on the couch, wondering what had just happened. Yes, it was the first time he had seen an actual werewolf in lycan form, after years of imagining just such a moment. He knew from his research that even in wolf form, lycans retained enough awareness of their dual nature to act consciously rather than react purely on instinct. That didn't make trying to touch a wolf whose human side had no use for Marc a good idea. If they were friends, if they had talked about it ahead of time, if the situation were different in any of a hundred ways, maybe Marc could have done it, but the impulse to do so now was inconsiderate and downright stupid. Fortunately Adenet had left before Marc could do more than take a step in his direction. Unless the shaman was a mind reader as well as a shape-shifter, he couldn't know what that step portended.

Marc took a deep breath and tried to concentrate on his plan for the days until the full moon. He needed to learn Adenet's magical signature and to see if any of the other werewolves had any signatures of their own, so he would be able to focus on Adenet during the ritual and not get distracted by anything else. If possible, he needed to see the grotto where the ritual would take place to get a sense of the flow of power there as well. All of that would have to wait for Adenet to return, though. Marc knew he was here on sufferance. He did not want to make it worse by doing magic in the shaman's house without permission.

# Chapter 10

THE COLD fall breeze did not bother Adenet when he was in wolf form, the bite of the upcoming winter meaningless through his thick pelt. He raced through the trees, lunging and veering along a path clear to none but him, letting loose all the tension brought on by having the strange wizard in his house. Even in this form, he still kept his mental hands buried in his wolf's ruff, controlling him. He could not afford to indulge in his wolf's fascination with the man. He had responsibilities to his pack and to his alpha. He had to stay in control and not make a mistake that could cost them everything they had left.

He scented a hare and swerved to follow its path, his body straining to catch it before it went to ground somewhere. He was hungry, and that made him susceptible to flights of fancy he would otherwise resist.

He caught the hare almost too easily, the capture enough to satisfy his hunger but not truly his need to hunt. He dropped his guard as he ate and his wolf took advantage, bolting free of his control.

He struggled to change back to human form. He would be cold in the woods with no clothes to protect him, but he could control himself better in that form. His wolf, though, had other ideas, bounding off after another hare, to take back to his mate this time, the better to impress him with Adenet's prowess and ability to provide.

The wizard smelled so good, so right. The wolf longed to tackle the man to the ground and rub all over him, covering the man in his scent and covering himself in the scent of the man. It wouldn't be enough for long, but it would be a start, enough to let the others know this man was *his*. Not that any but the alpha would even consider challenging the shaman for someone who had caught his interest, and the alpha already had a mate. No, this one was all for him, his to protect and cherish, his to claim.

The second hare fell to his prowess in a matter of moments. He ate that one as well, too hungry to wait. The woods were full of small animals. He would find another one, a *better* one to take back to his mate. One worthy of him.

His mate wasn't a lycan. Even with his wolf in control of his thoughts and actions, Adenet retained enough awareness to know he couldn't trust the mating instinct to bring his mate to him. He would have to woo the man and convince him to stay. A hare would be a good place to start. He couldn't get a deer on his own. He might be able to catch a duck if he was lucky and fast enough.

Adenet exerted all his control and forced the change. He shivered in the cold air, human flesh much more sensitive than thick fur, but he had to stop that train of thought before it took root any deeper than it already had.

Quelle saloperie. He did not have time for this, and even if he did, he could not have a male mate. He simply could not. The pack needed pups, and that meant mating with females. It didn't matter that everything about the wizard appealed to him, from his smooth, youthful skin to the enthusiasm Adenet had tried to disparage. It did not matter that every fiber of Adenet's being wanted to do exactly as his wolf had planned and race home with an offering between his jaws. He could not do it. He could not betray his vows to consider the good of the pack in everything he did. Even more than the alpha in some ways, Adenet was responsible to and for the pack. They looked to Lorens for leadership, but Adenet was their center, the one who guided them through the rituals that governed their lives.

If they had been a healthy, thriving pack the way they had been in Adenet's predecessor's youth, it would not have mattered so much. All those years ago, the pack was still strong enough for only the alpha to mate for procreation and for the others to mate as they pleased. No one would have noticed even if Adenet's predecessor had taken a male mate.

Then the birthrate had fallen and the alpha had decided to open the fertility rituals to the other mated couples as well, and then eventually to everyone, trying to boost the number of pups born each year. It had seemed to work at first, and then it had stopped, and now Adenet was stuck.

His shivering increased, so Adenet shifted back to wolf form. No matter how hopeless the situation seemed, getting sick because he had sat around naked in the woods would only make matters worse. He turned slowly toward home, trying to steel his resolve against acting on the awareness his wolf would no longer allow him to deny. He was still the master of his actions. He would control himself and do what was right for the pack. He had no other choice.

MARC WAS sitting on the couch when Adenet returned. His wolf whined softly, wanting to go curl up next to him, rub all over him, maybe even tackle him to the ground, but Adenet had already lost as much control as he intended to today. He went into his room and shifted back into human form, then dressed slowly, more casually than before. He had to work with the wizard, regardless of his feelings—or his wolf's feelings—on the matter.

"I'm sorry I disappeared on you like that," Adenet said as he walked back into the living room. "Sometimes my lupine side needs to run."

"I hope I didn't make you uncomfortable," Marc said. "I mean, I've read…."

"Maybe it would help us both if you forgot everything you read and dealt with what you see and experience here," Adenet said. "I've read some of the things mortals say about us, and believe me, they aren't true."

"None of them?" Marc asked, face falling in disappointment.

The expression tore at Adenet's soul. He scowled at his own reaction. "Most of them," he said. "We can change form, obviously, so that part is right."

"Are your senses as sharp in human form as they are in wolf form?"

"No, but they're sharp enough, sharper than a nonlycan's senses would be," Adenet replied, "at least based on what experience I have with nonlycans. More than how sharp they are, though, it's how we interpret that input. Even in human form, I can smell emotions on people. Fear is the strongest, but it's not the only one I can sense."

"How do you smell an emotion?" Marc asked.

"Strong emotions have a physiological component to them," Adenet explained. "They cause pheromones, and even in human form, we can smell and interpret those. It's like reading body language, only with a different sense."

"That makes sense, I suppose," Marc replied. "No superhuman strength?"

Adenet smiled at that. "No. We're as strong or as weak in our human bodies as you would expect of someone that size, just as we are as strong or weak in our wolf forms as those bodies will allow. Each form has its advantages, but they don't carry over."

"What's it like, having a wolf inside you?" Marc asked. "If that isn't too presumptuous of me. Is it strange being two entities?"

Adenet could not help his smile at Marc's curiosity and enthusiasm. "We aren't two entities," he said. "We're two halves of a whole, and most of the time we act in concert. It isn't him or me, it's just us."

"And when you don't act in concert?" Marc asked. "I can't imagine that kind of internal conflict."

"It's not any different than you debating a course of action with yourself, weighing options until you decide what's the best one," Adenet said. "Just because you don't have a second form doesn't mean you aren't ever conflicted about something."

"That's true," Marc said. "I guess I never thought of it that way."

"Ultimately it's almost impossible for us to be out of sync on something," Adenet said. "We only have one body, even if it has two forms, and that means we have to make a decision."

"Who usually wins?" Marc asked.

"It's not like that," Adenet insisted, ignoring the fact that today it had felt exactly like that. "Besides, as long as I'm not hungry or upset, the wolf pretty much ignores everything else that's going on. It's not like he cares about which car I drive or even what we have for dinner as long as there's plenty of meat. His drives are very basic—food, shelter, companionship."

Marc looked around the otherwise empty house. "You live alone, though."

"I have the pack. They provide companionship." It was even true. Just not completely true.

"I thought werewolves mated young and for life," Marc said.

"They often do," Adenet agreed. "Once they leave adolescence, the pack considers them old enough to find their mates and cement that bond, but that doesn't mean everyone finds their mate the first day or even the first year after they reach that point. Some people go for years without finding the right person. After all, the packs are understandably scattered, and we don't meet in large numbers very often. Some people never find the right person. Maybe their mate isn't a lycan and they don't ever meet, since we tend to be somewhat insular. Maybe their mate isn't a lycan and doesn't feel the call of the mating bond the way the lycan does. Things happen."

"That seems… sad."

"It is, but you can't miss what you've never known."

If that was not the biggest lie Adenet had ever told, he did not know what was. Even before he met Marc, he had felt the absence of a mate keenly. Now it tore at him because he had found the one his wolf wanted and he couldn't have him. He could not sit here talking to the one he longed for and not go crazy. "Shall I show you around the village? We should take advantage of the daylight while we can. It will be night soon, and I doubt your vision is as good as mine once the sun goes down."

Marc accepted the change of subject, not pressing for more information about the man opposite him. He was astute enough to sense the melancholy beneath the surface, but bringing it up struck him as a bad idea. He needed Adenet to trust him enough to talk to him about the upcoming ritual.

"Can we see the den where you do your rituals?" he asked. "I've always wondered what one would look like."

"Not today," Adenet said. "It's not inside the village, and you can't turn into a wolf to cover the ground more quickly." Marc's face fell and Adenet's wolf whined in protest. "We'll go tomorrow."

The words were out before he could stop them. He strengthened his internal barriers, pushing his wolf firmly back behind them again. He had to stay in control.

"The ritual will be the night of the full moon, right?" Marc asked as they walked out of Adenet's house. "Is there anything I should know? Anything I should do or not do?"

"Stay outside the circle," Adenet said. "You're there to observe, not participate, so you shouldn't be inside the circle. And don't interrupt. If you have questions, save them for later. I'll answer what I can when I can, but the middle of the ritual is not the right time."

"Of course not," Marc said immediately. "I wouldn't want to keep the ritual from working by disturbing your concentration. I know how much work magic takes."

Adenet frowned. "It didn't seem like work to the other wizards who were here."

"Eric Simonet and Vincent Jollet, right?" Marc verified.

"Yes."

"Well, for one thing, they've been doing magic a lot longer than I have, so maybe it gets easier. And then, it's them. They fought behind Serrier's lines for most of the war. They'd have to be incredibly powerful just to survive. I'm not like that. My ability only manifested a year ago. I can do what I need to, but it still requires concentration and a lot of effort, especially if I'm inside."

"Why would that make a difference?" Adenet asked, curious despite himself.

"Because my affinity is with air," Marc explained. "Free moving air, preferably. An artificial breeze from a fan is better than nothing, but it's still artificial. I have to draw more power internally, and I don't have all that much to begin with. Supposedly that will get better as I get more experience, but at the moment, if I'm inside, I can only do a few small spells before I'm exhausted."

"Then it's a good thing we do all our rituals outside," Adenet said before he could stop the words.

"From what I understood from Vincent's report, the only element missing from your grotto is fire," Marc said, "unless you have a fire going while you're doing your rituals, so I'd be fine even if I had a different affinity."

"We have candles or a fire in the summer, depending on the weather conditions, and a fire in the winter," Adenet replied automatically.

"Tell me more about the village, about the pack," Marc asked. "I feel like a kid in a candy shop. I've dreamed about this. I never thought I'd really get the chance to experience everything I'd only read about in books, though."


ADENET LAY in bed that night, vividly aware of the thickness of the single wall separating his room from the one Marc was using, and mulled over the afternoon and evening. Even aside from his wolf being convinced Marc was his mate, the wizard was not at all what Adenet had expected. He had expected someone more like the two men who had come to inspect the den—hard, closed, distrustful men worn down by life and magic. Instead he had gotten Marc.

Sweet, energetic, youthful, innocent Marc with the laughing green eyes and the light-brown hair and all the effervescence that had been lacking in Adenet's life for… well, forever, certainly since they had realized how serious the situation was for the pack. Adenet could tell himself intellectually that Marc was no more attractive than any of a hundred other men, but that didn't matter one bit to Adenet's wolf. The wolf had taken one look at the man and decided he was the most beautiful thing in the world. Period. Full stop. End of discussion.

Adenet shuddered when he thought about the upcoming ritual. Always before, he had been able to change into wolf form and participate as expected, the offer of sex enough to rouse his wolf even if Adenet had no interest in anything beyond the hopeful procreative outcome. Now, though, Adenet's wolf had one focus and one focus only—the man sleeping in the next room. The man who would be observing the ritual during the full moon, watching Adenet's wolf have sex with someone else, assuming Adenet could make his wolf go through with it.

Usually it was the other way around; Adenet normally stepped back once the words of the ritual were complete and let his wolf take control. He would not be able to do that this time. If he let his wolf take charge, the animal would bolt straight for Marc—and that would be the end of any kind of secrecy. Mating between incompatible species wasn't an option, but Adenet's wolf could change forms at will as well. He would be human in a heartbeat, naked and aroused and all over Marc before the other man knew what hit him.

Not the impression Adenet wanted to leave on the wizard, not to mention that he would probably end up flat on his ass from a spell. Marc might claim not to be a powerful wizard like some of the others, but Adenet was sure fear would boost his abilities enough for him to defend himself from Adenet's unwelcome advances. Even if Marc was gay, he would not be interested in someone like Adenet—older, bitter, tied to a dying pack.

If only Marc were a little less perfect.... Adenet rolled over with a grumbled curse. He knew that was his wolf talking. No one was perfect, no matter how much Adenet's wolf wanted it to be that way. Objectively, Adenet could see that Marc's forehead was a little too high and his teeth were a little bit crooked, but that did nothing to lessen the wolf's interest in Marc.

Realizing he would never be able to sleep with his thoughts in this much turmoil, Adenet rose and stripped. He would shift once he was outside, clear of the doors that were too complicated for his lupine self.

He made it almost to the front door before he heard the sound of feet shuffling into the room from the small kitchen.

"Wha... what's going on?"

"Nothing," Adenet said, turning his head but otherwise keeping his back to Marc. "I couldn't sleep. I'm going for a run. I can't open the door in wolf form, and my clothes disappear if I'm wearing them when I turn. I'd rather not have to keep buying new ones. Now, if you'll excuse me."

"Oh, um, yeah, sure." Marc stumbled over the words in a way that should not have been endearing, looking everywhere but at Adenet.

Adenet stifled a curse and opened the door, slamming it behind him even as he changed form and took off into the night.

On the other side of the door, Marc slumped onto the couch, trying to ignore the fact that he had reacted to the sight of Adenet naked like a teenager with his first skin mag. He had known the man was attractive. His suit and, later, his casual sweater had shown off the breadth of his shoulders, but they had not given Marc the slightest idea Adenet was hiding *that* beneath his clothes. Damn, the man was hot as anything: broad shoulders, trim waist, firm ass, thighs like oak trees.... Marc cleared his throat, trying to change the direction of his thoughts. He had no business lusting after a man—a werewolf—he had only met that afternoon, no matter how hot he was. He was here to do a job, not to fall in lust at first sight.

He was tempted to stay right where he was until Adenet came back so maybe he could get a glimpse of the front view this time, but that bordered on perverted, so he made himself get up and return to the room he had been assigned for the duration. If his dreams were full of a black wolf who turned into the most attentive lover Marc had ever had, nobody else had to be the wiser.

# Chapter 11

MARC HAD a hard time looking Adenet in the eye the next morning. Between running into him naked and then the dreams that had haunted him all night, he was acutely aware of the other man's presence, but he was afraid he would give away every thought in his head if he met Adenet's eyes.

His deep brown eyes the color of chocolate fondue....

Merde, he had it bad.

"What's the plan for today?" he asked, determined to keep things as normal as possible.

"You wanted to see the den," Adenet replied. "I thought we would hike there this morning so you can do what you need to do before it gets too late. You don't want to be traipsing around in the woods after dark."

"I doubt anything in the woods would go up against you," Marc said. He dared a glance in Adenet's direction as he spoke. "I saw you in your wolf form. Unless it was another wolf, maybe, nothing would stand a chance against you."

It must have been a trick of the light, but Marc swore Adenet's eyes changed color at his words, lightening to almost amber before returning to their usual dark brown.

"There are wild boars in the woods," Adenet said. "As a pack, we could bring one down, but I wouldn't want to face one alone."

"Do you hunt larger game as a pack?" Marc asked, smiling as Adenet handed him a cup of coffee. He took a sip and sighed in pleasure at the dark, rich taste.

"Sometimes," Adenet said. "Usually to mark a special occasion. A mating or something like that."

"I don't want to be presumptuous, but wouldn't it help morale if you hunted together more often?"

"What does morale have to do with it?" Adenet asked.

"Maybe nothing," Marc said, "but magic doesn't happen in a void. Even a wizard who points a wand and casts a spell is influenced by his or her physical and emotional state. It stands to reason that anything that might improve the cohesiveness of the pack could also improve your physical and emotional states as you begin the fertility ritual. What should be a joyful occasion has become a painful one. That can't be good for the outcome of the next one. If you can do something to increase everyone's optimism, maybe that will help."

"And if it doesn't?"

"Then you'll have had a good hunt," Marc said. "It's a good thing in and of itself, isn't it?"

Adenet nodded slowly. "I'll speak with Lorens when we get back from the den."

Marc finished his coffee quickly and took his cup to the sink. "I'm ready when you are."

Adenet looked pointedly at Marc's shoes. "Those will be ruined in five minutes. Do you have any boots?"

"Not that I brought with me," Marc said. "I could go get them. A couple of spells and I could be there and back in no time. If that won't make you uncomfortable, I mean. I wouldn't want to cast a spell here without your permission."

The thought made Adenet distinctly uncomfortable, but he didn't say that to Marc. "Go ahead," he said. "Although maybe you could cast the actual spell outside?"

"Of course," Marc said. "I'll be back in ten minutes, maybe less. I'm not exactly sure where my boots are. It may take me a few minutes to find them."

Adenet followed Marc outside and watched as the wizard drew his wand and cast a swift spell, disappearing instantly. He frowned a little at the casual use of power, but while Marc used magic at will, he had not been unaware of the repercussions—although not in the way Adenet had always been taught to consider them. He shrugged the observation aside. It was not his job to change the way Marc thought about magic.

He went back inside to pack some necessities. They might not be back in time for lunch, and while Adenet could shift and hunt if he got hungry, Marc didn't have that option. On impulse, Adenet tossed a change of clothes in the bag as well. He had not lost control of shifting since he left adolescence, but he had never tried to keep his wolf from its mate before either. Better safe than sorry.

Marc had returned by the time Adenet finished packing their lunch, and he leaned against the wall of Adenet's house in a way that made Adenet's wolf want to pin him there and take advantage of him.

"Let's go," he snapped, not about to linger in the face of temptation. His control of his wolf was good, but he still had his limits.

Marc followed Adenet into the woods, not at all sure what he had done to irritate the werewolf now. He had asked permission before casting the spells, had done them outside as requested, and had not even presumed to come back inside upon his return. He rolled his eyes at Adenet's back and did his best to keep pace. Even in human form, Adenet moved through the woods with an ease Marc envied and could not come close to imitating. He was a city boy through and through.

Well over an hour later, they arrived at their destination. Marc knew from what Eric and Vincent had told him not to expect an actual cave-like den, but their factual reports had not prepared him for the beauty of the grotto and its grove of trees.

"May I enter?" he asked Adenet, pausing on the edge of the circle.

Adenet nodded sharply, not replying in words, but Marc didn't even care as he walked slowly around the circle of trees. He didn't recognize most of them, but he could tell they were old and well tended.

He took a deep breath, letting the scents of earth and water fill his senses. He could see where the fires had burned at previous rituals, but the ashes were cold now. "How long has your pack used this den?"

"For as long as we've been a pack," Adenet replied. "The first werewolves came to this area with the Celts, well before the Romans reached this far north. There was already a thriving pack here when Caesar won the Battle of Alésia against Vercingétorix in 52 BC. The other French packs split from this one later, when our pack got too large for the territory we could claim and defend as our own."

"So thousands of years of werewolves have been conceived right here," Marc said, his awe clear in his voice.

"I don't know that they were all conceived here," Adenet said. "The ritual activates the fertility of those who participate, but while we are tied to the moon's cycle, not every female goes into heat at the same time. Once upon a time, the alpha would choose the pack's strongest females to participate in the ritual and would mate with them over the course of the month after the ritual as they went into heat."

"Everyone was descended from the same alpha?" Marc asked.

"Mostly," Adenet said. "You'd get the occasional male who would challenge the alpha or sneak around the edge of the den during the ritual. The packs remain on friendly terms, so there is always movement between them to bring in fresh blood, and the mated pairs could petition the alpha for the right to join the ritual. I'm not aware of an alpha ever refusing. He wouldn't have stayed alpha long, I would think. Strength is important, but wisdom is equally necessary to rule a pack. As birth rates declined, it only made sense to open the ritual to any who wanted to participate."

Marc nodded. "That does make sense, although I wonder...."

"What?" Adenet asked.

"Well, the ritual probably produces a finite amount of power. If you're spreading it over more people, that could make it less effective than if fewer people were trying to take advantage of it," Marc said. "I mean, take the spell I did to go home and get my boots. If I'm the only one I'm trying to move from place to place, it's a relatively simple spell, but if I'm carrying a lot of stuff or if I'm trying to move more than one person, it requires a lot more energy to do it. Could it be that you're overtaxing the power of the den and of your connection to it by trying to include everyone at once?"

"The birth rates declined before we opened the ritual to the whole pack," Adenet pointed out.

"I understand," Marc said, "but in terms of now, in terms of fixing the problem, maybe it would be better to limit it again, to concentrate power on a few people and see if that makes a difference. If it works, you could do the ritual again in a month and include different people since the people, at least the women, you included this time wouldn't be able to participate again right away."

"And if it doesn't work?"

"Then you've tried it and next month you go back to doing it the way you've been doing it," Marc said. "If it doesn't work, it doesn't matter whether you had one couple or fifty. If it does work, you have a baby on the way and can maybe have another one next month."

"I'll discuss it with Lorens," Adenet said after a moment's reflection. "I can make the suggestion, but the decree has to come from him. He will participate, of course, with his mate. If he agrees with your logic, it will be interesting to see who else he chooses to join them."

"Logically it would be the strongest wolves after him, wouldn't it?" Marc asked. "I mean, if you go back to the origins of the ritual, with the alpha mating with the strongest females to preserve the strength of the pack, then besides the alpha, you'd want the next most dominant male and female, and their mates, I guess, if they aren't mated to each other. For your pack, who would that be?"

"In pack hierarchy, I am second to the alpha," Adenet replied, "although for actual physical strength, some of the Guardians could probably overpower me if we were to make a contest of it."

"Well, of course you would have to be here," Marc replied. "Who would conduct the ritual if you weren't here?"

"Historically, the shaman conducted the ritual but did not take the power for himself," Adenet said. "That was reserved for the alpha, but that changed well before my time."

"So you and Lorens, Lorens's mate," Marc ticked off on his fingers. "You don't have a mate, though, do you?"

"No," Adenet said, refusing to acknowledge his wolf's agitation at his reply. Marc could not be his mate, no matter how much his wolf wanted otherwise. "Lorens would have to choose one of the unmated females to participate as well."

Marc's stomach fell. It would only make sense that Adenet would participate fully in the ritual, but hearing it confirmed still left an ache around his heart as he imagined Adenet curled around the body of a faceless woman, whether in wolf form or human. He pushed away the wish it could be him instead. He was neither female nor a werewolf. He had nothing to contribute to this process except his experience with magic, such as it was.

"Surely you would get some say in the process, since you would be the one sleeping with her," Marc blurted out before he could stop himself.

Adenet shrugged. "If she's not my mate, it makes no difference to me who she is. I will do my duty like everyone else."

"You make it sound like a chore," Marc said.

"In some ways it is," Adenet replied, cursing his honesty even as he spoke. "If I had a mate, it wouldn't be. It would be the expression of my feelings. Instead it's a physical release with no meaning behind it. It gets old."

"Maybe you shouldn't be the one to participate, then," Marc said, tucking away the longing in Adenet's voice for later reflection. The werewolf had said he did not miss what he had never known, but Marc wondered now if that was the full truth. "If we're looking for things that might be blocking the magic, maybe your reluctance is part of it. Yes, I know, it was a problem even before you became shaman, but if we're trying to test under ideal conditions, wouldn't it make more sense to pick a mated couple who want to have children?"

"I think everyone has given up hope," Adenet admitted.

Marc wanted nothing more than to pull Adenet into his arms, to offer comfort of some form or another, but the gesture would surely not be appreciated. He settled for a hopefully comforting hand on Adenet's shoulder. "That's why you came to us. That's why I'm here. To try to give people hope, to make it worth trying another time or two or ten, however many it takes to figure out the problem and fix it. I've been in love with the idea of werewolves since I was six years old and read a book that included them. I'm not going to give up. If I can't help you, I'll keep looking until I find someone who can. I don't want to be part of a world that doesn't include werewolves."

Adenet's wolf lunged at his control, wanting Marc more than ever at the touch of his hand and the heartfelt declaration. Adenet dragged him back by the scruff of his neck as he turned to look at Marc.

"Your eyes," Marc said. "They change color."

Adenet cursed silently. "Yes, that's my wolf," he said. "When my eyes change, he's there too, or he's in control, even if I'm in this form."

"Another one of those things they don't mention in any of the books I read," Marc said with a smile. "You can let him out, you know. I want to meet him too."

"I don't know if that's a good idea right now," Adenet said. "He's all tied up in knots because of the upcoming ritual. He'd probably end up rubbing all over you."

Adenet hated to lie, but he could hardly tell Marc the truth, and this way, if his wolf did get loose and rub all over Marc, Marc would chalk it up to the upcoming ritual rather than to the real reason.

Marc could think of worse things than rubbing up against the gorgeous wolf he had seen the day before, but he doubted Adenet would want to hear that, so he made himself laugh. "Poor thing. Is he going to be upset if you don't participate in the ritual except as the shaman?"

*Not with you here.*

"He'll get over it," Adenet replied.

THEY SPENT another hour at the grotto, Marc asking questions and even casting a revealing spell with Adenet's permission so he would know what the grotto looked like at rest. He could see traces of a brownish signature, probably Vincent's, along the rock wall at the back of the grotto, and then the prism-like aura of all the elements combined shimmering through the rest of the space. Adenet stood to the side of the spell, so Marc could not tell if he had a magical signature of his own, but he could wait until the ritual to determine that. Any signature other than those there now would be Adenet's when the time came.

"I brought sandwiches if you want to eat before we head back," Adenet said when Marc had ended his spell.

"I could eat," Marc replied, aware of his stomach rumbling. "Magic still takes a lot of energy for me."

Adenet pulled out two baguette sandwiches. "I've got ham and cheese or pâté," Adenet offered. "Which one would you like?"

"Either is fine with me," Marc said. "I'll take whichever one you don't."

Adenet's wolf wanted him to insist, to give Marc his choice first, but Adenet overruled him, taking the pâté for himself and passing Marc the ham and cheese. They ate mostly in silence, neither of them feeling the need to fill the space between them with empty chatter. Adenet was grateful. He was used to silence, and it would be hard to live with someone who could not let him have that time when he needed it.

The thought horrified him as soon as it formed. He was not living with Marc, not beyond the few days or weeks it took before Marc gave up and went home. He was not imagining the wizard in his life and his home longer than that. He could not set himself up for that heartache.

He finished his sandwich quickly and stood up, needing to be away from Marc and from the glances he caught the wizard sending his way. The man had said he was fascinated by werewolves—in love with them since he was six years old. It made sense he would study Adenet every chance he got. That did not mean Marc was interested in him in particular, not in the way his wolf wanted him to be.

"We can go back whenever you're ready," Marc said, rising and wrapping up the rest of his sandwich.

"You aren't finished," Adenet said.

"It's fine," Marc said. "I ate enough for now."

Adenet nodded as Marc moved to stand at his side.

"Does it look different when you're in wolf form?" Marc asked, gesturing to the woods around him.

"I notice different things when I'm in wolf form," Adenet said. "It's not so much that it looks different as that what I see as important is different. When I'm in this form, I'm watching the ground, making sure I don't trip over roots or branches or whatever might be in my way. When I'm in wolf form, those things aren't important. Instead I'm focusing on the signs of an animal's passage, any disturbance that might indicate someone from outside the pack has been here, anything I might need to see or notice as it affects the pack. It's not that I can't see those things in human form, but it requires thought, whereas it's automatic if my wolf is in control."

"If he's in control but you don't change forms, do you still see it?"

"That doesn't happen unless there's a reason for me to be in human form. He is more comfortable as a wolf."

"What would be a reason for you to be in human form with your wolf in control?"

Adenet shrugged. "Nothing I can think of, but stranger things have happened."

They had walked perhaps halfway back when Adenet's sharp ears picked up rustlings in the woods, too loud for a rabbit. The earlier conversation about boars in the woods came back to him, and he barely had time to drop his pack before his wolf took over and forced his shift. With the heightened scent of smell, he identified a deer rather than anything dangerous, but the relief was not enough to let Adenet wrest control back from his lupine half. The wolf was far too fascinated with Marc to give up so easily.

Marc had no idea what had provoked Adenet's shift, but he was not about to pass up the chance to interact with Adenet's other half. He held out his hand, not sure of the best way to approach the wolf. That was apparently all the offer the wolf needed, because he bounded to Marc's side and insinuated himself under Marc's hand.

Marc scratched at the wolf's ears, figuring the wolf would let him know if he did something it didn't like. The wolf tilted his head into the caress, so Marc scratched harder, staring into the amber eyes he had noticed earlier that morning.

"You're beautiful," Marc said, rubbing his hands over the wolf's muzzle and down his sides. "I got a glimpse of you yesterday, but up close you're just magnificent."

The wolf dropped to the ground and rolled to one side, offering the soft fur of his belly for Marc to pet. Marc knelt next to the wolf and attacked its belly enthusiastically, rubbing and scratching, everything he could do to encourage the wolf's closeness. Maybe it would have no effect on Adenet's attitude toward him, but Marc would take every chance he could to touch. This might be his only opportunity to touch a wolf.

The wolf knocked him over, climbed into his lap, and then tipped him backward, pinning him to the ground.

"Hi," Marc said, continuing to stroke the wolf's thick pelt. "You're a whole lot friendlier in this form."

The wolf could not reply in words, of course, but the little yip he gave at Marc's words made Marc smile. "What's Adenet's problem, then?" Marc asked, knowing Adenet would hear his words as clearly as the wolf. "He's not rubbing all over me the way you are. Or are you just the playful kind and he got all the serious genes?"

The wolf nuzzled Marc's neck, raspy pink tongue catching his jaw and cheek. Marc laughed again. "It's all good, buddy. I like you too."

He rubbed the wolf's muzzle, scratching under his chin.

He heard the rumble of contentment that would have been a purr if he had been stroking a cat instead of the magnificent wolf, and then just as suddenly as the wolf had tackled him, it bounded away from him. Marc sat up, confused for a moment until the wolf shifted back to human form again, giving Marc another glimpse of Adenet's naked backside.

"I have extra clothes in my bag," Adenet said, his voice as controlled as ever. "If you'll turn your back, I'll get dressed."

"You don't have anything I don't have," Marc muttered, but he turned his back nonetheless. "You can get your bag now."

He listened in silence to the rustling behind him.

"You can turn around now."

"What happens to your clothes when you shift?" Marc asked.

"I have no idea," Adenet said. "They disappear and aren't there when I shift back. I've learned to keep extra sets of clothes around or to take them with me. I don't shift accidentally very often, but he still surprises me on occasion."

"What set him off this time?" Marc asked curiously.

"I heard something in the woods," Adenet replied. "I'm far more capable of protecting both of us in wolf form than in human form. I may not be the most dangerous creature in the woods, but there are few that would want to tangle with me in wolf form."

"You know I can protect myself, right?" Marc said. "I mean, even if all I did was escape, I could get away from anything that attacked us, and I could even take you with me if I had to."

"That won't be necessary," Adenet said. "The only thing that would really be a threat to me would be a boar, and they're too slow to catch me even if they're stupid enough to try."

"Was it a boar?" Marc asked.

"No," Adenet said, "a deer, but I couldn't tell that until I shifted and could smell it."

"That is so cool."

Adenet was less sure of that. He had memories now of what Marc felt like beneath him. He had been in wolf form, not human form, so the contact had been more affectionate than amorous—but his wolf would be even more demanding now, wanting to feel more, touch more, taste more. Patience had never been his wolf's strong suit, except when they hunted as a pack. Maybe Marc had the right idea about organizing a hunt. He would suggest it to Lorens as soon as they got back to the village.

"YOU LOOK different."

Alain looked up from the book he was reading as he waited for Orlando to finish his meeting with Jean.

"Different how?" he asked Thierry.

"I don't know," Thierry said. "I'd say happier except you weren't unhappy, so that doesn't make sense."

"I'm certainly happy," Alain agreed.

"So what's different?" Thierry asked.

"Why does anything have to be different?" Alain asked, although he thought he knew.

"Because something is," Thierry insisted. "You can tell me what it is or I can keep bugging you about it."

Alain thought seriously about not saying anything. Jean had explained that the magic of the Aveu de Sang only worked once. Sebastien had claimed and lost his Avoué four hundred years ago. He and Thierry could not have the bond that allowed Orlando the freedoms they were now discovering he could enjoy. Thierry would not give up, though, and Alain had never kept secrets from his best friend.

"We discovered a new benefit of the Aveu de Sang," he said. "Well, Jean and Raymond did, but it works for us as well."

"I knew it," Thierry said. "I knew there was something they weren't telling us."

"And they made that decision for a reason," Alain said, "so don't go spreading it around."

"I won't," Thierry promised. "They're my friends too. Tell me about this new benefit."

Alain took a deep breath and tried to decide how to explain it. "Has Sebastien ever talked about feeling like he has to stay in control all the time or feeling like he's got a monster inside him or anything like that?"

"Not really," Thierry said, "other than talking about not feeding so much that it weakens me, but we already knew a vampire can feed as much as he wants from his Avoué without it causing problems."

"To hear Orlando and Jean talk about it, they're constantly having to control violent impulses to feed and keep feeding far beyond what a single person could survive," Alain said. "The way they describe it, only by being hypervigilant do they keep from becoming like that vampire we went up against during the war."

"The one who took great joy in torturing and killing the people he fed from?"

Alain nodded.

"But they aren't like that at all."

"No, they aren't," Alain agreed, "but apparently that requires a great deal of diligence on their part. Not that you'd know it to look at them. I didn't really know it even with the bond I share with Orlando, but when we actually talked about it, I could tell how serious Orlando was about his concerns. In his head—and Jean feels the same way—if they relax for even a few minutes, they risk going on a killing spree."

"And the benefit of the Aveu de Sang?"

"Even out of control, they don't want to hurt their Avoué," Alain said. "They can abandon all control, and nothing bad happens as long as we're around. It's like the presence of their Avoué is enough to call them back from the brink. Orlando might have been out of control, but he focused all that on me, and apparently I can contain that side of him even when he doesn't. He actually sleeps when it's over. Not just rests beside me, but really sleeps."

"And just what do you do to wear him out to that point?" Thierry asked with a knowing grin.

"Wouldn't you like to know?" Alain retorted.

"Yeah, I really would," Thierry said seriously. "I have a partner too, you know."

Alain's eyes narrowed. "I haven't forgotten, but this isn't a partnership thing, Thierry. You don't have an Aveu de Sang to keep Sebastien from draining you dry. Orlando can't kill me. He can't drain me dry and he can't hurt me. It's physically impossible for him to do something that would harm me. Sebastien doesn't have those constraints on him. He could hurt you or even kill you without meaning to."

"Not helpless here," Thierry said.

"Fine," Alain said. "He fed from me and we made love, but not just once. I swear it felt like it went all night long."

"How long did it actually go on?" Thierry asked.

"Hours," Alain said, "and that's not an exaggeration."

"How is that possible?" Thierry asked.

"It's the Aveu de Sang again," Alain said. "As long as we don't both come at the same time, it just keeps building and building and building until we finally can't take it anymore, and then when he keeps biting me on top of it…." He trailed off with a delicious shudder as the memories of the long nights of making love so Orlando could sleep washed through him.

"I can't decide if I want to smack you for the TMI or because I'm insanely jealous," Thierry said.

"You know he'd offer you the same bond if he could," Alain said.

"Yeah, I know," Thierry replied, "but he can't, so we both end up stuck with second best because the damn spell only works once. Whose fucked-up idea was that anyway?"

"Probably the same person who made it impossible for a vampire to turn his Avoué so there was no end for them but separation when the Avoué dies," Alain reminded him. "Yes, there are wonderful things about it, but it's not all sweetness and light. Orlando's going to have to watch me die someday."

"Wizards can't be turned anyway," Thierry reminded him. "He'd have to go through that even if you were just his lover."

"Yeah, but he can't leave," Alain said. "For as long as I'm alive, he has no choice because he can't feed from anyone else. If I wasn't his Avoué, he could go somewhere else, leave before I died."

"And how is that any better?" Thierry demanded. "He's so crazy in love with you that leaving would break him, and you know it, so don't think this would have any other outcome even without that brand on your neck. Stupid bastard."

"At least he'd have a choice."

Thierry's snort telegraphed his disbelief loud and clear. "So when Orlando drops his guard, so to speak, his two desires are feeding and fucking, right? He doesn't become some crazed madman intent on torturing everyone in his path, just on driving you out of your mind."

"I don't even think it's about me," Alain said. "I think he's learned to control desires that he's never been able to sate before—because what he takes from me, what the bond lets us share, goes beyond what any one person should be able to give him. Maybe even what his body could handle from multiple people if he were willing and able to consider that."

"What do you mean?"

"Way back when we were first forming the alliance and feeling out the partnerships, I remember Jean talking about overfeeding and how that could be as dangerous to a vampire as it was to the person they overfed from. Okay, maybe not quite as dangerous since the person would end up dead and Jean didn't specify what the consequences would be to the vampire. Still, the idea was there that a vampire needed to be careful about how much blood he consumed just like he needed to be careful about how much he took from any given person."

"And the Aveu de Sang protects Orlando from the dangers of overfeeding?"

"Exactly," Alain said, "and I don't know what Orlando would be like as a lover without the Aveu de Sang between us. We already had that bond before we ended up in bed the first time, but I can't seriously imagine that even a vampire's stamina would normally extend to hours of lovemaking. Even if he changed partners and each partner's lust fueled his, it still seems unlikely."

"So without the Aveu de Sang, it's dangerous for a vampire to truly sate himself on blood and impossible for him to sate himself on sex. Is that what you're saying?"

"Well, I'm guessing, not stating facts since this is all conjecture based on our experiences and a conversation between Orlando and Jean that Orlando won't share in detail, but it seems like a logical guess."

"Fuck logic," Thierry said, his voice harsh. "If this is something vampires need, there has to be another way to give it to them, or else why would the Aveu de Sang only work once? Why can't they form a new bond once the old one is gone?"

"Is it ever really gone, though?" Alain asked. "How long did Sebastien mourn his Avoué? Monsieur Lombard is still mourning his, and from what I understand, his Avoué has been gone fifteen hundred years. Maybe they don't want a new bond?"

"You're missing the point," Thierry said. "If this is something they need, then the Aveu de Sang being the only way to get it doesn't make sense. Why would you create a bond to satisfy a need in a way that makes it impossible to ever satisfy that need again once the Avoué is gone? I mean, maybe I can imagine some sickly sadistic wizard doing it, but why would a vampire agree to it?"

"Maybe he didn't know."

"I don't buy it," Thierry said with a shake of his head. "I'm not saying you're wrong about the Aveu de Sang giving you the benefits it does. It obviously has given you something special, and something newly special with Orlando, but I don't buy that it's the only way to meet those needs."

Alain sighed. "Don't do anything rash. Please? Sebastien would kill me for putting ideas in your head, and then Orlando would kill him for killing me, and then there'd be a *judicium* and Orlando's already had to sit through that twice, which is twice more than any vampire should ever have to do, and—"

"Shut up," Thierry interrupted. "I get the point. I won't do anything rash, but that doesn't mean I'm not going to find a way to give Sebastien the same options the Aveu de Sang gives you."

"Talk to Jean and Raymond," Alain said. "They know far more about it than I do. I just know what I've experienced with Orlando. Knowing them, they've spent the past week since Jean first mentioned it to Orlando digging through every scrap of information they can find to figure it out. Maybe they've found something I've missed. You know that kind of history stuff has never been my forte."

"Yeah, mine either," Thierry replied. "If it works, that's good enough for me. I don't need to trace a spell back to its origins in the Dark Ages in Transylvania or wherever the hell the spells we use come from."


ADENET APPROACHED Lorens's house slowly, taking slow, deep breaths to calm the turmoil that still lingered after his wolf's cavorting with Marc in the woods. It had felt good. It had felt *too* good, and that had Adenet worried. He did not need Lorens figuring out that something was bothering him, much less what was bothering him. He was not the average werewolf, he reminded himself. Of all the members of the pack, he had the best chance of controlling the signals he gave off and keeping Lorens from picking up on it. He simply had to stay calm and focused on the matter at hand, not the man he had left behind in his house.

His wolf perked up at the thought of going back and seeing Marc again, maybe even playing with him some more. Adenet pushed the urge back behind his barriers and firmly admonished his wolf to stay there. He knocked on Lorens's door and waited.

"Adenet, how are you?" Edine asked when she opened the door, allowing Adenet inside.

"Well," he replied, kissing Edine's cheeks in greeting. She might be his alpha's mate, but their friendship went back even farther than that. Adenet was one of the few wolves in their pack who still greeted her that way. None of the others dared to get that close to her.

"Lorens is meeting with the Guardians," Edine said. "Can I offer you something while we wait?"

"Merci, I'm fine," Adenet said with a shake of his head. "How are you, though? Lorens said you had been... upset."

Edine smiled at him, her face sad despite the expression. "Always the shaman, looking out for everyone else's well-being."

"I was your friend long before I became the shaman," Adenet reminded her.

"You were," she agreed, taking a seat on the couch. He sat in the chair across from her. They might have all been friends since they were children, but he saw no reason to give Lorens's wolf a reason to get more possessive than he already was.

"How are you?" Adenet pressed.

"I don't know anymore," Edine answered after a moment. "I dread the approach of the full moon now, knowing it will mean another ritual, another month of getting my hopes up, perhaps for nothing. I tell myself not to think about it, to simply enjoy being with my mate, but it's impossible not to think about it."

"You know the problem isn't with you, don't you?" Adenet said.

"How can you be so sure?" Edine asked.

"Because the ritual isn't working for anyone," Adenet said.

"We shouldn't have waited so long," Edine said, her anguish clear in her voice. "We thought we had all the time in the world, even with the small number of pups born each season. And now it's too late."

"It's not too late," Adenet reminded her. "Lorens went to get us help. The wizard who arrived yesterday has a lot of good ideas. I can't swear they'll work, but they're worth trying. We spent a long time this morning looking at options that might increase the chances of the ritual working. He's going to observe the next time, and maybe he'll see something as we go through it that hasn't occurred to him yet. We will find a solution, Edine. Lorens won't stop trying until we do, and I won't either."

"Thank you," Edine said, wiping at her eyes. "It means a lot to hear that."

The door to Lorens's study opened and two of the Guardians came out, giving Edine and Adenet respectful nods.

"Adenet, what brings you by today? I thought you'd be busy with the wizard."

"I was," Adenet said, "but he had some suggestions I need to talk to you about, if you have a few minutes."

"For that, I have all the time you need," Lorens said.

"Would you mind if I listened too?" Edine asked.

"Of course not," Adenet said. "We'll have to explain it to the rest of the pack anyway, once we decide on what we want to do."

When they were all settled in Lorens's study, Lorens turned to Adenet expectantly. "What did the wizard suggest?"

Adenet's wolf bristled at Lorens's use of Marc's profession rather than his name, but Adenet pushed the retort down. "Marc had a couple of different thoughts. The first is to do something to boost morale, to cheer people up. If we all go into the ritual with dark thoughts and sure it will fail, we could be creating a self-fulfilling prophecy."

"Did he have a suggestion for how to do that?"

"Indirectly, yes," Adenet said. "We should organize a hunt before the full moon for everyone in the pack able to run with us."

"Why?" Lorens asked.

"Why not?" Edine countered. "We hunt as individuals when we feel like it, but we haven't organized a hunt as a pack since… since Paul and Nathalie celebrated their mating, and that was at least two years ago."

"Hunting as a pack reinforces the bonds between us," Adenet went on. "It reminds us that we have to rely on each other for survival.

Maybe it won't make any difference in the ritual, but as Edine said, why not do it? It doesn't have to just be for celebrations."

"Okay," Lorens said. "We'll organize a hunt. Tomorrow night?"

"That's the night before the full moon," Adenet agreed. "That should be a good time."

"What else?"

"The other suggestion is the one I'm less certain of," Adenet admitted. "I can see the logic from Marc's perspective, from the way he uses magic, but I'm not sure it actually applies to us."

"What was his suggestion?" Lorens asked.

"He suggested we could be hurting our chances of success by spreading the power of the ritual over a large number of participants," Adenet explained. "He suggested limiting the number of participants in the hope of increasing the potential for success. He also suggested that only mated pairs should participate since the bond between them would add power to the ritual."

"You said you had doubts," Lorens said.

"The way he explained it, it requires more magic to move two people from place to place than one person," Adenet said, "which makes sense. It would be like lifting two books instead of one. From that perspective, if the ritual generates a finite amount of energy, focusing it on two or three couples instead of on twenty would increase the amount of energy each couple receives."

"That makes sense," Edine said. "So what's the problem with it?"

"We don't do magic the way a wizard does magic," Adenet said. "There is no waving of a wand and having magical energy flow out. We connect with the life force of everything around us in our rituals. When Marc talks about magic, he thinks about a finite resource that is his own strength. There's nothing finite about what we do."

"Are you saying we shouldn't listen to his suggestion?" Lorens asked. "I brought him here to help."

"No, I'm not saying we shouldn't listen to him," Adenet replied, "just that we should be realistic about the likelihood of this particular suggestion making a difference. It makes sense in his paradigm. It might not make a difference in ours."

"Then should we limit the number of participants this time?"

Adenet sighed. "I don't know. A part of me says it won't make a difference, but the other part of me says it can't hurt anything. If it works, whether because of Marc's suggestion or for any other reason, we're already a step ahead of where we were. If it doesn't, that's that many couples who aren't heartbroken because it didn't work, and we can include everyone again next month."

Lorens nodded slowly. "Edine and I will participate, of course. I can't ask my pack to do something I'm not willing to do. If we are only including mated pairs, you would only be there as our shaman. Are you comfortable with that?"

Adenet's wolf whined, insisting Adenet did have a mate—but mating with Marc couldn't help solve their fertility problem, so Adenet ignored him. "It will be fine. Choose the two or three other couples you think should participate and invite them. I will support whoever you choose in that respect."

ADENET BREATHED a sigh of relief when the door to Lorens's house closed behind him. Lorens hadn't noticed. Of all the wolves in the pack, Adenet had the best chance of hiding something from Lorens, but even he could only do so much. Fortunately, Lorens was sufficiently distracted by the issues of the pack's fertility not to pay attention to the pheromones Adenet was sure he was throwing off after his wolf's encounter with Marc in the woods.

He was restless, wanting to run, but if he shifted, if he gave his wolf that bit of control, his wolf would do one thing—run straight to Marc—which would only increase his problems. On the other hand, he could hardly return home. He needed space and solitude to think.

Not having anything else to do, he wandered aimlessly back into the woods until he found the glen where he would sometimes sit and meditate, near the stream that ran through the parc naturel.

He didn't like being out of sync with his wolf. It was a division of mind and body he could only maintain for a short period of time before he had to resolve it. In any other circumstances, he could have approached his mate and at least had an answer. If Marc did not want him, he would know and could move on out of necessity—but Marc had not acted uninterested as they walked back from the grotto earlier in the day. On the contrary, Marc had seemed quite taken with Adenet's lupine form, petting him, letting him knock Marc over and climb on top of him, even teasing him about being friendlier in wolf form than in human form.

Adenet longed for the freedom to give his wolf what he wanted, to come to Marc in his human form, both sides of himself in alignment as they offered Marc promises of a lifetime of devotion. Rationally Adenet could say it was too soon, but he had lived in a pack all his life, had always known how the mating instinct worked. A wolf knew its mate instantly. All of Adenet's concerns about the pack, the fertility ritual, all the reasons for holding back seemed flimsy in light of that knowledge, but Adenet had not reached his position as shaman of the dominant pack in Western Europe by chance or through lack of discipline. His pack needed certain things from him, and he would not let them down. He could not mate with Marc, not while everything was so uncertain. Perhaps if they resolved the fertility issues and the pack began to grow again, Adenet would reach a point where his participation in the fertility ritual could be purely facilitatory again.

If that happened, it wouldn't matter who his mate was. He could have a male mate. He could call down the power of the ritual and then sate the desire it evoked in his body with someone who meant something to him. All they had to do was get the ritual working again.

Adenet huffed at the thought. All they had to do…. Like it was as simple as Marc waving his wand. The problem hadn't developed overnight. Adenet was far too realistic to expect it to be solved overnight. If he were lucky, he might live to see the pack regain some of its former glory, but it would take time and everyone's participation, and that precluded Adenet from having an attachment that would keep him from doing his part.

His wolf could dream all he wanted. Adenet had to keep his feet firmly planted on the ground. He owed it to his pack.

MARC LOOKED up when Adenet came in. He had not felt comfortable going in the kitchen and helping himself. Despite Adenet's offer of hospitality, Marc knew Adenet didn't really want him there, and abusing the shaman's hospitality hardly seemed a way to improve the situation. It was getting hard to ignore his stomach, though.

"Have you eaten?" Marc asked.

"No," Adenet replied. "Did you?"

"I didn't want to dig through your cabinets without asking." His stomach growled audibly.

Adenet's wolf whined in protest at the thought of his mate being hungry. Adenet's own hunger made it harder to push down his wolf's insistence. "Let's see if we can find something, then."

Marc followed Adenet into the kitchen and waited to see how he could help.

"Would you mind chopping some onions and peppers?" Adenet asked, pointing to a knife and cutting board. "We can use them to season the steaks, since I didn't put them in marinade earlier."

"You had a few other things going on," Marc reminded him. "How did the conversation with Lorens go?"

"Well enough," Adenet said, digging in the refrigerator for the steaks. "He agreed to your suggestions. Now we just have to hope it makes a difference."

Impulsively Marc put his hand on Adenet's shoulder, even that contact enough to make him wish for more. As much as he had enjoyed cavorting with the wolf in the woods, he wanted the man more. "If it doesn't work, we'll try something else. I won't give up. I promise."

The dark eyes lightened, turning amber, and Adenet leaned forward suddenly and kissed Marc with all the pent-up longing of being denied his mate.

Adenet's lips were hot and hard on Marc's, stealing his breath with the unexpected kiss. Marc did not protest, though, not when it felt this good. He knew it was Adenet's wolf, not Adenet himself, who wanted him, but the body against his felt human even if Adenet's lupine side controlled his actions now. Adenet had said he and his wolf could not be out of sync for long, so perhaps that boded well for the future. Marc closed his eyes and gave himself over to the kiss, letting himself be folded into the embrace of the taller, broader man.

Adenet's hands moved over his back, pulling Marc closer, and Marc went willingly. Later he would wonder how this had happened so quickly, but right now it felt too good to question. The man—the werewolf—Marc had been watching since his arrival was kissing him like there was no tomorrow, and that was all Marc needed to know. He pushed aside caution and returned the kiss enthusiastically.

When Adenet's tongue brushed across his lips, he parted them, offering his mouth to the werewolf. Another time, when they knew each other better, he might reassert his own dominance, but for now, he would settle for being glad the werewolf had enough interest in men to be here with him, kissing him like his life depended on it.

When Adenet pulled back, Marc opened his eyes and saw Adenet's pupils flicker back and forth between amber and dark brown. He leaned back in for another kiss, but before he could make contact, dark brown won over amber and Adenet pulled away.

"I'm sorry. My wolf gets overly excited sometimes."

As excuses went, it was a shitty one, but Marc swallowed the twinge of pain at the dismissal. He and Adenet had to work together, and he had just made a promise he intended to keep. "Nothing to apologize for. I wasn't exactly pushing you away."

"You should," Adenet said. "I can't offer you anything."

"I don't remember asking for anything," Marc replied, keeping his voice as even as possible.

Even in human form, Adenet could smell the need and agitation on Marc's skin. His wolf howled inside him, straining to break free again, to satisfy the need and soothe the agitation. Adenet dragged him back by the scruff of his neck and held on for all he was worth. "If you'll finish with the vegetables, I'll make dinner."

Marc cursed the stubborn werewolf silently as he picked up the knife and diced the peppers and onion for Adenet to toss in the pan with the steak. He had no idea what had prompted the kiss—not that he was complaining—or what had made Adenet draw back, but he would worry about that later. Right now, he needed to focus on what he was doing and on not losing a finger in the process. He could figure out what to do about Adenet later, when he was alone in his room.

He handed Adenet the seasonings when he had them done and then leaned on the counter to watch as Adenet finished cooking. He had tried to be discreet when he studied Adenet before, but the kiss made him bold. It gave him the courage to stare openly at Adenet, learning every nuance of his body, from the black hair that nearly matched the color of his wolf's pelt, down his back to his broad shoulders and the rest of his gorgeous body. Marc didn't know how old Adenet was— over thirty but not yet fifty—but the life he spent outdoors as both man and wolf had hewn him down, leaving him all hard muscle without an ounce of fat to spare.

It was an ensemble that pushed all of Marc's buttons. His friends at university had teased him about his penchant for older men, but he had always laughed it off, telling them they did not know what they were missing. None of them had ever looked as good to him as Adenet did. His hands itched to touch in a way he could not explain. He had met men as attractive as Adenet before. He had probably met men who were objectively even more attractive than Adenet, but this need was new. He had never had trouble keeping himself in check when necessary. He had never felt like he would come out of his skin if he did not have some kind of contact soon. It was as disconcerting as it was arousing.

"Dinner won't be ready for another ten minutes," Adenet said without turning to face Marc. "Go take a walk or something until then. I can't concentrate with you staring at me."

Marc smiled at the thought that Adenet was as conscious of Marc as Marc was of him. "I don't want to take a walk," Marc replied. "I'd much rather stay in here with you."

"Don't push, Marc," Adenet said, his voice so low it reminded Marc of the growl of the wolf in the woods before he had realized he'd heard a deer, not something more dangerous, and had turned into the playful creature that had knocked Marc on the ground and rubbed all over him.

"Why not?" Marc asked. "You kissed me first, not the other way around."

The spatula landed on the counter with a loud clatter as Adenet whirled to face Marc. "And so because of one ill-advised kiss, you think you have the right to do whatever you want? You're still a guest here, and as such, I'd think some basic courtesy would be in order. Get the hell out of my kitchen, or I'll go and you can finish cooking dinner by yourself."

The unexpected anger caught Marc completely off guard, shattering his flirtatious mood. "Fine," he snapped back as he stomped toward the living room. He sank down on the couch where he had waited for Adenet earlier and wondered what had just happened. How had he gone from being kissed senseless to being sent from the room like an errant child?

More importantly, what did he do about it now?

# Chapter 12

THIERRY WAITED until after Sebastien had fucked him nearly senseless to bring up his conversation with Alain.

"Did you satisfy your hunger?"

"I took enough," Sebastien said, his voice husky from the groans and curses he had uttered while they made love.

"That wasn't what I asked," Thierry said. "If you could, if you didn't have to worry about it hurting me, would you take more?"

"It's a moot point," Sebastien said.

"Not to me," Thierry insisted. "If you aren't getting what you need from me, I think I deserve to know it."

"Now you're putting words in my mouth," Sebastien said. "You've given me everything I've asked for and more."

"But is it everything you need?" Thierry pressed.

Sebastien sighed and ran a hand through his longish brown hair. "You're getting at something. Why don't you just tell me what it is so we can hash it out and you can go to sleep?"

"What about you?" Thierry countered. "Will you sleep too?"

"Vampires don't sleep," Sebastien said. "You know that."

"According to Alain, Orlando has finally started sleeping," Thierry replied. "Really sleeping. He says if he can get Orlando to let go enough to actually drink his fill of blood, Orlando will fall asleep next to him. Of course, that could be because they've completely worn each other out too."

"Feeding and sex do tend to go together when you're paired with a vampire," Sebastien agreed, "but I still don't understand."

Sebastien did not show any signs of recognizing what Thierry had described from his own experiences with his Avoué, so Thierry tried another tack. "Let me ask you this, then. Do you ever feel like you've got this thing inside you trying to get out that would go on a rampage if you let it loose?"

"Every minute of every day," Sebastien admitted, "but nothing changes that. You weren't at the *judicium* for Couthon after the war ended, but monsieur Lombard said something that night that applies to every vampire. Couthon was mouthing off, implying we were all weak because we chose not to kill. Monsieur Lombard stood up, towering over Couthon, and put him in his place."

"What did he say?"

"He said it takes far more power and maturity to control our instincts to kill than to give in to them. I don't know Couthon's story, but from his appearance, I would guess he was turned when he was still a teenager. Late teens, probably, but still more boy than man. He never learned control, either because he didn't want to or because he never had anyone to teach him, and that lack of control ended with him bound in an open courtyard as the sun rose."

"I can't begin to imagine what that must be like," Thierry said with a shake of his head. He rolled onto his side, pulling Sebastien into a tighter embrace, heedless of the sticky mess between them. This was more important. "Never letting your guard down for a minute, never able to fully relax…. It's a wonder any of you are sane."

"Some days I think we aren't," Sebastien admitted. "Not so much right now, because I have you to help balance me out, to give me a stable life, which helps because I don't have to hunt. It's a lot easier to stay in control when I never get to the point of being dangerously hungry—but there were times after Thibaut died when I was sure I'd lose it, when pulling away from the body beneath me before I killed the person whose blood I drank was beyond me. I never killed anyone, thank God, but it came close a few times."

"What about when Thibaut was alive?" Thierry asked. He never asked about those days. He did not want to know about the man who kept him from having the same bond with his partner as Alain had with Orlando, but he needed to know.

"I couldn't kill Thibaut," Sebastien said, "but other than that, it was much like it is with you. I didn't have to worry about where my next meal was coming from."

Thierry could not help the vicious thrill he felt at knowing Sebastien had not shared with Thibaut what Alain had described.

"You never just let go with him?" Thierry pressed.

"It never occurred to me," Sebastien replied honestly. "You're getting at something, and I'm getting tired of you beating around the bush."

"Alain said he convinced Orlando to let go of all that self-control you all use to stay sane or whatever and that the Aveu de Sang let Alain calm him and soothe him," Thierry said. "Orlando could feed until he was truly full instead of just enough to survive a little longer, and when it was over, Orlando slept. I'm not your Avoué, but I am your lover, and I want to do the same for you."

"As much as I like the sound of that, I don't think it's a good idea," Sebastien said.

"Why not?" Thierry demanded.

"Well, first of all, there's the fact that I could kill you if I took too much blood," Sebastien pointed out. "And then there's the fact that I'm not sure I could take that much blood without getting sick. And finally there's the fact that I could hurt you, something Orlando can't do to Alain."

"There's also the chance you could take that much blood without getting sick and that you'd react the same way to me as Orlando does to Alain," Thierry replied. "How do you know it's the Aveu de Sang and not simply the fact that they love each other that made it possible?"

"I suppose it could be, at least the not hurting part," Sebastien said, "but that's a hell of a risk to take if you're wrong."

In the blink of an eye, Thierry disappeared with a muttered word and reappeared on the other side of the room. "Even if you were hurting me, even if you had me pinned down so I couldn't push you off, I can still get away from you. I'm not saying we shouldn't be careful about it. I'm just saying it's not as big a risk as you think it is."

"I'll think about it," Sebastien agreed after a moment. "Now come back to bed. It's cold in here, and if I'm cold, you have to be freezing."

Thierry walked back to the bed and climbed under the covers next to Sebastien, letting the warmth of the vampire's body, warmth that came from Thierry's blood circulating through the vampire's veins— that thought never failed to arouse Thierry—ease away the goose bumps that prickled his skin.

MARC HEARD the baying of the pack as they returned from their hunt. He had felt the anticipation building all day as the pack members went through their daily routines, cutting corners here and there to be sure they would be finished in time to join in. Marc had done his best to stay out of Adenet's way, not wanting to be responsible for keeping the shaman from participating. He had not forgotten their kiss in the kitchen the day before, though, and had high hopes for a repeat tonight. Adenet would spend the hunt in wolf form, probably with his wolf in control. Both times Adenet had shown any interest in Marc, in the woods and in the kitchen, his wolf had ruled his actions, regardless of the form he took. The amber eyes had clued Marc in to that once he calmed down enough from the kiss and the aftermath to think about it rationally.

Marc hoped a night spent hunting would put the wolf firmly back in control. After rising from the couch, he went to the door and opened it in welcome. He didn't know how long it would be before Adenet returned home, but he would be waiting when it happened.

As if summoned by his thoughts, the black wolf appeared at the threshold just as Marc regained his seat on the couch. Marc smiled at the magnificent creature and patted the space on the couch beside him. That was all the invitation the wolf needed, crossing the room with two quick bounds and landing on the cushions next to Marc. Marc didn't wait to be knocked over this time, lying back on the couch as he stroked the wolf's fur. The door still stood open, admitting the chilly night air, but Marc could not be bothered to care, not when he had a hundred pounds of silky-furred wolf to keep him warm.

"You are beautiful," Marc said as he ran his hands down the wolf's lean flanks, "but as amazing as you are, I'd really love it if you switched forms right now. It's a little hard to kiss you when you're in this form."

The wolf shimmered above him, Adenet's face taking the place of the wolf's, but the amber eyes remained unchanged.

Marc trembled in anticipation. When Adenet didn't immediately lean in for a kiss, Marc slid his hands into the dark hair that had replaced the dark pelt and pulled Adenet's mouth toward his. The encouragement broke whatever reserve had held the werewolf back, his lips claiming Marc's in a kiss far more feral and possessive than the one they had shared in the kitchen.

Marc responded in kind, meeting every movement of Adenet's lips and tongue with one of his own until he no longer knew who led and who followed. He only knew how good and right it felt to lie there beneath the naked body of the pack shaman, his hands still on the man's neck and shoulders despite the desire to go exploring, their bodies rubbing together with erotic friction.

Marc resented the constriction of the clothes he still wore, which kept him from feeling Adenet's skin against his, but he didn't want to take the risk of shattering the spell that held them in place by separating long enough to undress. If Adenet regained control of his wolf, he would almost certainly pull away, leaving Marc aching and unfulfilled. Coming in his pants would better than that.

Marc shifted a little beneath Adenet, making space between his legs for the werewolf to sink into so the ridge of Adenet's erection pressed more closely where it would do them both the most good. Adenet took advantage of the new position, slotting their bodies together so perfectly that Marc groaned into the kiss as Adenet moved against him. For a brief moment, Marc wished for his wand so he could cast a spell to make his clothes disappear, but even breaking the kiss to speak the words of the spell would have been more separation than Marc was willing to contemplate at the moment. Instead he bucked up against Adenet and kissed him harder.

Controlled as he was by his lupine side, Adenet knew only one thing: his mate returned his interest. He could taste it in their kisses, feel it in the hard flesh against his own needy cock, smell it in the scent of desire that rolled off his mate's body, ratcheting his own need even higher. He needed more of that scent, needed it all over his body, and that meant getting rid of the barriers between them. He reared back, hands flying over buttons and snaps, pushing fabric aside until Marc's chest and groin were bare to his eyes and hands. He covered the slim body with his own again, a growl escaping him as their skin touched for the first time.

Marc shivered at the sudden chill as Adenet pulled his clothing out of the way enough to find skin. Then the werewolf leaned over him again and chased away all the chill with the heat of his body. The low growl from the werewolf's throat nearly did Marc in, a pulse of liquid heat moving through his body at the possessive sound. He let his hands fall to the side and his head fall back, offering Adenet his full submission. He felt far more debauched lying there on the couch, his clothing pushed aside but not removed, than he would have completely naked, but Adenet felt too good against him for Marc to protest.

Marc could feel his balls tightening as Adenet continued to thrust against him, the hair of his treasure trail and groin providing another layer of pleasurable friction as their cocks slid together through the increasing slickness on their skin. Feeling bold, he ran his hands down Adenet's back, enjoying the play of muscle beneath his fingers. He grabbed on to Adenet's ass, urging him to move faster, to push them both higher, until they could not hold back any longer.

Marc shuddered as he climaxed, his whole body tensing and releasing with the sheer explosion of pleasure that sang along his nerves. Above him, Adenet kept moving, smearing the evidence of his release over their bellies, marking them both with their combined scent. Marc did his best to keep moving with him, to give Adenet as much pleasure as Adenet had given him, though he could only gauge how well he succeeded in the expressions that played across Adenet's face, the most unguarded Marc had ever seen him. Moments later a second rush of fluid coated his stomach, proof that Adenet had indeed found release. He collapsed on top of Marc, pinning him to the cushions.

Marc ran his fingers through Adenet's black hair, relishing the silky texture, and tipped Adenet's head toward his for another kiss. Their lips had barely touched when Adenet suddenly stiffened in Marc's embrace. Marc closed his eyes, not needing to see the shift from amber to chocolate to know that Adenet had regained control of his wolf and was pulling away.

"You don't have to go," Marc said, not opening his eyes. "I didn't want you to stop, so don't get some idea in your head that you took advantage of me."

"That doesn't make it right or a good idea," Adenet said, lifting off Marc and staring down at his disheveled—debauched—appearance. His wolf whined behind the shield he had thrown up when he had come back to himself after his orgasm. He could smell himself on Marc, overlaying the wizard's own scent, and the combination was a punch in the gut. His very naked gut. His wolf wanted him to lean down and lick Marc clean, to let Marc return the favor, but Adenet was back in control now, and one monumental lapse in judgment was enough for one day.

"Why not?" Marc asked, opening his eyes finally. "We're two consenting adults, the last time I checked."

"Not when my wolf acts without my consent," Adenet replied, getting to his feet. He squashed the regret he felt when Marc's open gaze clouded over. "Don't expect a repeat."

Marc wanted to rage at that, but he let it go. He had known Adenet's wolf was in control even before he had returned the first kiss.

"Then don't offer one," Marc replied, taking his time looking Adenet over from head to foot. He had seen the shaman naked from the back before, but this was the first time he had really been in a position to appreciate the front view. Adenet's chest was as well muscled as his back and covered with a light pelt of dark hair, no surprise given his other form. The strands currently stuck together damply, sending a fresh bolt of lust through Marc. The rest of his body was just as hard, including, Marc noticed, his cock. "You sure you won't come back and let me take care of that?"

Adenet scowled in reply and left the room.

Marc cursed under his breath. That had not been the reaction he was hoping for.

Adenet heard the muffled invective as he left the room, but he forced his feet to keep going, to take him into the bathroom and into the tub, which he slowly filled with hot water. He was sweaty from the hunt, sticky from the interlude with Marc, and throwing off the scents of lust—his wolf's—and shame—his own—like crazy. The combination was more than he could stand and stay sane.

He laid his head back against the cool edge of the tub, hissing as the chill of the porcelain bit at his skin. He grabbed the spray attachment and turned it on himself, washing away the chill and the smells. If only he could wash away the memory as easily.

Marc had felt so good beneath him, so willing and eager for Adenet's touch. He had kissed Adenet back like he meant it, like he wanted to be there, wanted everything the werewolf could offer and a hundred times more. Adenet closed his eyes against the curl of desire in his groin. His mate was on the other side of the door, clothes all in disarray, jeans pushed down around his knees, shirt pulled open enough to reveal skin, so eager for Adenet he hadn't even bothered to undress the rest of the way when Adenet had bared enough skin to satisfy him. All Adenet had to do was call his name, and Marc would come through the door, join him in the tub, and finish what they had begun in the living room. Adenet could claim his mate and nothing would ever separate them again.

It would be so easy, and that was what held him back. Easy did not make it right, and he would not betray his pack that way. He washed quickly, scrubbing at the dirt on his skin, real or imagined, until his body tingled in protest. He opened the drain to let the water run out, dried off, and went to his bedroom without looking to see if Marc was still in the living room. He could not take another encounter with the wizard tonight.

He only hoped tomorrow would be easier.

# Chapter 13

SEBASTIEN BIDED his time until he could be sure of finding Jean alone in the abbot's quarters. He knew Thierry would not lie to him, but Thierry's information was already secondhand, and Sebastien would not take any chances with his lover. He only hoped Jean did not kick him out the minute he started this conversation. They had only recently gotten back on speaking terms after four hundred years of distance, the root of which was the heart of Sebastien's current problem.

"Sebastien," Jean said when he opened the door. "I wasn't expecting company tonight."

"Do you have a few minutes?" Sebastien asked. "I need some advice, and I wasn't sure who else to ask."

"Of course," Jean said, stepping back so Sebastien could come inside. "I can't promise to have answers, but I'm happy to help however I can."

Sebastien nodded in understanding, walked into the living room area, and took a seat on the couch, trying to figure out how to ask what he needed to know.

Jean waited in silence as Sebastien gathered his thoughts, but when Sebastien remained silent, Jean finally prompted him. "Is something wrong with Thierry?"

"Not in the sense you mean, no," Sebastien said. "He wants the one thing I can't give him."

"An Aveu de Sang?" Jean ventured to guess.

"Yeah," Sebastien said. "How did you know?"

"Because I can't think of anything else you can't give him, unless he wanted kids," Jean replied. "And if that were the case, you wouldn't be here talking to me. You'd be talking to Alain and Orlando about how they got approved to be foster parents. The magic of the Aveu de Sang only works once. That's not something I can control. You know that."

"He knows it too," Sebastien said. "He doesn't like it particularly, but he knows it and accepts it. The problem is that Alain keeps telling him about new benefits he and Orlando discover to the Aveu de Sang, and so Thierry feels like he's somehow cheating me out of everything we could have in our relationship, as if the fact that I made the decision to offer that bond to someone else was somehow his fault." Neither man acknowledged the identity of Sebastien's Avoué, but it hung between them nonetheless, the specter of the man who had destroyed their friendship before it ever had a chance to start.

"So what do you need advice about?" Jean asked.

"Thierry said Alain talked about Orlando letting go of his control when they were alone together, feeding until he was completely full and then sleeping it off next to Alain," Sebastien said. "According to what Alain said, it's a side benefit of the Aveu de Sang."

"Yes, I know."

"Did Orlando talk to you about it?" Sebastien asked.

"No, I talked to him about it," Jean replied.

"What? How did you...? Oh," Sebastien said as he finally made sense of Jean's statement. "When?"

Jean chuckled. "Which of those questions would you like me to answer?"

"The last one, salaud," Sebastien said with a mock glare.

"After Raymond nearly died in the collapse here at l'Institut," Jean said. "He was still the president of l'ANS at the time and didn't feel like we could tell anyone because of the apparent conflict of interest. As long as he was president he had to appear impartial, regardless of the reality of our relationship. After he resigned, it just seemed like more trouble than it was worth to announce it. Raymond didn't gain anything from it since he was already my Consort, and his role in the war was enough to win the respect of the Cour. I didn't gain anything from it since the alliance, the equal rights legislation, and the benefits of the partnership had already cemented my place well enough that le jeu des Cours is little more than an annoyance for me right now. In a way, it would almost be harder to come back to it later than to remain a part of it even now."

"Wow, okay, that changes things," Sebastien said. "I was going to ask if you knew of any vampire without an Aveu de Sang who had ever managed to do what Orlando seems to have done or even if you'd tried it yourself, but if you have an Aveu de Sang, Raymond is as protected as Alain is."

"That doesn't mean I can't try to help," Jean said. "What exactly are you trying to do?"

"Keep Thierry from feeling like he's failing me," Sebastien replied immediately. "I've dealt with the instincts inside me since I was turned. I've gotten so I don't even think about it anymore. I know when I've drunk enough to sustain me for a few days, and I stop. Sure, there's a selfish part of me that thinks about what Thierry said and wonders what it would be like, but that's wishful thinking. I don't need it, and the thought of possibly hurting Thierry, even in the process of trying to give him what he wants, makes me sick to my stomach."

"Then maybe the better question is what Thierry wants," Jean said. "What does he think he isn't giving you that makes him feel like he's letting you down?"

"He's got this idea that I'm somehow not getting what I need from him," Sebastien said. "That because I can't gorge myself on him the way Orlando can with Alain, I must somehow regret our partnership or be looking for a way to get more. I've told him I don't feel that way, but he doesn't seem to hear me. He's started pushing every time I feed, insisting it won't hurt him if I take a little more, asking if I'm sleepy when I'm done, that sort of thing."

"Do you feel like you're holding back with him?" Jean asked.

"No more than I've ever done with anyone else," Sebastien replied, "and a lot less than I've done with some people."

"What about with Thibaut?"

The question hung between them for so long Jean was not sure Sebastien would answer.

"I loved Thibaut," Sebastien said slowly. "I mourned his death for a very long time, but looking back now, I never embraced the bond as fully as Orlando seems to have done. As fully as I would do if I could make one now with Thierry. Maybe that's maturity on my part, or an awareness of the fragility of mortal life that I was too newly turned to truly appreciate at the time. Maybe it's being with a wizard instead of a nonmagical man. Maybe it's just the difference between Thibaut and Thierry. I don't know. But to answer your question, no, I never fully let go with Thibaut either, always too aware of how much stronger I was than he could ever dream of being. I would never have hurt him intentionally—I couldn't have hurt him intentionally—but I would see bruises on his arms sometimes where I had gripped too tightly. He never complained and I never did it on purpose, but I always felt like I had to hold back my strength so I wouldn't do something unthinkable without realizing it."

"If Thierry is anything like Raymond, the thought that you're holding anything back will drive him mad," Jean said.

"Yeah, that pretty much sums it up," Sebastien agreed. "And I even get that to some extent. He fought a war. He's hardly helpless, but this is different."

"It is," Jean concurred. "I wasn't exactly thrilled with the idea the first time Raymond brought it up."

"What made you change your mind?"

"He didn't give me a choice," Jean replied honestly, though he kept the particulars to himself. Some things did not need to be shared.

"I find that hard to believe," Sebastien said with a laugh.

Jean did not return his smile. "He can be very persuasive," Jean said, "and you know how hard it is to deny your Avoué something within your power to give."

"I'm not any better at saying no to Thierry than I was to Thibaut," Sebastien said. "That's why I'm here. I have to figure out if there's a safe way to give him what he wants."

Jean sighed. "Then it depends on what he wants. It's not just about taking more. That's the side effect, I guess. The thing that makes the difference, that the Aveu de Sang makes… safe, for lack of a better word, is letting go of the self-control we use to keep ourselves within the bounds of propriety."

"I… don't think I'd even know how to do that," Sebastien said slowly. "Not after all these years."

"Raymond goaded me into it," Jean admitted. "I couldn't have done it on my own, not the first time."

"And when you did finally?"

"It was every bit as fearsome as I'd worried it would be," Jean said. "The thing inside me hates being caged. It's like a wild animal, intent on shattering my control, but for all the wildness, once it was loose, it wanted only one thing."

"Raymond?" Sebastien guessed.

Jean nodded. "And since the Aveu de Sang keeps me from draining him or otherwise hurting him, it got what it wanted, and when it did, it went to sleep, and so did I."

"I guess the question is what I would want if I relinquished all control and gave in to my basest instincts," Sebastien mused aloud. "If Thibaut were still alive or if Thierry were my Avoué, I would know the answer to that, but since neither of those things is possible, it could be anything."

"Blood and sex," Jean said "I highly doubt the desires would change. The only difference is the focus. For me, there can be no blood if not from Raymond, and at our basest forms, there's no difference between feeding and fucking, so of course it focused on him, the one person who could take everything I dished out and give me back everything I needed to be calm and in control again. It's a foreign feeling, but it's not a bad one after the first few times."

Sebastien could not stop the surge of envy at the smug satisfaction in Jean's voice. While Sebastien could not blame Thierry for a situation Sebastien had created by choosing an Avoué long before he knew anything of the partnerships, he did finally understand Thierry's sense of being denied something special because of that choice. "Could a single human withstand that without an Aveu de Sang?"

"I don't know," Jean said. "I wouldn't want to try it with a random person off the street, but the wizards' magic already makes them stronger than the average mortal. We saw that during the war when we fed far more often than we would have from any one person, and none of the wizards showed any sign of weakening because of it. If you try it, do it in such a way that Thierry can get away from you if he has to. He'll tell you his magic is enough, and maybe it is, but even that has limits in his strength. If you've weakened him too much from feeding, he may not be able to use his magic or not use it as effectively. And he may not realize he's reached that point until it's too late. It's not as if being with you is a hardship, and he's as likely to be drunk on the pleasure of it as you are."

"That's the part that scares me," Sebastien said. "Putain, sometimes I think it would be so much simpler if I hadn't given in to Thibaut."

Jean looked at him sharply. "What do you mean?"

"He wanted to be someone's Avoué," Sebastien said. "In hindsight, I think he would have preferred to be yours, but you weren't saying yes. He went looking for a vampire he could persuade. I was flattered and overwhelmed, and I didn't realize what he really wanted was to get back at you for saying no. Yes, I fell in love with him, and yes, I was happy with him, but if I had it to do over again, I wouldn't make the same choice. Not when I see what I have with Thierry now and realize how much more that is, even without an Aveu de Sang."

"I was angry for a long time about what happened," Jean said, as if that needed to be stated, "but now I see it was more at the loss of face, the fact that Thibaut had been mine in all but name, visibly and publicly mine, and then suddenly he wasn't. I had not been chef de la Cour for long at the time, and that was a blow I could have done without. I think that hurt worse than actually losing Thibaut, not that I would have admitted it then, or really until very recently. Meeting Raymond has been good for me in more ways than I can count."

"The wizards have been good for all of us," Sebastien agreed. "So, make it so Thierry can get away from me, you said?"

"I recommend magically reinforced ties," Jean said, his face so deadpan Sebastien could not decide if he was serious or joking.

Jean's expression did not change. "I can't quite believe you just told me that," Sebastien said. "You did tell me that, didn't you?"

"Not if you're going to say anything to anyone else."

"No, of course not," Sebastien said. "That goes without saying. I wouldn't say anything about any of this, well, except a little of it to Thierry, but I wouldn't even tell him that part. I mean, I'd have to tell him enough that he would put a spell on the ties, but I wouldn't tell him about you. He wouldn't believe me even if I did tell him."

"You'll have to tell him something."

"I'll tell him you suggested restraining myself in such a way that I can't hurt him," Sebastien said. "Isn't that how it started for you?"

"Close enough," Jean said. He had volunteered more information than he would to anyone else already. "It's what I would suggest even if I didn't have personal experience with it, because Thierry will be in far greater danger than you will be if things go wrong and you can't bring yourself back under control. He might not be stronger than you, but if you can't grab him, he can get away if he needs to. And if he doesn't need to, you'll know for future times."

"Yeah. This still makes me nervous," Sebastien admitted. "I can see so many ways it could go wrong."

"You don't have to do it," Jean reminded him. "You can tell Thierry you aren't comfortable with the risk and leave it at that."

"He won't leave it at that."

"He isn't inside your head. He'll only know what you tell him."

Sebastien shook his head. "No, he'll know. I guess I'll give it a try once and see how it goes, and then decide where to go from there."

"I know we haven't always been friends," Jean said, "but I'm here if you need to talk, if it will help to have another vampire as a sounding board."

"Thanks," Sebastien said. "I'll keep it in mind."


MARC FOLLOWED the five werewolves through the darkening evening. He had not been there when Lorens announced the change in who would participate in the ritual, so he did not know how they had decided which other couple besides Lorens and his mate would participate, nor why they had decided on one couple instead of two or three. Adenet had avoided Marc completely all day. Marc had tried a couple of times to talk to him, but Adenet had come up with one excuse or another, and Marc had left it alone until now. Perhaps after the ritual, Adenet would be less guarded and Marc could appeal to his wolf again. He knew that was underhanded, but the problem seemed to lie firmly with Adenet, and Marc was not above undermining his control to get to Adenet's wolf. Adenet had said it was not possible for them to be out of alignment for long. If the wolf wanted Marc badly enough, Adenet would come around in time.

Marc didn't know the other couple who loped through the woods beside Lorens and Edine. Of the five, only Adenet remained in human form. Marc assumed it was because Adenet would need his voice to complete the ritual.

They reached the grotto as night fell and the full moon rose overhead. Adenet kept his back to Marc as he stripped and set his clothes neatly aside. "Don't come inside the circle."

"I won't," Marc said, but his promise did not keep him from watching Adenet, drinking in the sight of the body that had pleasured his the night before. Reminding himself of his own task, he cast the revealing spell and studied the magic he could now see as Adenet completed his preparations, lighting a fire in the pit and gesturing for the other wolves to come inside.

As Adenet began to chant, calling on the Goddess to bless their ritual and grant them the gift of children, Marc focused on the ebb and flow of the magic, watching it swirl around the bodies in the circle. The chant continued and the power built and built until it swirled with gale force, but the wolves seemed unaffected by it. Even Adenet gave no sign of feeling any of it. Marc reached out, trying to guide it to establish a connection, but while the magic moved at his command, he couldn't make it connect to the wolves any more than Adenet seemed to be able to do.

Marc looked away as the chanting slowed and the two couples moved together to mate. They remained in wolf form, but Marc didn't need to see those moments of intimacy. Instead he focused on Adenet, who maintained his position, eyes closed as if meditating or perhaps continuing the chant silently. Marc wished he could see Adenet's eyes, but even if they had been open, he would not have been able to tell their color at this distance with only the light of the fire. The urge to step into the circle and take Adenet in his arms was nearly impossible to ignore. Nothing that would benefit the pack could come of their union, but the image of Adenet standing to the side as the other four wolves loved each other struck a chord deep in Marc's heart. Adenet didn't deserve to be isolated in this moment. He needed to be held, to be loved, to join in the celebration, even if his mating could bear no fruit.

The magic summoned by the ritual shimmered through the grotto, beckoning Marc inside. He took a step forward, too caught up in everything he was feeling to remember his promise at first, but the prickle of magic along his skin reminded him that the grove was sacred space and he had not been invited inside. He paced the perimeter, hoping for a sign from Adenet that he would be welcome, but the shaman never opened his eyes, never saw the offer on Marc's face.

Only after the two pairs of wolves curled around each other in repletion did Adenet open his eyes. The magic waned slightly, making Marc think Adenet's chanting could indeed summon and dismiss it, but that didn't explain why the shaman had been unable to direct it once he had raised it. It was a problem for another time, though, because Adenet was looking directly at Marc, and as the werewolf drew near, Marc could see the shimmer of amber in his eyes. He held out his hand in welcome.

Adenet stepped outside the circle of trees, all trace of magic left behind as he stood in front of Marc. Marc took a step back and Adenet followed, so Marc stepped back again, wanting to be out of sight of the wolves still curled together in the grotto. They looked asleep, but Marc could not change forms, and he did not have Adenet's disregard for his own nudity.

Adenet unbuttoned the jacket Marc was wearing, letting the breeze eddy around his torso. Marc shivered, wondering how Adenet could stand the temperature fully unclothed. He opened his mouth to ask only to find words impossible when Adenet kissed him, hard and deep and lush. Marc groaned into the kiss, circling Adenet with his arms and pulling him inside the jacket as much as he could.

He took a few more steps back until he ran up against a tree. He had a feeling he would need the support if Adenet continued as he was.

The baying of a wolf behind them startled Marc, drawing his attention back toward the grotto. He could see no movement there, so he focused on Adenet again, only to see that Adenet's eyes had changed color. A shiver went through him now, as if his human body only felt the cold when his human side controlled his actions. Marc pulled the jacket around him more tightly, offering the warmth of his body, but Adenet pulled away.

"I told you not to come in the grotto."

"I didn't," Marc said, stung at the accusation. "You came out to me."

Adenet shivered again. "I have to get dressed."

"And then we have to talk," Marc insisted, although he let Adenet go since it really was too cold to stand around naked.

"We have nothing to talk about," Adenet insisted.

"No?" Marc said. "How about the fact that your wolf jumps me every time he gets the upper hand? How about the fact that I'd really like it if you didn't pull away every time he does?"

"I can't give you what you want," Adenet said from the edge of the circle. "Go back to Paris where you belong."

Marc took a step forward, determined not to let it end this way, but the look Adenet sent him was full of such venom that he changed his mind and cast a displacement spell. He would have to return to pack lands for his belongings, but right now, he had to get away.

# Chapter 14

"MARC, WE didn't expect you back tonight. Isn't tonight the ritual?"

"Yes, it just ended," Marc explained to Raymond when the other wizard arrived to let him through the wards at l'Institut.

"You could have waited until tomorrow to report in," Raymond said. "Nobody expected you to report tonight."

"I know," Marc said, "but it's… complicated."

Raymond raised an eyebrow at him, and Marc sighed. "The shaman's wolf took a particular interest in me. The shaman doesn't share it. Things got a little out of hand after the ritual, and the shaman got upset. It seemed easier to leave than to risk making matters worse."

Raymond suspected that was still only half the story, but he left it alone. He did not know Marc well enough to pry. "How did the ritual go? Were you able to follow it?"

"I had no problem following it," Marc said, "and I could see the power raised by it, but it didn't seem to connect with the werewolves, even the shaman. I could poke at it, but I couldn't complete the connection either."

"So the power is there, the ritual itself is not failing, but something in the execution of it is off," Raymond mused. "And you have no idea what."

"It's like Adenet summoned the power but didn't know what to do with it or even that it was there," Marc said. "A complete disconnect between Adenet and the magic in the grotto."

"Not complete, or he couldn't have summoned it in the first place," Raymond said. "Perhaps something blocking the execution?"

"That would explain Adenet, but why would the other French packs have the same problem if it's just Adenet?" Marc asked. "I mean, I could understand if it was one shaman, one issue, but they're reporting that it's more widespread than that."

"If the alpha's attitude toward magic is any indication, that could be part of it," Raymond said. "It's hard to do magic when you reject the very thought of it."

"Adenet loosened up a bit about it while I was there, at least in regards to me doing magic," Marc said, "but I guess that's not the main thing."

"It's better than nothing," Raymond said, "but obviously not enough. Martin mentioned something about a British witch joining a pack of American werewolves. I think it might be time to track him down. We could keep poking at this and maybe stumble onto the solution, but it doesn't make sense to do that when we could potentially get an answer faster. If nothing else, we can find out if the problem is universal."

"I'm not sure my English is up to the task," Marc admitted. "It was never my best subject in school."

"Mine either," Raymond said, "but Martin is bilingual, and Orlando is British, even if he's lived in France for so long nobody can tell the difference anymore. Between them, we should be able to talk to the witch, or the alpha, or whoever it is we need to contact."

"It would depend on the witch's status in the pack," Marc said, glad his studies of everything he could find about werewolves were good for something, "but the safest way to do it without worrying about offending anyone is to contact the alpha, explain the situation, and ask for permission to talk with the witch. Once permission is given, then you don't have to worry about raising any hackles. If the witch has some status within the pack, like as their shaman, it might not matter as much, but we aren't in such a hurry that we can't wait to do it right. It will be a month before we can try another fertility ritual, even if the witch can give us the answer right away."

Raymond smiled at Marc's inclusion of himself in the pack. It should not have come as a surprise given the younger man's fascination with the species, but Raymond considered it a good sign. Whatever complications might have arisen with the shaman, Marc had not given up when he retreated.

"Martin has already returned to Autun for the night," Raymond said, "but we can ask him for more information first thing tomorrow morning. Hopefully by the time it's morning in the States, we'll have a phone number and can contact the alpha of the appropriate pack. We could have answers by tomorrow night."

"Do you really think it will be that easy?"

"No, probably not," Raymond admitted, "but any progress will be something to take back to Iserin and the pack, even if it's just to tell them we're researching other options."

"I told Adenet I wouldn't give up, no matter how long it took to find the solution," Marc said, "but that was before...."

"I won't pry," Raymond said, "but if you ever need someone to talk to, I've learned a few things about having a relationship with someone from a different magical race—with ideas about life and everything else that don't always mesh easily with my own. Jean isn't a werewolf, but he'll give anyone a run for their money in sheer stubbornness and occasional bullheadedness."

"Thanks," Marc said, "but there isn't really anything to say. Adenet doesn't want me, no matter what his wolf thinks about the situation, and I don't want to be the cause of more tension. He's under enough stress as it is. He thinks it's his fault somehow that the ritual keeps failing."

"He may be right," Raymond said. "Given what you described, whatever is blocking the ritual from working almost has to be with him. That doesn't mean it's intentional. Maybe he wasn't taught the right way to do it. Maybe he inherited the position but doesn't actually have the capability to fill it. That said, anything that adds to his stress can only complicate matters, which could be an argument for having it out once and for all and resolving whatever's between you."

Marc nodded slowly. "Let's see what happens tomorrow. It's not like I can do anything else about it tonight."

"The guest room you were using when you were here before is still made up for you," Raymond said. "I'll see you at breakfast."

"Thanks," Marc said, leaving Raymond alone in his office.

Jean came in almost as soon as Marc was gone.

"Is everything all right?"

"I'm fine," Raymond said, "but I'm not so sure about our young friend. I can't help if he won't confide in me, though, and tonight, anyway, he wasn't really interested in talking. I should probably warn you. We may have more werewolves around. Marc couldn't help resolve the problem himself, so I'm going to contact some American packs and see if any of them have any suggestions. Depending on what they say, that may mean a visit or more. It may take a werewolf to solve the problem."

"I'll deal with that if it happens," Jean said. "I promised after we had the misunderstanding with Iserin, and I meant it. I might not like it, but I'll deal with it."

"Thank you," Raymond said. Jean might be stubborn and at times bullheaded, but he was also the most loyal, giving man Raymond had ever known. The contradiction was endlessly fascinating. "We can't do anything about that until tomorrow when Martin returns from Autun anyway."

Jean grinned. "Then what should we do now?"

"I'm sure you can come up with some suggestions," Raymond said with an answering grin. He rose from his desk and stepped out into the hallway, locking the door behind them.

"I'm sure I can," Jean agreed, tugging Raymond toward their rooms.


ADENET CONSIDERED it an unexpected reprieve that Lorens didn't seek him out until after breakfast the next day. He did not expect it to continue now that Lorens had cornered him in his house.

"Where is Marc?"

"He left right after the ritual last night," Adenet said.

"Why would he do that?" Lorens asked. "Did something go wrong?"

"I don't know," Adenet replied. "I didn't ask."

Lorens's frown deepened. "This is important, Adenet. We have to figure out what's going on, and he's our best hope for that right now."

"You think I don't know that?" Adenet snapped. "I have done everything I can think of, taken every suggestion anyone has come up with, including him, to try to make this work."

"Then what happened last night? Why did he leave before you could talk to him?"

Answers chased themselves through Adenet's head. *Because I lost control of my wolf like a child, because my wolf pounces on him every chance he gets, because he makes me want things I can never have.*

"Why didn't you tell me he was your mate?" Lorens asked.

Adenet's stomach sank. He had known he couldn't put this conversation off forever, but he had hoped to delay a little longer. "I know my duty," Adenet said. "You don't have to worry about that. He knows nothing can happen between us."

"What are you talking about?" Lorens said. "If he's your mate, we should be celebrating."

"Lorens, he's male and he's not a werewolf. He can't be my mate."

"The last time I checked, we didn't have a prohibition against same-sex mates—and while we haven't had anyone petition to join the pack recently, we'd have no reason to turn him down if he did ask to join, whether he wanted to be turned or not."

"The pack's dying, and it's my fault," Adenet said. "I'm not going to make that worse by mating with someone who can't give us even the hope of children. I've failed everyone enough already."

"Fuck that," Lorens said immediately.

Adenet was so surprised by Lorens's reaction that he did not reply right away.

Lorens took his silence as permission to continue. "First of all, everyone knows the mating instinct is never wrong, which means he's your mate. Nobody gets to challenge that, and that includes you. Secondly, you don't know that the ritual's failure is your fault, but even if it is, even if every dire thought you've had about why it stopped working is right, denying yourself your mate, forcing yourself to go against your wolf's need for his mate, isn't going to fix it. And finally, being at odds with your wolf—I assume he was smart enough to accept Marc even if you weren't"—Adenet nodded—"then being at odds with your wolf is only going to make it harder for you to fulfill your role as our shaman, not easier. I can't believe I have to tell you that."

"It doesn't matter now," Adenet said. "He left, so it's a moot point."

"And why did he leave?" Lorens asked.

"Just drop it," Adenet said. "There's nothing we can do about it now anyway."

"You could go after him," Lorens suggested.

"And say what?" Adenet demanded. "The pack is dying. I don't have a life to offer him outside of that, and if I tried to make one, it would only make things worse here, and then I'd have that guilt eating at me too. He's fascinated by the idea of werewolves, not by me. He only noticed me because you made him stay here with me."

"So he *did* notice you," Lorens said. "That's a good start."

"It's a little hard to miss me when he's living under my roof," Adenet replied.

"That's not what I meant," Lorens retorted. "Did he give any indication of being attracted to you?"

"My wolf didn't give him a lot of choice," Adenet said. "Every time I changed forms, my wolf wanted nothing but to pounce on him and not get up."

"He didn't run away screaming," Lorens pointed out.

He had done far more than not run away, but Adenet had no desire to share those details, even with his best friend. "I told you, he's fascinated by werewolves."

"Then I guess it's a good thing you are one," Lorens said.

"He isn't one, though. He doesn't have a mating instinct."

"So you might actually have to do some work to convince him to return your feelings," Lorens said with a shrug. "That's hardly the end of the world."

"You're assuming I want him to return my feelings."

"He's your mate," Lorens said simply. "You can deny it for a while, but ultimately you won't be able to fight it. You can't be at odds with yourself."

"None of that changes my duty to the pack," Adenet said.

"There's more to life than duty," Lorens insisted.

"If we got the ritual working again and found out Edine still couldn't conceive, you'd give up on the idea of having children?" Adenet asked. He knew it was cruel, but he had to make Lorens understand.

"If it came to that," Lorens said slowly, "if we determined she would never be the mother of my children, I would do my duty and have sex with a fertile female, but Edine would still be my mate. Nothing touches that bond. Not even our deaths can touch it. And you realize in trying to persuade me otherwise, you just added to my argument. If you truly feel you must participate in the fertility ritual with a female, explain that to Marc. He might surprise you."

"And if he doesn't?"

"Then we deal with it," Lorens replied, exasperated. "You're obviously not listening, so I'm not going to keep beating my head against the wall, but you need to get *your* head out of your ass and claim your mate before you miss your chance and spend the rest of your life miserable because you could have had him and were too much of a coward to do anything about it."

Adenet nearly turned on his best friend at that, but he held himself in check out of deference to his alpha. "You don't know the first thing about it," he said in a low, tight voice. "Get out before I say or do something I regret."

Lorens stared at him for a long moment before doing as Adenet had ordered, leaving the shaman alone with his misery.

# Chapter 15

"I TALKED to Jean yesterday," Sebastien said when Thierry came to bed. "I hoped he'd have some suggestions or at least some reassurances for me."

"Did he?" Thierry asked, although the way Sebastien sat hunched over himself was not encouraging.

"He agreed it was probably a really bad idea," Sebastien said. "He reminded me of how much I could hurt you, even kill you, if I wasn't careful, but he has a partner too. He knows how stubborn wizards can be." Sebastien picked at the edge of the sheet, trying to work up the nerve to say the rest. "I need you to understand that I'm not asking anything of you. I love you, and I get so much more from being with you than I ever imagined possible. You're about to say I'm not getting what Orlando gets from Alain. I can see it on your face, but don't say it. Even with Thibaut, I didn't know I could have that—or maybe it only works with wizards as Avoués—but the point is I don't miss it because I've never had it. I've never thought about having it because I didn't even know it was possible. You don't have anything to prove to me. You don't have to do this to keep me or whatever off-the-wall thoughts might be going through your head. If we do this, it's because *you* want it, not because you think I do."

"It's not just about you not missing it," Thierry said, rubbing his hand over his face as he tried to figure out how to explain. "Orlando is more relaxed, more comfortable in his skin because of this. He can sleep. Maybe he never missed it before because he didn't know he could have it, and maybe it's a 'luxury,' but it's one he's benefiting from, and not just in some intangible way. He's healthier and happier because of it. I want that for you. I want to give that to you."

"And if you can't?"

"At least I'll know we tried."

Sebastien studied Thierry's face for a moment, taking in the unwavering determination in the set of his jaw and brow. "In that case, we'll need a couple of your ties."

"What?"

"Your ties," Sebastien said. "We'll try it, but only on the condition that you tie my hands and use magic to strengthen the fabric so I can't get free. If the blood madness gets to be too much, you'll be able to get away from me, and don't say you could always cast a spell. What if you were already too weak? What if I kept you from speaking? I would never do it if I were myself, but I won't be. If I do what you want, it won't be me in bed with you anymore. It will be the monster everyone fears my kind is."

"This really isn't necessary," Thierry began.

"Maybe, maybe not, but it's the condition I'm placing on my agreement," Sebastien replied. "You can tie my hands, and I'll try to do what you want, or you can choose not to tie them and we'll make love like we always do, and it will be wonderful, and I'll never have to worry that you'll hate me once you've seen the nightmare inside me."

"I could never hate you," Thierry insisted, leaning forward to kiss Sebastien tenderly. "I love you, remember?"

"That isn't the issue," Sebastien said. "Get the ties or not. It's your choice, but I won't do this without them."

Thierry rose on silent feet and crossed the room to pull two ties out of the closet.

Sebastien offered his hands, stretching out on the bed and finding a comfortable position for his arms. It might not be comfortable later when he inevitably started fighting the bonds, trying to take more than anyone could be expected to give, but at least he would start out the night at ease. Thierry tied him in place. Sebastien tugged on the ties experimentally. They would hold for now, but he did not trust them against his full strength.

"Reinforce them," Sebastien said, "and the bed frame as well. As strong as you can make them."

Thierry frowned at him, but he did as Sebastien asked, casting a spell on the ties and bed frame. Sebastien could feel Thierry's magic tickling along his skin, not affecting him directly but present. When the sensation passed, Sebastien tugged again, already feeling a difference in the way the ties gave. He pulled harder, not quite full strength, but far more than a mortal would be able to do, and the cloth and wood held.

"Are you sure this is what you want?" Sebastien asked one more time.

"I'm sure."

Sebastien nodded and closed his eyes. "Then God help us all."

For the first time since he opened his eyes as a vampire to find himself held in place by the strong arms of his maker and forced to hold back rather than lunge out of the room into the city full of people, all of whom he could smell so vividly he could almost taste them, Sebastien sought the bloodlust instead of rejecting it. He might have regretted how easy it was to give up that control if he could have thought of anything beyond the pulse of the man just out of arm's reach and the need for blood that rose up inside him. The intensity of it scared him to the point that he considered trying to pull it back under his control, even now, but he had promised Thierry. He fought the bonds, but they held, keeping him from reaching for his prey.

"Sebastien?"

The snarl that left the vampire's throat at the sound of its name, the name of the weak, puny mortal it had been, only proved that it had left humanity behind. It lunged for the hand that came near its face, its fangs scoring skin. The taste of blood only enraged it more.

"Take it easy," the man above it said. "I'm right here. I'll give you what you need."

"What are you waiting for?" the vampire demanded, its voice rough and cruel.

It saw the surprise and unease on its victim's face, but it could not be bothered to care. The man had one purpose and one purpose only: to provide enough blood to extend the vampire's existence another day.

The man leaned down, obviously intending to kiss the vampire. It let its target get close enough for their lips to touch, the contact familiar in a fleeting, unimportant fashion, the thought gone in the face of the need for blood.

The moment the man deepened the kiss, the vampire took what it wanted as well, its fangs piercing the man's lip and drawing blood. It could taste the shock and the bite of pain—but the mortal's distress was not its concern, not when it could also taste the power in this man's blood. It fought the ties around its wrists, needing to get free, to gorge, to take that power into itself.

In its distraction with the bindings on his wrist, the vampire lost its grip on the man's lip and the man pulled away.

"Stop fighting, Sebastien," the man said. His voice was close enough to the vampire's ear for it to feel the rush of air from its breath, but not close enough for the vampire to reach him. "You know I'll give you what you want."

The vampire snarled again at the sound of the meaningless mortal name. It owed the restraints around its wrists to that human side, which usually kept it under lock and key, and to the blond man who hovered over it even now. They would pay for confining it, the man in blood and its other half in anguish when the man was dead. The vampire would have its revenge for this confinement.

The man was smart enough not to try to kiss it again, but his hand settled near the vampire's mouth. It took advantage, driving its fangs into its victim's wrist, enjoying the hiss of pain from the mortal who thought to confine and tame it. It would show the world the folly of that thought. It would break free and take its due.

The blood in its mouth tasted sweet, layered with love, devotion, and determination. The vampire might even have enjoyed the flavor under other circumstances, but with the use of its hands denied him, its emotions ran too deep for it to focus on anything other than consuming enough blood to break free. It did not know how the mortal had managed to bind it so completely with nothing but cloth, but it would regain its strength. When it did, nothing would stop it from regaining his freedom.

The mortal used the hand not currently at the vampire's mouth to caress its body, obviously expecting the gesture to be both welcome and soothing. It could not pull away, bound as it was, but it snarled at the man's familiarity. It had not invited the contact, had not allowed the intimacy. *It* was in control of the situation, not its victim.

"Just relax and let me love you," the man urged. "I'm your partner, remember? I want to take care of you. I want to give you what you need."

The words barely penetrated the fog of rage and bloodlust, raising a faint niggling of recognition, but the vampire ignored it. It did not want paltry emotions holding it down any more than it wanted the restraints that bound its wrists. It tore at the flesh against its mouth, shredding it so it could draw more blood. The man hissed in pain, only adding to the vampire's satisfaction. It would show the mortal the error of his ways. It would wring him dry and leave his lifeless husk behind.

"Sebastien, stop," the man said, pulling his wrist away. "Don't do this."

The vampire merely snarled as it lifted its head as far as it could and fought its bonds. It grinned in anticipation when it heard the sound of wood fracturing. It would be free soon.

The man leaped back, muttering something under his breath. The vampire felt a rush of power over its skin, but it had no effect except to raise goose bumps. When it pulled on the restraints again, though, it found far less give than before. It thrashed harder on the bed, trying to escape. Its prey was getting dressed again, and that was unacceptable.

"I'm sorry," the man said. "I should have listened to you."

Its howl of rage echoed through the empty room as the man closed the door behind him.

THIERRY COLLAPSED against the wall of the corridor outside his and Sebastien's rooms. He had not expected it to be easy to tame Sebastien's wild side, but he had not expected to lose his lover entirely. Alain had talked about Orlando's inhibitions disappearing. He had not mentioned him losing all humanity, all reason. He shuddered as he listened to the increasingly animalistic sounds coming from the room behind him. He had no idea what it would take to bring Sebastien back to himself, but he could not do it alone. He would have to swallow his pride and ask Jean for help.

He could not shake the sense of impending doom as he walked the two flights of steps to the abbot's quarters and knocked on the door. He only hoped they were there. He did not want to end up chasing them all around l'Institut—or around the country if they were elsewhere.

Fortunately Raymond answered the door almost immediately.

"Thierry, we didn't expect to see you this evening," Raymond said, opening the door wider and inviting Thierry in. "Is everything all right?"

"No," Thierry replied bluntly, "and I don't know how to fix it. I'm hoping Jean can help."

"I'll get him. Have a seat."

Thierry sat for a moment, but the nervous energy running through him was too much for him to sit still. He rose again to pace in front of the huge marble fireplace as he waited for Jean and Raymond to return. It only took a minute, but in Thierry's agitated state, it seemed to last forever.

"Bonsoir, Thierry," Jean said when he came in. "Raymond said something was wrong?"

"I should have listened to Sebastien," Thierry said without preamble. "It was a disaster, and now he's tied to our bed, out of his mind, and I don't know how to get him back."

Raymond's eyes widened slightly, but Jean shook his head. "Start at the beginning and tell me what happened, as much as you can."

Thierry took a deep breath, trying to calm himself. "Sebastien agreed to try letting go of his control, the way Alain said Orlando had been able to do, but he insisted I tie him to the bed first and reinforce the rope and the bed with magic so he wouldn't be able to get loose. I did it because he asked and he'd know if I hadn't, but I didn't think it would be necessary. I figured he'd be a little rougher, a little more voracious than usual. I didn't expect to watch every ounce of humanity drain out of him. I didn't expect the animal he became."

"I keep telling you, all of you, that beneath the veneer of civilization, we are the monsters from your worst nightmares. Maybe next time you'll listen to me," Jean said with a resigned sigh. "You got away from him, obviously, which means the bonds held. Is he still in your room?"

"They almost didn't hold," Thierry admitted. "I had to reinforce them again when the bed frame started to crack, but yes, when I left, he was still tied up. I put a spell on the door too, so even if he gets loose, he won't be able to get out of the room."

"Can you help him?" Raymond asked Jean.

"Yes," Jean said, "but it won't be pleasant. Thierry, tell Raymond what he needs to know to undo your spells. Sebastien tasted your blood. If you go back in there, it will only enrage him more, and your magic won't work on him to protect you if he gets past me."

Thierry didn't like the idea of anyone else seeing Sebastien the way he had been when Thierry fled, but he didn't know what else to do. His presence had not soothed Sebastien as he had hoped it would, and his magic would have no effect on his partner, so he was essentially useless.

"The door is a simple locking spell, something any wizard with a little skill could undo, and the spell on the ties won't keep you from undoing them. It was just to keep the ties from ripping."

Raymond nodded. "We'll take care of him. Don't worry."

Thierry did not tell them how pointless trying not to worry would be. He was sure they knew.

"WHAT WILL he do when we let him loose?" Raymond asked as he and Jean approached the door to Thierry and Sebastien's room.

"Lunge at you," Jean said. "He's starved for blood, out of control, and probably as angry as hell. I'm nothing but another impediment, and if he's as out of it as Thierry said, he won't recognize me as his friend, his chef de la Cour, or anything but competition. If your mark were visible, he might hold back, but as it is, he probably won't remember that I told him about us."

"I wondered when Thierry mentioned reinforced ties," Raymond said.

"It was the only way to keep them both safe," Jean said with a shrug. "Sebastien won't say anything to anyone."

"Not even in his current state?"

"In his current state, he probably doesn't even remember the conversation," Jean said, "and if he does, he still doesn't have anyone to say it to except us."

"Are you ready?" Raymond asked, his hand on the doorknob in preparation for unlocking it.

"This isn't something you're ever ready for, but putting it off changes nothing. Let's go."

Raymond cast the spell to undo the lock and opened the door. Sebastien still lay on the bed, fighting the ties holding his arms to the point that his wrists were bleeding. Raymond took a step toward him, intending to release his arms so he would not get hurt worse, but Jean stopped him with a sharp motion of his hand. Raymond hovered apprehensively at the foot of the bed as Jean approached the head of the bed and grabbed Sebastien's jaw with unforgiving fingers. Raymond winced at the sight of them digging hard into Sebastien's skin, but it seemed to get the other vampire's attention.

"Stop," Jean ordered. "This isn't who you are. You're already going to hate yourself when you regain control. Don't make it even worse."

Sebastien tried to jerk his head away from Jean's hand, but Jean followed him, his fingers tightening until his knuckles were white with the strain. "Look at me," Jean said with a shake of his hand. "Come on, Sebastien. I know you're in there. Focus on my voice and get control of yourself again."

The vampire on the bed—Jean would not insult Sebastien by thinking of this creature as his friend—snarled and tried to snap at Jean's wrist with his fangs. Jean slapped him hard. "Control yourself, Sebastien," he repeated. "Get it together so we can release your hands and you can go make Thierry feel better."

For a moment Jean saw a glimmer of Sebastien in the wild eyes that refused to meet his, but it was gone a second later. Without releasing his grip, Jean turned back to Raymond. "Go to the door, release his bonds, and get out. Don't come back in until I call you, no matter what you hear. I'll let you know when it's safe."

Raymond thought that sounded like a spectacularly bad idea—but since he had no better suggestions to offer, he backed away and did as Jean requested, shutting the door behind him with a locking spell as he stepped into the hallway.

Jean didn't look to see when the ties around the other vampire's wrists released, but he didn't need to. The moment the enraged vampire regained his freedom of movement, he grabbed Jean's wrist, trying to force it away from his face.

Jean released his grip and took a step back, bracing for the other vampire to come at him. Jean knew he was stronger, even while in control of himself, than his adversary would be while out of control, but that did not mean the fight would be an easy one, especially if Sebastien's guilt kept him from siding with Jean in trying to gain control over his madness again.

The vampire lunged at him, trying to shove Jean aside so he could reach the door and freedom, but Jean blocked him, catching him in a tight hold and capturing his jaw. The body in his arms still struggled, but Jean caught his arm as well, forced it behind his back, and drove him toward the wall.

"Stop fighting me."

He thought Sebastien fought him less then, but he was not ready to risk it. He would wait until Sebastien could speak and promise him he was in control again. He pulled the wrenched arm a little higher. "Talk to me, Sebastien. Tell me you're coming back."

The hiss he got in reply was the answer he needed. He released Sebastien's jaw and pressed the man's shoulders harder against the wall, not quite banging his head against the plaster, but almost. "Sebastien."

The body beneath his arms went limp. "I'm here." Sebastien's voice was wrecked, but the voice was his again, not the random rage of a vampire out of control. Jean relaxed his hold a little, although not his guard. Sebastien stayed where he was, so Jean took a step back.

Sebastien took a deep breath. "Is Thierry safe?"

"He's in my office with Raymond," Jean said. He hoped Raymond had returned to sit with Thierry, although if he knew his partner, both wizards were outside the door instead.

"I didn't hurt him?"

"No," Jean said. "He got away before you could do any serious damage. He was upset but not hurt."

"Thank you," Sebastien said. "I'd like to be alone now."

"Are you sure that's a good idea?"

"No, but it's the only one I have right now," Sebastien said. "Please."

"All right," Jean said, "but if you change your mind, you know where to find me. Don't deal with this alone if you don't have to."

Sebastien nodded. Jean wanted to push for more of a response, but he had already gotten more than he expected. He patted Sebastien's shoulder and left him alone.

When the door closed, Sebastien sank to the floor, pressed his forehead against the wall, and wished, not for the first time since he was turned, that he could still cry.

# Chapter 16

"ALLÔ?"

"Bonjour, it's Raymond Payet from l'Institut Marcel Chavinier."

"I know who you are, monsieur Payet. Do you have news for me?"

"Some," Raymond said. "Marc felt unable to help after observing the ritual, so at the suggestion of one of my staff, we contacted a shaman from a werewolf pack in New York who has some background in magic as well. His pack is not experiencing the same problems you have reported, and he's willing to come see if he can be of assistance in sorting out the problem. He can be here by Friday if your pack is willing to welcome him and his mate into your territory."

"You really think this will help?"

"Marc is of the opinion that the problem is indeed a magical one, but he was unable to intervene because the magic seems not to work with werewolves the way it does for us. Tristan Northland, the shaman, is both a werewolf and a witch. If anyone has the right combination of skills, it is he. The only two conditions over his arrival are your agreement and that his mate be allowed to accompany him."

"Does he speak French?"

"A little," Raymond replied. "I have a colleague who is French Canadian and who has volunteered to translate if necessary. It will mean an extra wizard around as well, although Martin will probably not stay. His partner in Autun is already not happy about his going in the first place."

"Another vampire?"

"Another chef de la Cour," Raymond replied with a chuckle. "They're coming out of the woodwork."

"Will Marc be returning as well?" Iserin asked.

"He would like to," Raymond said, "but if that's a problem—"

"No, no problem," Iserin interrupted, making Raymond wonder why Iserin wanted Marc back so badly. "He should come back and finish what he started."

The insistence struck Raymond as odd, but he let it go without asking. Marc had made it clear he did not want to talk about it, whatever it was, and Raymond would respect that as long as it did not interfere with him doing his job.

"Then I will contact Tristan again and tell him we will meet him in Paris on Friday. We will bring him to the pack as soon as he is recovered from the trip."

"We will wait for your call."

Raymond said good-bye and hung up. He wondered what he had gotten himself into, bringing a British witch and an American werewolf into a French pack's territory, but he hoped the desperation of the situation would smooth over most of the issues.

MARC STOOD patiently—mostly patiently—outside of customs in Charles de Gaulle airport, holding up a name placard as he waited for the two werewolves from the States. Raymond had insisted Marc accompany him and Martin, since Marc had the most firsthand knowledge of the pack. Marc was not sure how much faith to put in Martin's report that Sterling "could get by" in French and that Northland had studied it some in school, since Martin had only spoken English with them on the phone. The conversation could get tedious if the Canadian wizard had to play translator constantly, not to mention that Martin's partner might have something to say about that. Marc spoke a little bit of English, but he had no illusions of being able to discuss the intricacies of magic with it. It was probably beyond him even in German, which he spoke better than English.

The pair, when they approached, were every bit as remarkable as Marc had worried they might be. Sterling was the older of the two by more than a few years, blond, polished, and professional even after a transatlantic flight, his French far more than "getting by" as he introduced himself. Northland—"Please, call me Tristan"—was handsome in a way that could only be called beautiful: brown eyes, olive skin, tumbled mahogany curls. Sterling was a lucky man, and from the possessive way he kept Tristan close at hand, Marc guessed he knew it. Tristan's French was far less polished than his mate's, but he had no problem following the introductions.

"We have two choices," Raymond said after they had all shaken hands. "We can take the train and have Jean meet us in Autun, or we can use a spell and be there in the blink of an eye. It is entirely up to you. Not everyone is comfortable traveling by magic."

The two werewolves exchanged a glance before Northland replied, "A spell will be fine. We have spent more than enough time traveling already."

"We have rooms waiting for you at l'Institut," Martin said. "The pack isn't expecting you until tomorrow, so you'll have time to rest and recover from your trip."

"A shower would be much appreciated," Sterling said. "It was overly warm on the plane."

"Just a few more minutes," Raymond said, drawing his wand. "If you're ready, messieurs?"

When everyone nodded, Raymond cast the spell, taking all five of them back to l'Institut. Marc took a silent moment to marvel at the wizard's power, but he had learned to keep his enthusiasm to himself. Raymond thought nothing of it, and most of the wizards he worked with were so used to him that they did not mention it either.

When they arrived at l'Institut, Jean was standing in the courtyard next to a vampire Marc did not know. He couldn't have said how he knew the man was a vampire, but he would have put money on it. Given the way the vampire's gaze fixed on Martin, Marc figured he must be Martin's partner—the chef de la Cour of Autun.

Marc had learned enough from Raymond about how poorly werewolves and vampires interacted to worry what would happen next, but while Sterling tensed beside him, Northland seemed unconcerned. "You must be monsieur Bellaiche," Northland said, his French accented but understandable. "I have looked forward to meeting you."

"The pleasure is mine," Jean replied in English, to Marc's surprise. He had not known Jean spoke any English. "Welcome to l'Institut Marcel Chavinier. I hope you and your mate will be comfortable here."

"I'm sure we will be," Northland replied. "Benjamin, come meet the vampire I was telling you about."

"Enchanté," Sterling said, offering Jean his hand. His voice suggested some edginess, but he didn't back away or bare his teeth or do any of the other things Marc had seen as aggressive or defensive behavior from wolves.

"Come, let me show you your rooms," Raymond said, breaking the tableau. "We will talk more after you have a chance to refresh yourselves."

He led them toward the hostellerie, where guest rooms had been set up. Marc let them go without him, noting Martin did the same, gravitating instead toward his partner.

"IF THERE is anything you need, please ask," Raymond said as he opened the door to the suite of rooms destined for the two werewolves. "I know you won't be here for long before you head to pack lands, but we want you to be comfortable while you're here."

"Everything looks lovely," Northland said. "Where shall we meet you when we've had a chance to settle in?"

"If you're hungry, it will be lunchtime soon and we could meet in the réfectoire, or if you prefer to rest first, you can come by our office later."

"We will join you for lunch," Sterling replied. "It's not good for us to go too long without eating. It makes our wolves hard to control."

"Benjamin, stop trying to scare them. You make it seem like we're going to turn into monsters."

"We have enough experience with those without any more," Jean said with a tense smile.

"Now who is trying to scare people?" Raymond scolded. "We will look for you at lunch in about half an hour, then."

"What was that all about?" Raymond asked when they had left the two werewolves alone.

"Nothing," Jean said. "Sterling. They are… different, not like I expected."

"Northland wasn't born a wolf. That could be the difference. I don't know Sterling's story, but just as no two vampires are exactly alike, I'm sure no two werewolves are identical. Perhaps that is what you were sensing."

Jean shrugged. "Perhaps. Do you think they'll be able to help us?"

"It's too soon to tell for sure, but Northland is in training with his pack's shaman, and he says they have had no problems like the ones reported here, so I'm hopeful he'll be able to find the problem and fix it. I would love to attend a ritual he conducts to see the differences, but I doubt the werewolves would agree to let you accompany me."

Jean hesitated a moment. "If it means that much to you, go without me. As you regularly remind me, you are hardly defenseless."

"Are you sure?"

"If there's something you can learn from it, you need to see it. You'd always regret it if you didn't go."

"I love you."

Jean smiled. "I know. I love you too."

"What changed your mind?"

"Sterling made the comment about controlling their wolves, and it made me think about controlling my own inner beast. It might not be able to take physical form—but without an Avoué to calm it, it can take control completely away from a vampire's rational side, as we saw with Sebastien. Maybe there's something to be learned from them as well. Or if not for us, for my kind, anyway, since I have you to keep me in check."

"Talk to Sterling," Raymond suggested. "He didn't raise your hackles the way Iserin did. Maybe you can figure out why."

"I'll do that after lunch," Jean said. "I imagine you and Northland will be holed up in the office all afternoon discussing magic and rituals with Marc. I'll show Sterling around the grounds and see how it goes."


AFTER LUNCH, Martin, Marc, Raymond, and Tristan—he had become Tristan over lunch, his friendly smile and joyful laugh making it impossible to call him anything else—returned to Raymond's office to discuss magic.

"Would you like to see the grounds?" Jean asked Benjamin when the wizards had left. "They'll be at it for hours, if I know my partner."

"He is your mate as well, is he not?" Benjamin asked.

"For most paired vampires and wizards, it is one and the same."

"Yes and no," Benjamin said. "Your scent is different, deeper, than what I smelled from the others in the room at lunch. I don't mean to pry, but I find I make fewer gaffes if I ask instead of assuming."

"It's a logical policy," Jean agreed, "but in this case, you are asking about something we have chosen not to share with anyone else. Yes, we have an extra bond. No, we don't talk about it."

"Then we will talk of other things," Benjamin said easily.

"How did you meet Tristan, if that's a story you're willing to share? A British witch and an American werewolf. It hardly seems a likely match."

Benjamin chuckled. "No, but a fated one. Tristan's ancestor cursed an ancestor of mine, turning him into a werewolf along with all his descendants. Tristan broke the curse."

"But you're still a werewolf, aren't you?"

"I am," Benjamin replied. "I discovered a different attitude about it after I lost my wolf. The thing I had always hated made me who I was and brought Tristan to me. It was hard to hate anything that brings me such joy. Would you have met Raymond if you had been mortal?"

Jean laughed at the ridiculousness of that thought. "I was turned in the year 911. I would have been nothing more than a footnote in the records of a now defunct monastery if I hadn't been turned."

"And yet because you were, you have a mate who gives you great joy," Benjamin pointed out.

"How do I make peace with that other side of me?" Jean asked. "I can't change forms, but if I let go of my control, the results are anywhere between frightening and disastrous."

"You have to answer that for yourself," Benjamin said, "since I know nothing of the ways of vampires, but I learned something after I met Tristan. My wolf and I want the same thing. Him. And as long as we have him, both sides of me are content. You should ask yourself what you have to gain and lose by finding a balance with yourself."

"I know what I have to gain," Jean answered honestly, "but I watched what happened earlier this week when a vampire lost control. He nearly killed his partner, would have if he could have gotten to him, and when he came back to himself afterward, the guilt of it crippled him. I can't afford to be crippled. I'm chef de la Cour, the alpha of the Paris vampires, if you will. They look to me for leadership, and any sign of weakness could cost me my position or worse."

"TELL ME everything you can about what's going on with the pack," Tristan said when everyone had settled in Raymond's office. "If I don't understand something, I'll ask and Martin can translate."

"I don't know how much Martin has already told you."

"Start at the beginning," Tristan said. "Even if I hear it again, you might say something differently or have a different insight. The more information I have, the better."

"A few weeks ago, Lorens Iserin, alpha of the local pack, came to l'Institut asking for our help," Raymond began. "They haven't had a live birth in a number of years and not even any stillbirths in the past three years, but that's the tip of the iceberg. The pack has shrunk from its height of two hundred fifty to less than fifty people now, with fewer and fewer pups born each year. Marc has an interest in werewolves, so we tapped him to visit the pack and see what we could learn and what we could do to help."

"What did you learn?" Tristan asked.

"The grotto where they do their rituals shows no sign of its power being depleted," Marc reported, "which was our first thought."

Tristan chuckled. "It wouldn't be. Werewolves are like witches in that respect. We don't create or use up magic. We just channel it. What is your element?" he asked, looking at Raymond.

"Water."

"And what would you do in the middle of the desert?"

"Struggle," Raymond admitted.

"I wouldn't," Tristan replied, "because I'm not tied to any one element or center of power. In any natural space, there is power I can channel to serve my purposes. So their circle is functional."

"The circle is functional," Marc confirmed, "but they seem unable to channel the magic they raise with their ritual. I could see the build of power, but it didn't connect with them, and I couldn't make it connect. I tried, but whatever is needed to bridge that gap, I didn't know how to do it."

Tristan nodded. "No one can make the connection for anyone else. It comes from within."

"Does that mean it's hopeless?" Marc asked, thinking of Adenet and the pain on his face each time he talked about the rituals and the pack. "It can't be."

"No, it isn't hopeless," Tristan said. "It's a skill that can be taught. The pack has a shaman?"

"Yes, Adenet Silaire."

Tristan looked at Marc sharply. "What is he to you?"

"He's the pack's shaman."

"Not what I asked," Tristan pressed. "Your scent changed when you said his name."

"I... I'd hoped I might be his mate," Marc admitted, "but he made it clear he doesn't want me."

Tristan laughed. "Remind me to tell you later about stubborn wolves and their determination to ignore what's good for them when they think it's not good for the one or ones they love. I've seen it enough times to tell you to listen to the wolf, not the man."

Marc let Tristan's words reassure him. He had already agreed to go back with the embassy from the Onondaga pack. Maybe he would try a little harder with Adenet.

"What do you think the problem is?" Raymond asked, bringing the conversation back to the original topic.

"I'm guessing, of course, until I get there and see, but my own experience with werewolves has shown that they're somewhere between distrustful and downright fearful of magic. My pack was fortunate that its shaman didn't fall into that trap and continued to nurture the den and circle and kept the pack thriving without mentioning the word magic. My brother's pack had been without a shaman for a time, and they suffered for it. Not in fertility, but in other ways."

"They are certainly distrustful of magic," Raymond said. "The shaman didn't want the alpha to ask for our help."

"And once he got it?" Tristan asked, looking back to Marc. "How did he deal with it?"

"He asked me not to cast any spells in his house or in the grotto, but he didn't refuse any magic otherwise.'

"That's a step in the right direction," Tristan said. "Now we have to build on that until he is comfortable being the one channeling the magic for his pack. I'll tell Ben we may be here awhile."

"Will you be able to stay?"

"Not indefinitely, but our shaman is not quite ready to retire, and Benjamin's business can run without him for a few weeks. His assistant doesn't usually get the chance to do much of anything. He can earn his pay while we're here," Tristan replied. "We can see this through."

"YOU CAN come in," Sebastien said when he heard the door open. He knew it was Thierry because no one else would have come in without knocking. "I won't hurt you again."

"I wasn't worried about that," Thierry said. The despondency in his voice was enough to get Sebastien's attention. He lifted his head and looked over at his partner, who was hovering in the doorway. "I was afraid you wouldn't want to see me."

"I'm the one who nearly hurt you, not the other way around," Sebastien said. "Why wouldn't I want to see you?"

"Because I practically forced you into the situation, even when you kept saying it was a bad idea," Thierry practically shouted. "This is my fault, and I don't know how to fix it."

"There's nothing to fix," Sebastien said. "You didn't do anything wrong."

"And yet you're lying there looking miserable and you won't meet my eyes, and I feel like everything we had is slipping through my fingers and I can't stop it."

Sebastien swallowed hard. "You'd be better off letting it slip through your fingers. You've seen what kind of a monster I am. If I thought I could control it, if I thought we could control it, maybe it wouldn't matter, but Jean had to take me down and force my submission before I could get the better of that thing."

"God, is that what you think I saw?" Thierry asked.

"What else is there to see?"

"You," Thierry said. "You live with that inside you constantly, and in the three years I've known you, you've never so much as cracked until I pushed you into it. I know three years is nothing compared to the length of time you've been a vampire, but it's certainly long enough to give me plenty of idea what living with you would be like, and let me tell you, it's not living in fear that you'll lose control and act that way again. The only time you've ever shown any sign of that side of you is when I pushed you into it. I'm many things, but I'm not stupid enough to do that again, which means you don't have anything to worry about. And neither do I."

"So that's it?" Sebastien said. "Just like that, everything is forgotten?"

"Not forgotten," Thierry said, "because I don't want to forget the mistake I made. And not forgiven, before you suggest that. There's nothing for me to forgive, because you did nothing wrong. But behind us, at least."

Sebastien didn't see how it could be that simple, but the way he saw it, he had two choices: accept Thierry's forgiveness, even if

Thierry would not use that word, or argue and possibly drive him away in a way his loss of control had somehow not done.

"D'accord, but if I didn't do anything that requires forgiveness, then neither did you. We made a decision. It was a mistake. We've accepted that, and we'll move on together."

"But I—"

"No buts," Sebastien said. "You had good intentions when you suggested it. I had good intentions in trying it. What's done is done. I'll let it go and stop dwelling on it if you'll do the same, but every time you start to feel guilty, I get to blame myself too, so think about that before you start."

"That's not playing fair," Thierry complained, but he had a smile on his face, the most relaxed Sebastien had seen since before their experiment began. "I'm supposed to make you feel better, but you're supposed to let me feel guilty for nearly screwing things up."

"Not in this lifetime," Sebastien retorted. "At least, not over this. Maybe next time you do something stupid, we can talk about it again."

"Hey! Who says I'm going to do something else this stupid?"

"Not me," Sebastien said. "I'd be perfectly happy never to be in this kind of a situation again."

# Chapter 17

MARC STOOD silently as the two groups of werewolves went through all the protocols associated with requesting permission to enter the territory of a different pack and welcoming important visitors and every other formality they could think of—as far as Marc was concerned, anyway. He held his tongue and let Benjamin's surprisingly good French pave the way for Tristan, all the while refusing to look at Adenet, who stood in his usual place at Lorens's side. Marc worried Lorens would give away Marc's place under Adenet's roof, because it made far more sense to have the two shamans together—but Lorens made no such offer, inviting Tristan and Benjamin to stay with him and his mate instead and leaving Marc to return to Adenet's guest room.

Adenet, however, had no time for Marc. Instead he followed Lorens, Tristan, and Benjamin to Lorens's house. Marc debated joining them, but he hadn't been invited, so he let them go without him. He would observe when he could so he could report back to Raymond if there was anything the other wizard needed to see, and he would hope for the best when Adenet returned home later.

Much to his surprise, Edine appeared at the door to Adenet's house mere minutes after Marc had let himself back inside. "You didn't join us," she said. "Tristan is asking for you."

"I didn't realize I was needed," Marc said. "Of course I'll come."

They entered Lorens and Edine's house to find Adenet and Tristan engaged in much the same argument Marc and Adenet had undertaken soon after his arrival.

"We can't *do* magic," Adenet insisted.

"Then how do you explain turning someone into a werewolf?" Tristan retorted. "Even if you don't consider the fertility rites as magic, what about a turning? Binding a mortal's soul to the soul of a wolf? That is magic. And before you argue with me, I was turned. I know what it feels like, what it takes. I nearly died because the pack turned my twin and not me, but our souls were too tightly linked, and so Will had to backtrack through the process to help me complete it."

"I've never turned anyone," Adenet admitted. "No one has petitioned to join the pack since I became shaman."

"It doesn't matter what you have done," Tristan said. "It matters what you can do."

"Nothing," Adenet muttered.

"That's not true," Marc interjected. "I watched you summon the magic in the grotto at the last ritual. It rose at your call."

"Did it work?"

"I... I couldn't tell," Marc prevaricated, "but you didn't do nothing or there would have been no reaction in the grotto."

Tristan nodded. "Then we need to go out to the grotto and see what we can figure out. Marc, will you come with us?"

"It will take longer if I do," Marc said. "I can't change form and run through the forest the way you do."

"Cast a spell and meet us there," Tristan suggested. "I know you can."

"Adenet has asked me not to do magic around the grotto," Marc replied. "I've tried to respect the pack's concerns."

"You have nothing to fear from Marc's magic," Tristan told Adenet. "Wizards use magic differently than witches or werewolves, but magic is magic. His spells won't interfere with your abilities. They may even heighten them."

Benjamin said something in English that Marc did not quite catch, but Tristan seemed to pay him no attention, keeping his eyes fixed on Adenet.

"Don't enter the grotto," Adenet repeated. "As long as you arrive outside the circle, you can cast the spell."

"Thank you," Marc said. "Are we going now?"

"If our guests are willing," Lorens said. "The sooner we determine what needs to be done, the sooner we can find a solution."

"We will change and meet you outside?" Tristan verified.

"Yes, we will gather there," Lorens agreed.

Adenet rose and left the house quickly. Tristan gestured for Marc to go after him. Benjamin's muttered "Don't meddle" was clearer this time. Marc grinned as he hurried after Adenet. The other shaman's encouragement gave him hope that perhaps his assessment of Adenet's wolf's reaction to him had been accurate.

"Adenet," Marc called after the shaman. "Wait."

Adenet stopped, but his expression was hardly welcoming.

"I'm sorry I left the way I did," Marc said, catching up with him in the middle of the village square. "I should have waited and talked to you instead of just disappearing."

"You're under no obligation to be here," Adenet replied, his voice cool. He resumed walking home.

"No, I'm not," Marc agreed, "but that doesn't excuse my behavior. I want to be here. That's why I came back. I want to help if I can, and even if I can't, I want to be here for what does work for Tristan."

"Then why are you here with me?" Adenet demanded. "I don't have anything to teach you."

Marc sighed. "Because I'm not interested in Tristan except as a shaman. I'm interested in you."

Adenet glared at him. "I'm not interested in you."

"Your wolf is," Marc countered.

"We aren't having this conversation."

"Why not?" Marc insisted as they entered Adenet's house. "Pretending doesn't solve anything."

"It doesn't matter what I want," Adenet replied, "whether you like it or not. I need to change. Lorens and the others are waiting for me."

"Do you want me to take a change of clothes for you?" Marc offered, knowing Adenet would have to change back to human form to attempt any hint of magic. "It's no problem to carry them with me."

Adenet hesitated a moment before shaking his head. "None of the other wolves will be dressed either. We don't have hang-ups with nudity."

Marc accepted the explanation willingly enough, especially because it meant he would have another chance to see Adenet unclothed. He might have felt bad about his prurient interest, except it was already on the table. He *wanted* to be Adenet's mate, and Tristan seemed convinced he could be. He would have to find a moment to take the witch up on his offer to discuss stubborn werewolves. The week Marc had spent at l'Institut, wishing he could share this thought or that observation with Adenet, had been enough to convince him to give it another try—this time with intent instead of casually.

"Then I'll just get my coat and meet you at the grotto."

Adenet nodded sharply before disappearing into his room. The wolf reappeared a few minutes later. Marc held out his hand, hoping the change in form would put the wolf in ascendance. To Marc's delight, Adenet bounded over to him. Marc knelt and hugged the furry body close. He scratched the soft ears and kissed the tip of the long muzzle. The wolf licked his neck in greeting, knocking him onto his back. Marc stayed where he was, tipping his head back in submission as the wolf pinned him to the floor.

"I'm back now," Marc promised. "I won't leave you again. You just have to help me convince Adenet, okay?"

The wolf whined and licked Marc's neck again. "Go on, now," Marc said. "Lorens, Tristan, and Benjamin are waiting for you. I'll meet you at the grotto. I won't leave this time."

The wolf growled softly and rolled off Marc, then padded to the door. Marc opened it for him and glanced back to Lorens's house, where three other wolves waited. Marc recognized Lorens from the fertility ritual and guessed the chocolate-brown wolf was Tristan and the other black wolf was Benjamin. Even once Adenet joined them, Marc had no problem telling them apart. Benjamin was taller through the shoulder, but Adenet was broader through the torso and haunches. As Marc approached, he saw that their eyes were different as well: Benjamin's a silvery ice-blue while Adenet's were the warm amber Marc already loved.

"I'll meet you at the grotto," he repeated.

The four wolves loped off, Lorens in the lead.

"Adenet is a very stubborn man."

Marc looked up in surprise to see Edine standing in the doorway.

"I had noticed that," Marc said slowly, not sure where the conversation was going.

"Don't give up on him. Lorens and I would like him to be happy again."

"And you think I can make him happy?"

"If you can't, no one can."

It was not an answer precisely, but Edine had already turned to go back into the house. Marc rolled his eyes. Now he really needed to talk to Tristan. He was the only one who seemed willing to give Marc straight answers. That would have to wait until after their visit to the grotto, though. Marc closed his eyes and pictured the spot outside the grotto where he had observed the fertility ritual.


TRISTAN LOOKED around the grotto and winced. The circle of trees had been tended into perfect submission, but he felt no sense of personal connection between the shaman standing beside him and the grove. At home, their circle positively resonated with Ian's presence. The phenomenon was less marked in Will's circle, but he had only been the shaman of Richard's pack for a year. "How long have you been shaman?"

"Ten years," Adenet replied.

Too long for there not to be a lingering signature. Tristan ran his hands over the trees, the earth, looking for the herbs that would usually grow nearby, if not in the circle itself.

"Does sage or rosemary grow here?"

"I think so," Adenet replied.

"Then why don't you have any in the circle? They would help purify the area and ward off negative emotions."

"We've never used herbs that way," Adenet said, "at least not in my memory."

Tristan took a minute more to look around. "I think it's time to start. We need sage, rosemary, lavender, peppermint—or any kind of mint if peppermint isn't native to this area—and valerian root. We'll need to collect some for a cleansing ritual to help rid both the pack and the circle of all the lingering pain and grief associated with it from the failed rituals. We'll also need some we can transplant here for future use. The herbs will grow in power if they're rooted here in sacred space."

"In the grotto?" Adenet asked, looking horrified. "But we've worked so hard to tend it."

"In all the wrong ways," Tristan said. "I'm sorry to say that, but the power of a circle is in its fecundity, not its formality. You've turned it into a perfectly pruned royal garden instead of a riot of natural life and beauty. We need to unleash that power again and help you reestablish a connection to it."

"I don't know if I've ever had a connection to it," Adenet admitted. "I learned the words by rote, but what you're describing... it has no place in what I've always believed."

"The choice to listen or not is yours," Benjamin said, speaking for the first time since they arrived at the grotto, "but I've seen what Tris can do. At my behest, he sundered my wolf from me, when I thought that was what it would take to break the curse I had always lived in fear of, and when that wasn't the solution, he moved heaven and earth—and the local pack—to merge us again. His ways may not be the same as yours, but you could do far worse than to listen to him."

"We have nothing to lose," Lorens said, looking at Adenet.

"What do we need to do?"

"Do you have a ritual knife?" Tristan asked. "It's a power boost to work with your own tools. I left mine at Lorens's house because I can't carry it in wolf form, but if we are collecting herbs, I would want to get it."

"I don't know," Adenet said. "If I do, no one ever explained what it was or how to use it."

"Then we should return to the village," Tristan said. "We will gather my tools, see what you have, and get what we need. We have a few days before the waxing moon. While we will need some preparation time, if we gather the herbs tomorrow instead of today, it should make no difference."

"I can take you all back," Marc offered. "It's not far."

"That would be appreciated," Tristan said before Adenet or Lorens could reply. "It's not far, as you said, but I'm not recovered from the trip yet. I'd rather save my energy for herb hunting."

Adenet wanted to refuse on principle, but the happiness in Marc's expression silenced him. He could not make himself extinguish that joy. "What are we waiting for?"

Marc's smile widened and he drew his wand. Adenet expected some sense of movement, but other than a slight disorientation as his feet touched the ground outside his house, he felt nothing.

"Thank you," Tristan said. "I'll gather my tools and clothes and we'll sort through your cabinets, Adenet. If we can't find what we need, we may have to take a trip to town."

"Depending on what it is you need, Raymond might have it or know where to find it," Marc suggested. "He works magic as a wizard, not a witch, but he would surely know where to find any magical items."

"We'll keep that in mind," Tristan promised, "but if there are tools left from previous shamans, they would have a connection to the circle and the pack that new tools couldn't have. We want to arrange things as much in our favor as possible."

Marc followed Adenet back to his house, trying not to be obvious about staring at the lycan's bare backside, but he was only human. He could not stop himself from watching the play of muscle beneath skin.

Knowing Tristan and probably Benjamin would be there shortly, he did not say anything to start the conversation he and Adenet needed to have, but he could still show his willingness to support Adenet as a mate would by staying at his side as he worked on his craft.

Adenet disappeared into his bedroom and returned a few minutes later fully clothed. "I don't even know what we're looking for," Adenet said, staring around the room.

"Was this the previous shaman's house?" Marc asked.

"It was," Adenet said. "I apprenticed with him until his death. He had no family, so everything came to me."

"Did he have a box or a chest or anything he kept for supplies?"

"No, nothing I ever saw."

"I imagine you cleaned out the cabinets and closets, but did you check the attic or the cellar?"

"No. I didn't need the space, and there was always something more pressing to do."

"Then we'll start there," Marc said. "If he didn't show it to you, he may not have known what they were. They could have been there for decades."

Adenet opened the trap door that led down to the cellar. Marc could smell the mustiness in the air, the staleness of having been closed up for so long.

"Any idea how we'll know if we find it?" Adenet asked.

"Not really, but Tristan talked about a knife, and if it's intended for magic, it could be inscribed with runes or other symbols of power. We'll set aside anything that looks likely and let Tristan give his opinion when he gets here."

"You like him."

"I respect him," Marc corrected as Adenet loomed nearer. Marc thought he caught a flash of amber in the dark eyes. "He is obviously a skilled witch, and I hope he can teach us what we need to know."

"Us?"

Marc stifled a sigh at the thought he had not intended to voice. "I have as much to learn here as you do," he backpedaled. "His approach to magic is completely different from mine."

"Could you do magic the way he does?" Adenet began looking through boxes and crates, brushing aside layers of dust and cobwebs as he searched.

"I don't know," Marc replied honestly, "but even if I can't, even if everything I learn is theoretical, I'd still like to know."

"Adenet? Marc?"

"We're in the cellar," Adenet called back, climbing up the cellar steps enough for his head to pass through the door into the kitchen. "We thought there might be something down here."

Tristan and Benjamin found him and joined them in the cellar. With all four of them looking, they finished checking everything fairly quickly.

"Let's look in the attic," Marc said, determined not to let his disappointment at not already finding the tools show.

Adenet led the way up to the equally dusty and cluttered attic. They quartered the room and began searching again.

Marc reached the far corner of his section and brushed the dust off the top of an old wooden chest that sat on top of an equally dusty table. The surge of power through his hand shocked him. He pulled back and dusted the lid to reveal a series of runes he could not read. "Adenet, Tristan, Benjamin. I think I've found it."

The three werewolves joined him under the low eaves of the roof. "I could feel the power in it when I started to wipe the dust off, and those runes definitely aren't modern."

"Open it, Adenet," Tristan said.

"You should do it," Adenet stalled. "You know what to do with what's inside. I don't."

"You are the pack's shaman," Tristan said with a shake of his head. "It's your place to touch them. I would take them if you handed them to me, but I would never take them from the box unless the situation was desperate."

Adenet swallowed hard and opened the lid of the chest, slowly, half-afraid of what he would find inside.

A curved knife as long and wide as his finger lay at the center of the box, surrounded by an assortment of other items.

"There are your tools," Tristan said with a reverent smile. "Why don't we take them downstairs where it's warmer and see what else is in the chest?"

Adenet signaled his agreement and hefted the chest, surprised at how heavy it was. They tramped back down the stairs to the kitchen. "When we've collected the herbs, you'll want to purify your tools the same way you'll purify yourself and the circle," Tristan said, "but for now, let's see what we've found."

Adenet took out the knife, studying the curved blade. The metal itself bore no marks, but the bone handle was covered in intricate carvings.

"That is a very old boline," Tristan said. "May I look at it more closely?"

Adenet offered it to the other shaman, hilt first. Tristan took it, his eyes widening in surprise. "And a very powerful one. I don't know what happened that your pack stopped using it, but these are priceless implements."

"We are the oldest pack in Western Europe," Adenet said. "We came with the ancient Celts. There has been a pack for as long as there has been a record of people here."

"What else is in the chest?" Marc asked, his curiosity getting the better of him.

Adenet pulled out another knife, this time with a straight blade— an athame, Tristan said—a mortar and pestle, a ritual chalice, and a scuffed flint stone.

"You have all the tools you need," Tristan said when the chest was empty. "Ian has a staff, but it's more the symbol of his position than a necessity for a ritual."

"Wait," Marc said. "I think I saw something like a staff in the cellar."

He hurried back down the cellar stairs, found what he had assumed was a walking stick, and brought it back to the kitchen.

"See the carvings?" Tristan asked. "They represent your pack, your territory, and your role. Now we take your boline and mine and we go find the herbs we need."

"I'll skip that, if you don't mind," Benjamin said. "You know I can't tell one plant from another."

"May I come?" Marc asked. "I don't have a boline, but I'd like to see how it's done. I can carry things for you if you want to shift at any point."

"We won't," Adenet said even as Tristan said, "Of course you can come. You might know something about the local area that I don't."

"I'm not from le Morvan," Marc said, "but I want to learn everything I can while you're here. I may not get another chance."

"I'm only a phone call away," Tristan promised. "Even if I can't come back, I can discuss whatever you'd like on the phone or online."

They left the village to go into the woods, looking for the herbs Tristan said they needed.

"How do we even know where to begin?" Marc asked as they walked.

"Eventually, Adenet will have all the herbs he needs growing inside his circle," Tristan said, "but for now, we will have to search. If we can't find any, we may have to buy and plant some, but it's always better to find herbs growing locally."

"How do you know which herbs to use?" Adenet asked.

"Experience, a good mentor, and a lot of research," Tristan said. "Flora is my gift, so I can sometimes tell what a plant will do by touching it, but unless it's an emergency, I try to research it as well. The Internet is your friend, especially since you haven't had years to learn through experience. As we walk today, I'll see what else I see. While we need the ones on my list for the purification ritual, we can bring others back to plant in the grove as well for later use."

They walked a bit farther before Tristan found a lavender bush, nearly faded from the autumn chill, but with a few flowers still hanging on. He showed Adenet how to harvest the blooms with his boline. Then Tristan gently uprooted the plant and handed it to Marc. "Will you carry this one for us?"

Marc took the plant and held it close.

They spent the next three hours traipsing through the woods, but when they returned, they had found everything on Tristan's list.

"It's too late to return to the grotto tonight to plant these," Adenet said.

"Not if I take us out there," Marc offered. "We could be there, plant the herbs, and be back in no more than half an hour. Unless there is more to planting them than just putting the roots in the ground?"

"No, nothing like that," Tristan said. "I'm willing if you are."

Adenet hesitated a moment, but Tristan hadn't seemed concerned about Marc doing magic near the grove, and Tristan was far more knowledgeable than Adenet had ever claimed to be. "Not inside the circle."

"Of course not," Marc said, drawing his wand. "*Déplacez!*"

They planted the herbs scattered around the grotto at Tristan's direction. When they were done, Marc started back to where he had cast the displacement spell before.

"Wait," Tristan said. "Why can't you do magic here?"

"Because Adenet asked me not to."

"Why don't you want to add his power to power of this place?" Tristan asked Adenet.

"It's sacred ground."

"It is," Tristan agreed, "but his spell does not defile that. If he were trafficking in dark magic, twisting people's will to his own or some such thing, perhaps you would have cause to worry, but the simple spell he uses to take us from place to place has no malice in it."

"I would never do anything that might despoil the grotto," Marc promised.

"So cast the spell," Tristan said.

Marc looked to Adenet for permission. Tristan might say it would do no harm, but this was Adenet's grove, not Tristan's. Adenet nodded slowly, so Marc cast the spell to take them home.

TRISTAN HANDED Adenet a sachet filled with the herbs they had gathered two days earlier. "Normally your mate would help you purify yourself before a ritual, but since you have never done this before and since I will be helping with the ritual as well, I will tell you how it's done."

"I don't have a mate," Adenet replied automatically.

"Oh really?" Tristan drawled. He could hear Benjamin's voice in his head telling him not to meddle, but Tristan ignored it. Part of his responsibilities as shaman included supporting and encouraging mated pairs, and the turbulence of his own mating made him particularly sensitive to the challenges other pairs faced. "That isn't what your wolf thinks."

"That's none of your business," Adenet snapped.

"Maybe, maybe not. You asked me here to help. If you can't work in concert with your wolf, you won't reap the full benefits of the ritual. I can teach you all the right words and gestures, but if you can't channel the power raised by the ritual because you've tied yourself in knots, all my teachings will be useless."

"I'm not tied in knots. What should I do with this bag of herbs?"

"Use it in your bathwater," Tristan said. "Wash your body completely and then rinse in cold water. When you are dry, change and go to the grove. I will purify myself and meet you there."

Adenet entered the bathroom and ran the water as hot as he could. He dropped the bag in the water, smelling the scents of the herbs as they blended together in the steam. They smelled fresh, clean, like a new beginning. Adenet hoped that was what tonight would be. He stepped into the nearly scalding water, pushing aside thoughts of anything except his hopes for the upcoming ritual. Purification, letting go of negativity—he needed to concentrate on all that was good, not on everything that had gone wrong and that he could not have.

"HAVE I mentioned how wonderful I think it is that you're here and helping this way?" Benjamin asked as Tristan undressed to join him in the herb-infused bath water.

"Once or twice," Tristan said with a smile as he climbed into the tub with his mate. "Tonight won't be enough."

"What will be?" Benjamin asked, sluicing water over Tristan's skin. He knew they would not make love before the ritual, but he never passed up a chance to touch his mate.

"Adenet accepting that Marc is his mate and that he has nothing to fear from the power their combined magic will raise," Tristan replied. "He can't function as a shaman if he isn't true to himself."

"What's holding him back?"

"What holds any werewolf back?" Tristan asked. "Fear, perhaps the fact that Marc isn't a wolf, that he's a wizard, perhaps even that he's male in a pack that's obsessed with fertility."

"Not without reason."

"I didn't say it was," Tristan replied, leaning back against Benjamin's strong chest. In public he might be the shaman, the central figure of their partnership, but in private he was content to let Benjamin take care of him. "But think how different our courtship would have gone if we'd had Ian to guide us sooner."

"You don't know that it would have made any difference," Benjamin said.

"Maybe not, but if he'd been there pushing us to stop messing around and complete our mating, we might have broken the curse without it nearly killing you. If Will had truly known Richard was his mate, maybe they would have broken Sienna's spell more quickly. And maybe not, but maybe it wouldn't have hurt him so much in the process."

"And maybe it would have made him overconfident. Maybe it would have sped up your half of the curse and nearly killed me faster, before you had time to figure it out. Don't meddle, Tristan. They have to figure it out for themselves."

"Part of my job as shaman—"

"It's still meddling, and they won't thank you for it. Do the ritual tonight, prove to Adenet how much power could be at his command. Show him what he's missing and maybe that will bring him around, but don't bring up Marc."

ONCE AGAIN Marc stood alone outside the grove as the shamans began their ritual. Marc was not part of the pack, of the need for purification or cleansing away the old, although a part of him wished he could stand at Adenet's side as Benjamin stood at Tristan's. Marc watched as Adenet moved around the grove, preparing it, using the old flint from the chest to start the fire instead of a match as he had done before. The full pack had gathered this time instead of just the two couples from the previous ritual. Marc could feel their anticipation. For the first time in years, they felt hope. Marc prayed to whatever deities might be listening that they would not be disappointed. He did not know how much more their hearts could take.

When the fires were lit, Adenet began the chant, echoed by Tristan. As before, Marc could see the power called by their words, could watch it eddy through the grove. Unlike the last time, the flow had direction, winding around Tristan and Adenet. Marc held his breath, waiting to see the connection that had been missing during the fertility ritual.

The sheer magnitude of it lit up the night in Marc's eyes, though he saw no sign that the werewolves noticed. Tristan gestured for Adenet to begin smudging the grove with the bundles of sage they had prepared. Adenet left Tristan's side to light the herbs in the ritual fire. Marc expected the eddies of power to shift with Adenet's movement, to follow him around the grove as he carried the smoking herbs and continued the chant to banish all negativity, past grief, and fear, but the connection with the source of power stayed with Tristan.

Marc nearly left then, his own disappointment so contrary to the point of the ritual that he feared tainting their hope with his frustration. He could not bring himself to abandon Adenet that way, though. He had no idea if the shaman could sense the difference between the way Tristan worked and the way he did, but if he did, Marc would be there to support him. Since Tristan's arrival, Adenet had been too busy for Marc to catch him alone, but Adenet had accepted Marc's help at every turn and had even started looking for Marc. It was a small step, but

Marc considered it progress. Whether he could turn that progress into the mating he desired remained to be seen.

He had spent the days between the fertility ritual and Tristan's arrival reviewing his sources, checking everything he could find about werewolves and their traditions about mating. Tristan had implied that he believed in Marc's hopes, but Marc had not found the time to speak with him alone since they arrived back on pack lands and Tristan had met Adenet.

Before Tristan's arrival, Marc had found nothing in his research to suggest that he could not mate with the shaman, either because he was male or because he was not a werewolf himself. Tristan had a male mate, though Benjamin was a werewolf, and from some comments Tristan had let drop, Marc understood that Tristan's brother was both shaman of his own pack and mate of the pack's prince. Surely if the two brothers could have male mates in such lofty positions, Adenet could do the same. Marc had only to persevere, to show Adenet his love and support, to prove himself worthy of being part of the pack. He had no real thought of being changed, not with his own magic tied to a human form, but he could be a member of the pack as Adenet's mate if they would accept them.

He could do this. He *would* do this.

Marc realized with a jolt that Tristan was drawing the ritual to a close. The pack dispersed slowly, smiles on the faces of those in human form, relaxation clear in the body language of those who had shifted. The mood in the grotto was as light as Marc had felt it since his arrival. Even Adenet seemed more relaxed as he scattered the ashes of the herbs under Tristan's direction. Marc waited patiently, determined to act as much like Adenet's mate as the werewolf would allow. Benjamin had not left the grove when the others did, although he stayed to the side out of Tristan's way, so Marc would do the same unless Adenet specifically told him to go.

"What did you think?" Tristan asked as they finished and began walking back toward the village.

Marc did not offer to take them magically. The contemplative spirit of their walk seemed to fit the mood after the ritual.

"I would never have thought to do it myself," Adenet admitted, "but even if I had the idea, what you did was more complex than what I was ever taught. The herbs, the knives, and all the rest… it's an entirely new way of approaching what we do, at least to me."

"Tonight's ritual is a first step," Tristan agreed, "to teaching you what you need to know and to repairing the damage done by neglect, but I think it was a good first step. The auras of the pack were lighter, free of grief and hopeful about the future. It's an essential first step because you cannot rebuild the pack in a day or a month. Even if the fertility ritual is successful when we try again in three weeks, it may only be one or two pups. It may still 'fail' for more couples than it succeeds for."

"What happens next?" Adenet asked. "You said a series of rituals at each stage of the moon leading up to the next full one."

"Yes, the new moon, the moment of rebirth, will be the time to reconsecrate the pack to the grove and the grove to the pack, to reconnect the pack's life force with the power represented by your sacred space."

"And then?"

"One step at a time," Tristan said with a shake of his head. "We will see how the first one goes, and then we can decide what will be next. Part of being a shaman is taking stock of the situation and then taking steps to address it, whatever that situation may be. It's far more than simply going through the motions of a ritual at the prescribed time because that's what you've been told you're supposed to do. Sometimes the situation calls for improvisation or even breaking completely with your established rhythm. Your pack has to trust you to make those decisions."

"I don't even know how to make them myself," Adenet protested. "There's so much I've never learned."

"I'll teach you what I can while I'm here," Tristan promised, "and even after I leave, I'm only a phone call or an e-mail away."

"You could stay."

"For a few weeks," Tristan said, "until I'm sure you're on the right track, but I have a home and a pack of my own."

# Chapter 18

"I HAVE some questions."

Jean looked up from the book he was reading to see Thierry at his door. "I'd be surprised if you didn't, although I may not be the best person to answer them."

"Sebastien can't or won't. Orlando doesn't know the answers. You're the oldest, most well-read vampire I know, so you're it."

Jean gestured to the chair opposite of him. "What do you want to know?"

"Why does the Aveu de Sang only work once?"

Jean coughed. "That was not what I was expecting."

"But it's the root of the problem," Thierry said. "We see all these benefits, some which even Sebastien didn't know about from his previous relationship, so it seems like there would be all these reasons for the bond to exist, but then there's the part where it only works once. It doesn't make sense. I can understand it not working again while the first Avoué's alive, or even while the vampire is grieving his Avoué's death. I'm not cruel, but to have that, to get all those benefits and then lose them only to never be able to regain them… that's the cruel part."

"More than one vampire agrees with you," Jean said, "which is one of the reasons so few of us make a bond even when we find a lover for a time."

"But that doesn't answer my question. Why does it only work once?"

"I don't know," Jean said. "The spell is an ancient one. Marcel told us that when Alain and Orlando made their bond. I've found references to the spell in the oldest books, but never with any mention of its creation. By the time we had texts to record it in, or at least from the texts we have extant, it was already known and both feared and revered, but nowhere is it explained."

"But you're sure it only works once? What would happen if a vampire tried to make a second one?"

"You would end up with a painful burn and Sebastien would be exiled from the Cour," Jean replied.

"But why?" Thierry's voice rose in frustration. "Why would a second bond require him to be exiled? None of this makes sense."

"You're assuming he wants a second Avoué," Jean said.

"He told me once before, soon after the war ended, that he would make me his Avoué if he could," Thierry said. "At the time, it was enough that he said the words. Now it's not enough anymore. There has to be an explanation, and if there isn't, then the spell should work again or there should be some other way to give him the benefits of it."

"I don't have an answer," Jean said. "I wish I did."

"So I'm just supposed to give up?" Thierry demanded.

"I didn't say that," Jean replied with a slow smile. "I said I didn't have an answer. I didn't say you shouldn't look for one."

"I wouldn't even know where to start."

"My library is open to you," Jean said, gesturing to the books behind him. "There are other places you can look as well. And perhaps the answer lies within your own lore. A wizard created this spell, for all that a vampire must carry it out. Sebastien can't have a second Avoué, but there may be other options for you to explore."

"I'm not a researcher or a historian," Thierry protested.

"How badly do you want this?" Jean asked seriously. "You're proposing something no one has dared to explore before now. You want something that we've always believed is impossible. Maybe we're wrong. Maybe there is a way. But if there is, no one has found it before."

"Necessity is the mother of invention and all that," Thierry said with a sigh. "Is that what you're saying?"

"More or less. We've said more than once how much has been lost because our kinds parted ways, and how much might have been gained had we not. Maybe this is only the beginning."

"Will you help me?" Thierry asked.

"In any way I can, but remember that while I may know about vampires, I know even less about magic and spells and wizards than you claim to. Raymond will be more help than I could be."

"Will he help?"

"You'll have to ask him."


THREE DAYS after the purification ritual, Marc was at his wits' end. Far from continuing to look to Marc for help, Adenet had returned to going out of his way to avoid spending any time alone with him. Marc had had enough.

"You said you'd tell me about stubborn werewolves," Marc said, seeking Tristan out. "I thought things were getting better, but my stubborn werewolf seems to be avoiding me."

"Part of that is my fault, even though I didn't mean to make him avoid you," Tristan said. "He's realized how much he has to learn, and I'm trying to squeeze a lifetime of knowledge into a few weeks of mentoring. I'll try to leave him a little more free time."

"I don't want to take him away from your lessons. I want to help, but I don't know how."

"By being patient right now," Tristan replied. "In the course of a few weeks, he's met his mate, learned that he has to do magic, and realized he doesn't know how."

"So I really am his mate?"

"Yes," Tristan said. "Benjamin says I shouldn't tell you, that you need to work things out for yourselves, but Adenet needs you. He's fighting his wolf, and the internal conflict upsets his balance. You work hard as a wizard to promote balance around you. He needs to preserve it inside, and right now, he doesn't know how. He needs you for that."

"How do I help him?"

"Seducing him is always an option, if you can get him alone, but it won't be enough to seduce his wolf. Adenet has to accept your mating as well, and he's proven remarkably good at ignoring what his wolf wants."

"Do I have other options?"

"You can try talking him into it before you seduce him," Tristan said, "but I've found it's easier to convince a stubborn man when his wolf is already on your side."

"Benjamin?" Marc said with a grin.

"And Richard, my brother's mate, and Alex, the alpha of my pack," Tristan said with a chuckle. "Their own mates seducing them, not me, of course."

"Of course."

"Richard was under the spell of a powerful witch. His mating bond with Will finally broke her spell. Benjamin was cursed to an unhappy marriage and then to life alone until our mating bond broke the curse not only for him but for his descendants."

"And your pack's alpha?"

"Is just a stubborn alpha," Tristan said, "and his mate is the only one who can sway him. If you're going to be Adenet's mate, you may as well learn how to manage him now. You can't always get your way, but a werewolf is fundamentally incapable of making his mate unhappy without a damn good reason."

SEBASTIEN HESITATED outside the door to Jean and Raymond's office, his embarrassment and guilt warring with his need to atone for his behavior. Thierry had forgiven him, but Sebastien still could not let it go.

"Jean?"

"Come in, Sebastien. I wondered how long it would take you to come find me."

"I owe you an apology."

"You really don't," Jean replied. "You didn't hurt me."

"I tried."

"You'll have to try harder than that. If anyone should apologize, it's me. I shouldn't have told you what I did. I should have told you not to try it."

"We needed to know," Sebastien said with a shake of his head. "The partnership bonds give us so much, more in some ways even than the Aveu de Sang gave me. We needed to know the limits."

"I don't know how to separate them," Jean said. "I mean, I know what seemed to be added when we made our Aveu de Sang, but I don't have anything to compare it to."

"There are the obvious things," Sebastien said, "the benefits we all get from the partnerships that have nothing to do with the Aveu de Sang."

"Walking in sunlight and all that," Jean agreed, "but that's the same regardless."

"It's little things," Sebastien said. "With Thibaut, I always wondered what he got out of our Aveu de Sang. With Thierry, there is no doubt what he gets from our bond. I don't have the sense of where he might be or of his emotions when I'm not feeding the way I did with Thibaut, but everything with Thibaut felt one-sided. He wanted something, and I moved heaven and earth to get it for him."

"And now Thierry is moving heaven and earth for you."

"Maybe that's just a difference in personality, but it feels like it's more than that. It feels like Thierry's attachment to me is as profound as mine is to him."

"He said something when we were planning l'Institut about the partnership bonds completing wizards in a way nothing else did," Jean remembered.

"Yes, he's said that several times," Sebastien agreed. "It shouldn't hold true for me. I should be able to say that no relationship can compare to my Avoué, but I can't say that. Yes, there are elements missing from my relationship with Thierry, like being able to sense him or being able to keep him on edge and making love for hours, but if Thibaut walked in here today, I'd stay with Thierry."

Jean shook his head. "I'm not doubting you," he said quickly when he saw Sebastien's scowl. "I'm trying to imagine feeling enough with someone else that I would let Raymond go. I can't. I can't envision a more all-encompassing relationship."

"But Raymond is a wizard. Thibaut wasn't."

"You think that makes a difference in the Aveu de Sang, not just in the addition of the partnership bond?"

"I don't know," Sebastien said, "and there's no way to know since I can't form a new one to compare them. All I can do is remember how I felt at the time and what I see in you and Orlando. It's more."

On impulse, Jean stood and poured two glasses of cognac. "Can you taste it?"

"Of course I can't," Sebastien said.

"No, try and see," Jean insisted, "because I can now. I've been able to for about a year, but I don't know if it's the Aveu de Sang, the partnership bond, or both."

Sebastien took a sip and shook his head. "Nothing."

"Could you taste anything besides blood when you were with Thibaut?"

"Not that I remember," Sebastien said, "but that was a long time ago, and resources were in short supply. I wouldn't have wanted to waste something that would feed Thibaut by eating it myself."

"Yes, but it's some evidence of a difference. I couldn't taste the cognac until after Raymond became my Avoué. You can't taste it still, and you couldn't then, so there is a difference when your Avoué is a wizard."

"The question, then, is why."

"And are there others?" Jean added. "Did you even try letting up on your control when you were with Thibaut?"

"No," Sebastien said, "it never would have occurred to me to try it. Even knowing I couldn't hurt him, I would have worried about frightening or disgusting him. I was bound to him, but I never completely trusted that he was bound to me."

"And yet you trusted Thierry that much."

"He saw far worse during the war than me out of control," Sebastien pointed out. "If he could deal with that, this was nothing in comparison."

"Is that really enough?" Jean asked.

"No," Sebastien said, "but I knew it wouldn't scare him away. He can't walk away from me any more than I can walk away from him, even without the Aveu de Sang. Even with that monster inside of me who didn't recognize him."

"So the partnership bond draws you together, maybe even keeps you together, but it's the Aveu de Sang that allows... forces... helps... our inner beasts to focus on one person instead of rampaging?"

"At least if that person is a wizard," Sebastien said.

"Then the solution to your problem is to find another way to force that recognition. One of the werewolves said something about being soothed by his mate and that helping him find balance within himself. Maybe we can learn something from their mating ritual, something that would allow you a second chance."

"Will they tell us?"

"I don't know, but it couldn't hurt to ask."


"FOR THE ritual tonight to work, you have to be the conduit for the power," Tristan told Adenet as they prepared the herbs and tools they would need. "I can assist you, whether now or in the grotto, but you are the pack's shaman. I can't create a connection between them and the grove because this isn't my pack."

"I've learned so much since you came," Adenet said. "I'm sure I'll be able to do it."

"Just remember that your power doesn't come from the outside but from inside, from your heart," Tristan said. "Be true to that, and everything else will fall in place."

"I don't think I could be any truer to myself than helping my family."

"And your mate?"

"Now is not the time," Adenet snapped. "I have a ritual to perform and a pack to help. I can't afford to be distracted."

Tristan sighed and let him go when he stormed out of the house. He shook his head at the stubbornness of werewolves. One of these days he was going to find one who could be reasonable, even if it killed him. He already knew what the outcome of the ritual would be. He needed to talk to Lorens. Fortunately the alpha was easy to find.

"I've changed my mind about tonight's ritual," Tristan told Lorens. "Adenet has come so far the past week, and I don't want to set him up for failure. We still have the waxing moon before it's time for the fertility ritual again. We can bring the pack back to the grove next week. Tonight Adenet needs to face his abilities on his own."

"What aren't you telling me?" Lorens said.

"He's holding himself back," Tristan replied, "and he won't admit it so he can fix it. I have a plan to force him to admit it and help him to fix it, but the pack doesn't need to see it. They've only begun to have their faith restored. They don't need to have it shaken again." Benjamin would accuse him of meddling, but this had gone beyond Adenet and Marc's relationship. Adenet's refusal was hurting his entire pack, and Tristan could not allow that to go on. Besides, Tristan had a history of meddling in things, and where would he and Benjamin be if he had not meddled in Benjamin's life?

"I want to be there," Lorens said.

"I'd advise against it, but you are the alpha here. I can't make you do anything."

"Why would you advise against it?"

"Because Adenet has his pride," Tristan said, "and the more people around watching him, the harder it will be to force him to admit that he can't do what he needs to do until he stops pretending Marc is not his mate. Is that going to be a problem for the pack?"

"No, and furthermore, he knows it, the idiot. I told him weeks ago that we would accept Marc into the pack as his mate."

"If all goes well, he'll have accepted that fact by tomorrow."

"And if it doesn't?"

"I'll worry about that if it doesn't. The grove isn't stocked with blankets or furs for a mating. Does the pack have special ones, or should I grab some from my bed?"

"I'll take care of it," Lorens promised. "The grove will be prepared for their mating if you can get them to cooperate."

Tristan hoped his plan worked. If it did not, he would have to listen to Benjamin scolding him, and he could think of far more pleasant ways to pass the time with his mate.

"WHERE IS everyone?" Adenet asked when they reached the grotto and no one else was there.

"Back in the village," Tristan said. "Tonight it will just be you and me."

"Why?"

"Because you still have things to learn, and your pack doesn't need to see you learning them."

"You couldn't have taught me earlier?"

"I tried. You weren't listening. Start the ritual. Prove to me you can do this."

Adenet took a deep breath and cleared his mind as Tristan had taught him, focusing on centering himself before beginning the chant to summon the power they would need for the ceremony. He could feel the tingle of it over his skin, much as he had the night of the purification ritual, which gave him hope he would be able to do what Tristan expected of him. He took a moment to toss the herb packet into the ritual fire, perfuming the air with smoke and incense.

The scents called to his wolf, bringing his other half closer to the surface than usual, but remembering Tristan's advice, Adenet did not try to suppress his wolf. Instead he tried to bring his other half into the ritual, but his wolf had one focus only: the wizard standing quietly outside the circle of trees. Adenet stifled a curse. Tristan had said no one would be there but the two of them, yet Marc ghosted around the edge of Adenet's consciousness.

"If you had claimed him already, his presence would add to your strength, not distract you," Tristan said, "but since you haven't, you'll have to work around it. You've raised the power you need. Now use it."

Adenet tried to connect with the magic summoned by his call, but it remained elusive.

"Concentrate," Tristan ordered.

"I'm trying."

"Not hard enough."

Adenet spun toward Tristan, but before he could take the first step, Tristan raised his hands. "Being angry with me doesn't help. The power is inside you. You just have to let it out."

Adenet tried again to meld his will with the power he had summoned, but he still felt nothing. No resonance, no reaction, nothing.

"I can't do it," he said, dropping to his knees in defeat. "Tell Lorens I'm sorry and to find another shaman."

"It doesn't work that way," Tristan reminded him. "This is your pack, your heart, your responsibility. If you don't do it, it won't be done."

"Then I guess the pack is doomed."

"It doesn't have to be. Everything you need is right here waiting for you. You just have to find the courage to accept it." Tristan cast a meaningful glance into the woods before shifting into wolf form and leaving Adenet alone in the grotto.

Marc's stomach churned as he watched Tristan leave the grove. He knew what Tristan wanted him to do, but now that the time had come, his nerves had returned. Tristan and Adenet had not dispersed the magic summoned by the ritual, which made Marc wary of approaching. Once the circle was closed, crossing into it without invitation could be dangerous. He could not leave Adenet to suffer alone, though, so he channeled his own magic around him as a shield and stepped into the grove.

"Don't give up," he said softly, kneeling next to Adenet's naked form. He wanted to pull the shaman into his arms, but he was not sure of his welcome, especially not now.

"You shouldn't have seen that," Adenet said, his voice cracking.

"Why not?" Marc asked. "I had my share of failures before I learned to control my magic. Why should I be concerned that it's taking time for you?"

"Because it's not a question of control. I can't do anything with it."

"You summoned it," Marc said. "If you didn't have the ability, you couldn't have done even that much. We'll keep trying. We'll figure it out. If Tristan can't help you, we'll find someone who can."

"I don't deserve your faith in me."

"You don't get to make that choice for me," Marc said, leaning forward to kiss Adenet. "My heart is mine to give where I will."

Adenet felt his wolf surge against his shields at the tender words, and Adenet finally stopped fighting. Tristan believed accepting Marc as his mate would make a difference. Lorens didn't care that his mate was male rather than female. His wolf ached to claim Marc. The only thing holding him back was his own blind stubbornness. Doing things his own way had gained him nothing. Maybe it was time to listen to everyone else. He captured Marc's lips with his own, laying claim to his mate's mouth. He nearly laughed with the joy of those words. His mate! Only the need to keep kissing Marc kept him from it.

Marc ran gentle hands over Adenet's shoulders. He had touched before, but only when Adenet's wolf had been in control of his actions. The eyes that stared at him now from Adenet's beloved face alternated between chocolate and amber, both halves of the man he had fallen in love with there with him. He tipped his head back, offering his submission to his mate.

Adenet nipped softly at the bared throat, needing to claim but not to hurt, never to hurt. Not Marc, his sweet mate who believed in him when everyone else had given up, who refused to let him give up, who knelt beside Adenet now in all his beauty. He needed skin, needed more than just the darkening bruise on Marc's throat to identify Marc as his, but they could not do that here. The overhang that formed one side of the grotto provided shade in the heat of the day but no protection from the other elements. They could not keep furs and supplies for mating there. When he glanced over toward the den where the pack's mating rituals were always celebrated, though, he saw the darker shadow of something piled against the stone cliff.

"Come with me," he said, urging Marc to his feet. Marc followed with such eagerness that Adenet had to stop and kiss him again even before they reached the pile of furs set out to couch their union. Marc met Adenet's tongue with his own, kissing him back with wanton abandon. Adenet growled into the kiss and pulled Marc against him, rubbing their lower bodies together repeatedly until Marc was panting into his mouth.

"There are furs to keep us warm if you don't mind staying here, or we can go back to my house," Adenet offered, resting his hands on Marc's hips. He itched to strip Marc bare, but given the chill of the night air on his own skin, it might be too cold for Marc. He wanted his soon-to-be lover's agreement before he began.

"Matings would normally take place here, wouldn't they?" Marc asked.

Adenet nodded. "At least the formal ceremony, although that includes the physical act as well. It's not usually the first time the couple has made love—it's symbolic, normally—but yes, it would take place here."

"Then we should stay here," Marc said. "I don't want anyone to challenge our mating in the morning."

"No one would," Adenet promised, "because the only people within the pack who might challenge a mating are the shaman and the alpha. I'm participating, and someone had to bring the furs out here. It must have been Lorens. If he were going to object, he wouldn't have helped us now."

Marc nodded and dropped his jacket to the ground beside the pile of furs. He reached for the hem of his sweater, but Adenet batted his hands away and removed it himself. Marc made himself relax and give control over to Adenet. Of course Adenet would want to be in charge. He might not be the pack's alpha, but he was still a dominant male within the pack. Marc found the thought incredibly arousing.

Adenet bore Marc back onto the pile of furs, adjusting them so they provided his mate some protection from the cool wind. He did not cover them completely, though. He needed to see as well as smell, feel, taste, and hear his mate the first time they made love. His wolf would settle for nothing less. As Marc squirmed on the furs to get comfortable, Adenet decided his wolf was the smarter of the two. He should have done this weeks ago.

He trailed his fingers over Marc's chest, feeling the smooth skin and the way Marc twitched beneath his touch. He paused for a moment at Marc's nipples, circling them teasingly. Marc gasped and arched into the contact, making Adenet glad for the flickering light of the fire that limned Marc's skin in gold and let Adenet's lupine vision pick up the details of Marc's constantly changing expression.

He lowered his head and nipped at the tightened nubs, rubbing his cheek back and forth against Marc's smooth skin so that his stubble tickled Marc's chest.

"Merde," Marc gasped. "Do that again."

Adenet chuckled and then tantalized Marc's other nipple for a moment before leaning back up to kiss Marc again. He could not get enough of his lover's mouth, of the taste and smell and feel of his mate beneath him. He wanted to rush; he wanted to drag it out as long as he could. He needed Marc now, but he needed the connection to last a lifetime.

Marc's body opened beneath his fingers, hot and lush, beckoning Adenet inside. He leaned down, needing the taste of his lover on his tongue. Marc cried out as Adenet licked the tip of his erection, enjoying how Marc's back bowed as Adenet continued to lavish pleasure on him. Adenet's wolf drank up the sounds, and Adenet gave him free rein. He wanted to make Marc climax, but his patience was gone, lost in the inferno that burned between them, lighting up the night. At first he thought it was a trick of his imagination, but when he looked toward the fire and then back at Marc, he realized the glow surrounding them was not coming from the fire but from them.

From him.

He threw his head back and howled in victory, the sound more muted from his human throat than it would have been in lupine form, but it did not matter. He was here with his mate in their sacred grove, touching the power that had been denied him up until now.

"I'm sorry," he said, leaning up to kiss Marc. "I shouldn't have fought this. I should have grabbed it with both hands and held on for dear life."

"What are you waiting for?" Marc asked with an equally joyful grin. "You didn't miss your chance. I'm still right here with you."

"Yes," Adenet said, smiling down at his mate. "Yes, you are."

As their bodies joined, Adenet felt the power inside him increase, doubling back in on itself with each thrust of his hips against Marc's groin, with each ingress into his mate's body. Even in the cool night air, sweat sheened his body as he burned with the sheer force of the power raised by their connection. A single glance revealed all the same signs in Marc: the blown pupils, the flushed cheeks, the parted lips, the harsh breaths sawing in and out of his chest. This was not sex. This was mating, in all its primal, unfettered glory, the way it had been intended to be celebrated, the way Adenet had always been too blind to see. He spared a thought for the other mated pairs in his pack, hoping they had felt this sense of connection with their mates at least once in their lives. Then Marc clenched around him and all thought of anything other than joining with his mate fled. Adenet's wolf took command, pulling back and flipping Marc onto his hands and knees. Marc moved at his urging, dropping his forehead onto his forearms, his perfect ass offered up for Adenet to plunder. He licked the luscious curve and nipped at the underside of one perfect cheek before mounting Marc again, joining their bodies once more in a rush of perfect harmony that only magnified the resonance between them. Marc cried out sharply, his body spasming around Adenet's shaft and then going limp. Adenet pounded into him, feeling the pinnacle approaching and, with it, a rush of power so strong he was sure he would explode from it.

"Give it to me," Marc whispered from beneath him. "Give the power to me."

Adenet nodded, words beyond him as he focused on the man beneath him, pushing the magical energy out through his fingers as they stroked Marc's hips, through his lips as they traced the curve of Marc's spine, and through his cock as the rapture inside him surpassed the limits of his control. Marc cried out with the force of it, but he never faltered beneath Adenet's onslaught, physical or magical. When Adenet finally collapsed across Marc's back, bearing them both down onto the sticky furs, Marc shifted enough to turn and face his lover.

"Can you see it?" Marc asked softly.

Adenet opened his eyes and saw what Marc was talking about: a ribbon of gold joined their hearts.

"Did we do that?"

"You did that," Marc said. "You created that bond with your power. I accepted it with mine, but it came from you. Do you understand what that means?"

"It means my pack finally has the shaman it deserves."

Marc smiled. "And I have the mate I deserve."

Adenet doubted that, but he already knew he would spend his life striving to be worthy of that one simple statement. "I love you."

Marc's smile widened. "I hoped you might. Your wolf certainly seems to."

"His view of the world is a little simpler than mine," Adenet said. "Food, shelter, a mate… not much else matters."

"I can think of worse ways to live."

Adenet considered that for a moment. "Go to sleep," he said after a moment. "You wore me out too much for any kind of philosophical discussion."

"*I* wore *you* out?" Marc teased. "I'm pretty sure you were the one wearing me out."

Adenet rolled his eyes and tucked Marc's head beneath his chin. "Go to sleep."

Marc chuckled and closed his eyes. He could win that battle tomorrow.

ADENET STIRRED beneath the furs, his wolf rumbling inside him with contentment at the scents of sex and Marc. His mate. Home, safety, love, every good thing all rolled up in one sweet, sexy package. Marc snuggled closer, not quite waking. Adenet shifted so that Marc's head rested more comfortably on his shoulder and pondered what would happen next. He had failed to complete the ritual the night before, but that was before his mating. He knew what magic felt like now, had felt it coursing through him as he gave his heart into Marc's care and took Marc's heart for his own. He had no idea if anyone beyond the two of them had seen or felt the outpouring of magic, but it had lit up the night. Even now, fine tendrils of gold joined his chest and Marc's, as quiet as their bodies, but Adenet suspected the breathtaking effervescence would return if he woke Marc and made love to him again.

The night was giving way to dawn, too late to complete the ritual Tristan had planned, but Adenet suspected what he and Marc had shared more than served the purpose of the original ritual. Adenet could feel the vibrant pulse of life all around him, in the air, in the grove, and beyond. He might have technique still to learn, but the connection Tristan described as essential was now in place.

Marc stirred, opening his eyes to stare at Adenet. "I didn't dream it?"

"No, *amans*, you didn't dream it. I'm done fighting my wolf and you."

"Good," Marc said, leaning in for a kiss.

Adenet returned the embrace lazily, exploring Marc's mouth. He could feel the hum of passion between them, waiting to wake, but he ignored it. This soft, tender kiss meant far more right now.

"We should talk about what happens now," Adenet said eventually.

"What do you mean?"

"You have a job in Paris, a life there," Adenet reminded him. "And I have responsibilities here."

"There's not a thing in Paris I can't leave behind," Marc said immediately. "A dinky apartment I could barely afford and a few acquaintances."

"Your job," Adenet reminded him.

"I've been thinking about that," Marc said. "I could go back to l'ANS and the job I was doing there, but really, anyone with a little magical background could do it. I'll have to talk to madame Valour and Raymond, but I had an idea for a job more suited to my unique… situation." He ran his hand over Adenet's chest, tangling his fingers in the soft pelt there.

"Your situation?" Adenet said with a chuckle.

"I am the only wizard in France mated to a werewolf," Marc said. "I think l'ANS needs an official emissary to the packs, to promote goodwill and avoid or help solve future problems."

"And you'd volunteer, of course."

"Of course. I have a unique perspective, after all."

Adenet laughed more openly. "You make a very persuasive argument."

"I'd probably have to spend some time at l'Institut," Marc said. "Unless you'd be comfortable with Raymond and some others coming here from time to time."

"We'll have visits from the other packs as well," Adenet said, "or else we'll have to visit them. I don't know what has broken the connection for them. Or maybe it's not a block so much as ignorance, because no one I talked to does anything like what Tristan has shown us—which makes sense, since our pack has always trained other shamans. Either way, we need to share Tristan's knowledge and our own experiences."

"Not right away," Marc said. "We need proof that it's working again."

"Edine and Lorens will be happy to provide that, and I can think of more than a few other couples as well."

"Will it be a problem that I can't shift forms?" Marc asked.

"No, it won't be," Adenet promised. "First, we wouldn't be able to have children of our own anyway. Lycan or mortal, we're both still men, so unless you're planning on sleeping with someone else, our participation in a fertility ritual would be purely symbolic."

His wolf howled at the thought of anyone else touching his mate, but Adenet ignored it. He thought he knew Marc's answer, but he needed to hear it confirmed.

"Symbolic sounds perfect to me," Marc said. "I don't want anyone else. I haven't since I first laid eyes on you."

"Good. We mated as werewolf and wizard, not two werewolves. Tristan was changed without it affecting his abilities, but it was an accident. I mated with you as a wizard, and I think that dynamic, fresh blood, a fresh perspective, is good for the pack and good for me. If you want to be changed, I won't stop you, but I don't need it. You are perfect for me just the way you are. If something went wrong, if your brand of magic affected the process differently than Tristan's, I could lose you, and I don't want that."

Marc squeezed him tight. "I've been fascinated by werewolves all my life. I dreamed of meeting a pack, but I never imagined I'd find one to be a part of. If the pack will accept me as your mate without me becoming a werewolf, then that's the choice I would make."

"They'll accept you or we'll petition another pack to accept us instead," Adenet swore, "and if no pack will have us, we'll think of something else, but I don't think it will come to that. Lorens was pretty clear when he realized we were mates. I don't think there will be any problem with him accepting you."

"Should we go ask him?"

"Later," Adenet said, his wolf's need for his mate growing too strong to ignore.

Marc rolled onto his back with a joyous laugh and pulled Adenet down on top of him.

# Epilogue

ADENET MOVED with confidence as he traced the sacred circle, chanting a wordless tune to summon the power of the Goddess as Tristan had taught him. He knew the other shaman was somewhere in the gathered throng, but he was a face among many, not the focus tonight. Tristan had questioned the wisdom of that, but Adenet knew the block was gone. Marc stood at the ritual fire, ready to assist Adenet as necessary, but even that was more for form than necessity, a way to show the pack that Marc had a part to play in their lives as well.

At Adenet's nod, Lorens stepped forward, Edine at his side, the king and his Consort ready to receive the blessings of the ritual and to hear the petitions of the pack. Adenet closed his eyes and drew on the power he had summoned, feeling it flow through him and out to the very edges of the grotto. *This* was what he had been born to do, and now, thanks to his mate, he could fulfill his duties. He felt as much as heard the murmur of surprise that ran through the pack as they, too, experienced the brush of magic for the first time. When it had settled again, Lorens spoke into the firelit night.

"Tonight as the moon waxes, growing fuller again, we gather in our sacred grove to celebrate Adenet's good fortune."

Adenet stepped in front of Lorens and Edine, going down on one knee in homage before his alpha. "What tidings would you share with the pack?" Lorens asked.

"I have found my mate," Adenet said, his voice firm with conviction, "and would petition the pack to accept him into our midst as a wizard, as a man, but most importantly as my heart and my strength, the foundation on which I will serve this pack for the rest of my life."

Marc had protested that last bit when Adenet had told him what he intended to say, but Adenet knew the truth. He drew power from their mating. Without it, he would be just another wolf.

"Marc, join your mate."

Marc moved to Adenet's side, the chill breeze biting into his skin away from the protection of the overhang and the ritual fire, but it would be worth it to have the blessing of the pack.

"Has Adenet spoken true? Do you accept him as your mate?"

"With all my heart," Marc swore.

"And will you pledge your life as well to the service of the pack?"

"I offer all that I have and all that I am," Marc said.

"I accept your fidelity," Lorens replied. "What says the pack?"

The roar of approval from the pack surprised Marc. He had not expected them to refuse, but their enthusiasm warmed his heart.

"Rise and take your place at your mate's side."

Marc stood, Adenet doing the same at his side, and they joined hands as they walked back to their place by the fire. Marc barely listened as others approached Lorens with requests of various kinds. Nothing else mattered in the face of his acceptance into the pack.

"Well done."

Marc looked away from Adenet in surprise. "Raymond?"

"Adenet thought you might like a wizard as witness as well. Jean chose to stay outside the grove, but he sends his congratulations also. Enjoy your mate. We'll see you at l'Institut in two weeks, not a day before."

"But—"

"Don't argue. A honeymoon is a grand tradition. Everything we need to discuss can wait until then."

"Thank you," Marc said. "For everything."

"Don't thank me," Raymond said. "I didn't do anything."

"You gave me the chance."

Raymond smiled. "Then you're welcome." He drifted back into the crowd.

Marc turned back to Adenet.

"Yes, I heard," Adenet said softly. "I won't complain about having you to myself for two weeks, though Tristan still has things he wants to teach me and we have the fertility ritual when the moon is full, so I'm not sure how much of a vacation it will really be."

Marc smiled. "I don't need a vacation. I just need my life with you."

The final Partnership in Blood novel

# *Partnership Reborn*

## By Ariel Tachna

All his life, wizard Raphael Tarayaud has dreamed of a vampire—first as a friend, then as a lover. His search for his missing soul mate brings him to the attention of Sebastien Noyer, one of his childhood heroes. While Sebastien isn't his soul mate, he could be the perfect partner for Raphael's best friend Kylian Raffier.

As strange coincidences mount up, Raphael offers his research expertise to try and help Kylian and Sebastien understand what is happening to them, though the more he learns, the less he likes it. But it won't keep him from fighting with everything he has to secure Kylian's future.

When he finally meets Jean Bellaiche, former chef de la Cour and grieving widower, the meeting is disastrous, but Raphael can't let it go. He doesn't stand a chance with Jean—who could compete with the ghost of Raymond Payet?—but nothing can stop him from dreaming.

# Chapter 1

*Thirty years later*

"TELL ME again why we're doing this?"

Raphael Taravaud looked up from his perusal of his closet, where he had been searching for the perfect shirt to wear when they went out. Kylian Raffier, his best friend since childhood, leaned casually against the doorframe, looking far too good for Raphael's peace of mind. Kylian had long, straight black hair and just the hint of a beard, exactly the kind of man Raphael would go for, except for one small detail: Kylian wasn't for him. He had tried more than once to translate that into words everyone else could understand, but he had never managed, even to his own mind. He could only say that he knew. The very essence of his being cried out for its mate, and Kylian was not it.

"Because I've looked everywhere else I can think of," Raphael replied. "The same vampires show up at l'Institut practically every time they have their dinners, and none of the others want partners. He's out there somewhere, Ky. I just have to find him."

"So you're going clubbing in Paris in the hope of miraculously running across him, and you're dragging me with you because I have nothing better to do on a Friday night than follow your sorry ass around from club to club," Kylian scoffed. "This is your worst idea yet."

"Then come up with a better one," Raphael challenged. "You think I enjoy this? You think I enjoy walking around feeling like half of me is missing?"

"You're so damn sure," Kylian said with a shake of his head. "How do you know this?"

"I don't," Raphael admitted, because for Kylian, he would try again to do what he had yet to manage for anyone. "I just know something's missing—and from everything I've learned about partnerships, that's what it feels like, except my partner isn't here. You remember some of the accounts we studied of partners who were separated during the war, or later for various reasons? How the bond helped them find their partners again by sense alone? I have that sense. I feel that tug, except I've never met the man on the other end. I've tried following it, but it's too nebulous to lead me anywhere."

"You're so sure it's a man. What are you going to do if it's a woman?" Kylian teased.

"I guess I'll learn to like tits," Raphael said with a shrug, but he was not worried. He could not explain the connection he had felt—and missed—for as long as he could remember, but he was done waiting for his partner to find him by conventional means. His vampire was out there somewhere, and he was going to find him. Whatever it took.

"I still say you're setting yourself up for disappointment," Kylian said. "Even if you find your partner, the kind of bond you're looking for is incredibly rare. It wasn't just any separated partners who found each other again by sense alone."

"Not as rare as it used to be," Raphael replied. "There were two in the previous generation."

"And one is dead, and the other now lives completely retired from society," Kylian reminded him. "Not a great recommendation for anyone considering that choice."

"But what grand love stories they were!" Raphael said. "Like you wouldn't jump at the chance for that kind of love if it came your way."

"*If* being the key word," Kylian said. "But if it came my way, I'd think about it. I'd discuss it with my partner and maybe we'd consider it, but it's a huge step. You know the stories. When Alain Magnier died, Orlando St. Clair sat at his grave until the sun took him, and when Raymond Payet died, Jean Bellaiche collapsed with grief. He's hardly been seen in thirty years. I'm not sure I'd want to do that to someone I loved."

"It's better to have loved and lost...."

"Is it?" Kylian challenged. "I'm not so sure, if that's the price for that kind of relationship. I can't think of any vampires who have found a second partner, and some of them lost their partners forty or fifty years ago."

"Which is nothing to a vampire," Raphael pointed out. "Even most of the young ones are hundreds of years old."

"They still have to live each day," Kylian said, "and you're talking about them watching the person they love grow old and die while they remain unchanged. It's not all hearts and flowers. There's self-sacrifice in that kind of commitment."

"Your grandmother only had ten years with your grandfather before he died, and she never remarried. Do you think she regrets those years for a moment?" Raphael asked.

"No, I know she doesn't," Kylian said.

"Then why are you so sure the vampires regret it?"

"You said it yourself. It's the same batch of vampires every time they have a dinner at l'Institut, and they are all newer vampires who haven't had a partner before. Can you think of a single instance where a vampire has taken a second partner after the first one died?"

"No, but I don't know every vampire or every pair. I'm sure there are some," Raphael insisted. "And even if there aren't, I don't need a vampire who had a partner before. I just need a vampire to be my partner now."

"And so you're going to drag me around Paris to every club vampires are known to frequent in the hope of meeting the one vampire who might be your partner and getting him to feed from you, and you're going to do all this hoping said vampire doesn't hate you for trapping him into a partnership without realizing you're a wizard before he feeds from you," Kylian summarized. "This may be your most brilliant plan yet."

"Sarcasm doesn't become you," Raphael retorted. "If I had an idea for a better plan, believe me, I'd go for that instead—but I have to do something."

"Why?" Kylian demanded. "That's the part of this I just don't get, Raph. I don't understand why you feel like you have to do this."

"Because he's missing," Raphael said. "I don't know how else to explain it, but he's out there somewhere instead of here beside me where he's supposed to be. Don't tell me it makes no sense. I know it makes no sense. There's no way I should miss someone I've never met, but I do. I look for him without thinking when I want to share good news. I reach for him during the night, only to find empty space next to me in bed. I dream about him without quite being able to see his face, but I can tell you everything else about him. He's thin but wiry, not tall, like maybe he was turned generations ago when people didn't grow as tall as average now. He's serious, but I know there's a wicked sense of humor underneath that."

"If you do manage to meet and recognize him, what then?" Kylian asked. "You have this all built up in your head of how he'll be and how things will work, but this isn't a story in some book. This is reality, and you don't know that he'll return your interest. Even if he's never had a partner before, even if he's not opposed to the idea of having one, you still have to win him over, and you're talking about doing it after you've tricked him into feeding from you and creating a bond he may not want."

"I don't know, all right?" Raphael said. "Are you happy now? I have no idea how it's going to work out, but I have to do something. If you have a better idea, I'll take it."

Kylian shook his head. "Not really. The only thing I can say is, tell him what you are and what you want before he bites you the first time. I know it's a great story about St. Clair and Magnier meeting in the cemetery, and St. Clair biting Magnier and just knowing they were meant to be together. I've read the accounts just like you did, and the idea that their love was so all-encompassing that St. Clair couldn't go on alone adds to it, but that's not the only account we studied. Many of the others, even the ones who settled into solid bonds, said they wouldn't have done it if they'd known what they were getting into before they started. It goes against everything we stand for to trap someone into a relationship that way. When the war was going on and the partnerships were first forming, they didn't know what they were doing. You do."

"I can't lose him," Raphael said.

"If you trick him into a relationship, how do you expect to keep him?" Kylian replied.

Raphael slumped onto the bed. "I don't know. I just know I have to find him."

"So we'll search," Kylian said. "We'll keep looking until we find him. Just tell him the truth before he bites you. You can seduce him if it feels right. You can both walk away from that, but neither of you can walk away once he's bitten you. What if you're wrong, and you end up hating him? You'll be as stuck as he is."

Raphael knew Kylian was right, objectively anyway, but he had lived with his phantom lover from his earliest memories. As a child, the man in his dreams had been a playmate rather than a lover, but his first wet dream had featured the same faceless man he searched for at every dinner he attended at l'Institut Marcel Chavinier and in the face of every man he met wherever he went.

"Just promise me you'll think before you rush into anything," Kylian said when Raphael didn't immediately reply.

"I promise," Raphael said. He could give Kylian that much. Not much else, but at least that much.

"IT'S TIME, Sebastien," Angélique said.

"It's past time," Sebastien agreed, "but it's still all I can do to drag him here twice a week. Do you really think he'll agree to go hunting with me? It's only been thirty years. If I take him to the clubs, he'll be recognized, and he'll argue that being out in public will set him up in opposition to Fabienne."

"That's bullshit, and we all know it," Angélique insisted. Jean would never challenge the new chef de la Cour, and Fabienne would hand the Cour back over to him in a heartbeat if he wanted it. "Yes, he might be recognized in some of the clubs, but he was never one to frequent them, even before Raymond. He ran the Cour, but in a city this size, not everyone chose to attend meetings. He's not as recognizable as he used to be. Scout out some of the smaller clubs. There's bound to be one he can go to."

"You realize we could be doing this for nothing. Monsieur Lombard has lived in retirement for far longer than Jean."

"You didn't," Angélique retorted. "Either time."

"Thibaut wasn't a wizard, and Thierry wasn't my Avoué," Sebastien countered.

Angélique snorted. "So more than ninety years of sharing his life, his bed, and his blood doesn't count? Pull the other one."

Sebastien scowled at her, but he could not deny that what he had shared with Thierry had surpassed even what he had shared with his Avoué. They had no name for the bond they had created between them—more than a partnership but not an Aveu de Sang, because that magic only worked once—but their bond had given him peace of mind, if nothing else. Sebastien's inner beast had recognized Thierry after they completed their private ritual. Sebastien had learned to relax again after that, finally free of the fear he would lose control and hurt Thierry again.

"It's not the same."

Angélique didn't look convinced, but Sebastien let it go. She had enjoyed her partner, and David had been totally devoted to her, but she had always kept the upper hand and kept one small step back so that David's death saddened her rather than gutted her. Sebastien envied her occasionally, but then he remembered all the joy of his years with Thierry and pitied her instead.

"Since you brought it up, I assume you have suggestions for clubs I should look into," Sebastien said.

"As a matter of fact, I do."

He chuckled when she pulled a list from under the pillow of the divan she was reclining on and handed it to him. The list contained ten clubs, neatly annotated in her elegant handwriting. "I'll check them out."

SEBASTIEN ALMOST turned around to leave the first club on Angélique's list before he ever made it in the door. He had decided not to announce his presence, as so many of the vampires did at the clubs, choosing instead to join the line of people waiting to get inside. The bouncer had come down the line, checking IDs, and stopped cold when he saw Sebastien's name on his ID card. "Sebastien Noyer? *The* Sebastien Noyer? Why are you in line out here? You don't have to wait."

"It's fine," Sebastien demurred. "I don't mind waiting with everyone else."

"No, no, I insist. My boss will have my job if he finds out I let you wait out here. It's spring, yes, but it's not warm yet. Please, come inside."

Sebastien let the bouncer lead him to the door, ignoring the whispers of the people he passed. He did not see a way out of going inside now that he had been identified, unless he created an even bigger scene. He could do that, but he had hoped to avoid attention. Protesting would only draw even more. He would take this club off his list for Jean, though, because if they recognized his name, with as little as he had been in the public eye in the later years of Thierry's life, they would know Jean instantly, and that defeated the purpose. Jean would never consent to go somewhere he might be recognized.

The inside of the club was nicer than Sebastien had expected, the walls done in understated dark wood rather than in the garish colors many of the clubs currently favored. Sebastien had seen fads come and go in his long existence. The colors would go out of style in a year or a decade. If the club stayed open long enough, it would not need to redecorate in a year or two as styles changed. The bar area itself resembled any of a hundred other bars around the city, but the young man propped up against the bar resembled no one Sebastien had ever seen before. A jolt of lust hit him before he could tear his gaze away.

He made it halfway across the room before he realized he had moved, but his new position allowed him a better view of the young man's face. Sebastien had never been good at guessing age, but he would have put the man between twenty and twenty-five, old enough to be legal but young enough to make Sebastien feel ancient.

*You* are *ancient,* he told himself, *no matter how young you look.*

It was not the man's age or physical beauty that held Sebastien's gaze as he kept staring. No, it was the look on his face, a mix of cynicism and amusement, as if the man could not decide if he wanted to laugh at or scorn the world around him. Sebastien had not seen that particular expression in thirty-three years.

Bile rose in his throat at the thought. He had begun hunting again since Thierry died, refusing to break his promise to Thierry by isolating himself as Jean had done, but those assignations had been about feeding his body, not about replacing Thierry. No one could replace Thierry, just as Thierry had not replaced Thibaut. Sebastien accepted that he might meet someone and fall in love again, but it was too soon. Even more importantly, he would not sully Thierry's memory or his new relationship by claiming someone purely because he reminded Sebastien of Thierry.

*Maybe a woman this time*, he thought as he focused his gaze elsewhere. The mortals in the club appeared of an age with the one who had caught Sebastien's interest, all of them dressed to draw attention, either with collars missing or turned down to show the smooth, enticing skin of their necks, or with plunging décolletage to offer even more. He had fed well the day before. He should not have been hungry again, but the sight of so many nubile young bodies on offer whetted his hunger, and he felt his fangs drop. The club would not suit for Jean, given the way Sebastien had been recognized, but Sebastien was already here. He saw no reason to deny himself a taste of one of the succulent offerings.

"Hunting, Noyer?"

"What else would I be doing here?" Sebastien summoned his best polite smile for the vampire who had called him by name.

"I don't know, but these aren't your usual hunting grounds."

It took Sebastien a moment to place the vampire, but he finally recognized Stéphane, one of the vampires who had challenged Jean frequently at the beginning of the alliance. He had never found a partner, if Sebastien remembered correctly.

"I wasn't aware you'd become as territorial as a werewolf," Sebastien drawled. After all the help the Morvan pack had given him and Thierry, the comparison would not have insulted him, but the other vampire would not take the words so lightly. He bared his fangs threateningly, but Sebastien ignored him. His bond with Thierry had not lifted him outside le jeu des Cours, but his years with Thierry and as Jean's right hand had cemented his position in a way this upstart could not hope to threaten.

"Is there a problem?"

Sebastien turned to smile at the bouncer who had escorted him out of the line and inside. "No problem. I was just deciding where I wanted to sit," he said.

## Partnership Reborn

"I'll clear a spot for you at the bar," the bouncer offered. Sebastien refrained from shooting a triumphant look back at the vampire he had just bested. Jean had taught him that it stung the loser more if he did not even acknowledge his victory.

Don't miss how the
story started!

# *Alliance in Blood*

Partnership in Blood:
Volume One

By Ariel Tachna

Can a desperate wizard and a bitter, disillusioned vampire find a way to
build the partnership that could save their world?

In a world rocked by magical war, vampires are seen by many as less
than human, as the stereotypical creatures of the night who prey on
others. But as the war intensifies, the wizards know they need an
advantage to turn the tide in their favor: the strength and edge the
vampires can give them in the battle against the dark wizards who seek
to destroy life as they know it.

In a dangerous move and show of good will, the wizards ask the leader
of the vampires to meet with them, so that they might plead their cause.
One desperate man, Alain Magnier, and one bitter, disillusioned
vampire, Orlando St. Clair, meet in Paris, and the fate of the world
hangs in the balance of their decision: Will the vampires join the cause
and form a partnership with the wizards to win the war?

Don't miss what
happens next in

# Covenant
# in Blood

Sequel to *Alliance in Blood*
Partnership in Blood:
Volume Two

By Ariel Tachna

The wizards and the vampires have forged an alliance based on blood
and magic, hoping to turn the tide of the war against the dark
wizards. A few wizard-vampire bonds are as successful as Alain
Magnier's and Orlando St. Clair's, but some are much less so,
leading to arguments, resentment, and outright fights between the
allies despite their mutual goals.

Following his best friend Alain's example, Thierry Dumont determinedly
forms a partnership with vampire Sebastien Noyer, despite the wizard's
discomfort with being so close to a vampire—a man—so soon after his
wife's death. But they find that desperation may be the key to forming
a covenant that works: Thierry and Sebastien are almost immediately
devoted to one another's safety.

With new strength behind it, the Alliance's leaders move to announce
its existence to the whole world, hoping to rally support against the
dark wizards who threaten to destroy life as they know it. Struggling to
find its way in the expanding war, the Alliance discovers that despite its
advantages, the partnerships are affecting the balance of magical power
in the world, which may be an even bigger threat than the war itself.

The story continues in

# *Conflict in Blood*

Sequel to *Covenant in Blood*
Partnership in Blood:
Volume Three

By Ariel Tachna

As the Alliance wizard-vampire partnerships grow stronger, the dark wizards feel the effects and become increasingly desperate to find enough information to counter them, unaware of the growing strain of the blood-magic bonds on the wizards and vampires alike.

The conflict is spreading. The strife of uncomfortable relationships, both personal and professional, is threatening to tear up the Alliance from the inside, despite the efforts of Alain Magnier and Orlando St. Clair, Thierry Dumont and Sebastien Noyer, and even Raymond Payet and Jean Bellaiche, leader of the Paris vampires, who is fighting to establish a stable covenant with his own partner so he might lead by example.

As the war rages on and heartbreaking casualties mount on both sides, the dark wizards keep searching for clues to understand and counter the strength of the Alliance, while the blood-bound Alliance partners hunt through ancient prejudices and forgotten lore to find an edge that can turn the tide of the war once and for all.

# Don't miss the epic finale:

# *Reparation in Blood*

Sequel to *Conflict in Blood*
Partnership in Blood:
Volume Four

By Ariel Tachna

The war is at a fever pitch with both sides stretched to the limit, when the dark wizards score a shocking victory and capture Orlando St. Clair. Haggard with worry and grief at the separation from his lover, Alain fears that even if they find Orlando, the vampire's heart and mind may be far too broken to save.

Knowing the Alliance teeters on the brink, Christophe Lombard, the oldest, most powerful vampire in Paris, leaves his self-imposed seclusion to join the fight. Alain's lost friend Eric Simonet, who betrayed him to join the dark wizards, is faced with a choice between revenge and redemption. And Jean, enraged by Orlando's capture, faces the most agonizing decision in his unlife as the final battle looms: Will their actions lead to the shattering of the Alliance or the salvation of the world?

A Partnership in Blood novel

# *Perilous Partnership*

By Ariel Tachna

A year after the end of the war that brought them together, Raymond Payet and Jean Bellaiche have found a balance in their relationship: Jean drinks only Raymond's blood; Raymond sleeps only in Jean's bed. The demands of their public roles as president of l'Association Nationale de Sorcellerie and chef de la Cour of the Parisian vampires keep them busy dealing with fallout from the war and the alliance, particularly the not-always-successful partnerships between vampires and wizards.

The foundation of an institute to research and educate wizards and vampires about the implications of the partnership bonds only adds to those responsibilities. When political factions, both vampire and mortal, oppose their leaders' decisions, the stress begins to affect Raymond and Jean's deepening relationship. And when political opposition turns to vandalism and then to violence, they'll have to find a way to reconcile their personal and professional lives before external and internal forces pull them apart.

A Partnership in Blood novel

# *Reluctant Partnerships*

### By Ariel Tachna

Thanks to the efforts of Raymond Payet and l'ANS, vampires now have the same legal rights as mortals, and research at l'Institut Marcel Chavinier is focusing on the mysterious partnership bonds between wizards and vampires. But the battle for public opinion rages on. When Detective Adèle Rougier encounters Pascale Auboussu, a shy young woman turned into a vampire against her will, Raymond and Denis Langlois, chef de la Cour nearest the crime, fear a public relations nightmare.

The vampire responsible for Pascale's turning must be brought to justice, but Denis is distracted by an unlikely potential partner—Canadian researcher Martin Delacroix, who is spending a year's sabbatical at l'Institut—and Denis's lingering feelings for his deceased lover prompt him to reject the bond. There's no denying the attraction between them, though, and the allure of companionship is nearly as strong as Denis's grief.

Growing familiarity and yearning for a true mate may induce Adèle and Denis to soften their stances against new partnerships, but Adèle will have to accept a deeper intimacy with Pascale when she has never considered a relationship with a woman, and it will take a near-deadly attack to make Denis admit his most hidden desires. Now he has to hope Martin will be willing to stay.

ARIEL TACHNA lives outside of Houston with her husband, her daughter and son, and their cat. Before moving there, she traveled all over the world, having fallen in love with both France, where she found her husband, and India, where she dreams of retiring someday. She's bilingual with snippets of four other languages to her credit and is as in love with languages as she is with writing.

Visit Ariel at her website: http://www.arieltachna.com or on Facebook: https://www.facebook.com/ArielTachna, or e-mail her at arieltachna@gmail.com.

# THE PATH
## ARIEL TACHNA

http://www.dreamspinnerpress.com

# Lang Downs Series

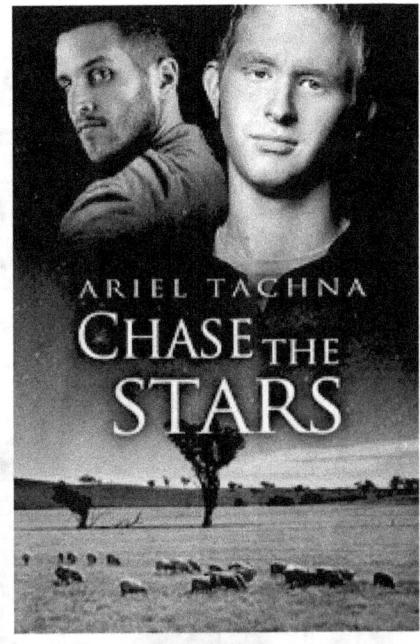

http://www.dreamspinnerpress.com